Matthew Langley had gone about a mile when he heard hoofbeats behind him around a turn. He pulled up, thinking someone was coming from the wagons. When he turned, Chavez and four soldiers were galloping around the bend. The Mexican immigration officer grinned broadly when he saw Langley, and when they reined in, they had him ringed.

Langley knew he was in the country without authorization, carrying contraband property. It was also apparent that Chavez liked the look of his horse. Two of his men had their muskets trained on him, and when Chavez ordered him to produce the land grant he had been seen with in Nacogdoches, he handed it over in its oilskin pouch.

Chavez smiled a thin smile. "You shall not need this again, señor," he said coldly. "Now drop your rifle and step down from that horse."

That was too much. Langley brought his rifle up level and was drawing the hammer when one of the men clubbed him behind the ear. The next moment he seemed to be slowly floating down to the hard ground below. . . .

FOR THE BEST OF THE WEST—
DAN PARKINSON

A MAN CALLED WOLF   (2794, $3.95)
Somewhere in the scorched southwestern frontier where civilization was just a step away from the dark ages, an army of hired guns was restoring the blood cult of an ancient empire. Only one man could stop them: John Thomas Wolf.

THE WAY TO WYOMING   (2411, $3.95)
Matt Hazlewood and Big Jim Tyson had fought side by side wearing the gray ten years before. Now, with a bloody range war closing in fast behind and killers up ahead, they'd join up to ride and fight again in an untamed land where there was just the plains, the dust, and the heat— and the law of the gun!

GUNPOWDER WIND   (2456, $3.95)
by Dan Parkinson and David Hicks
War was brewing between the Anglo homesteaders and the town's loco Mexican commander Colonel Piedras. Figuring to keep the settlers occupied with a little Indian trouble, Piedras had Cherokee warrior Utsada gunned down in cold blood. Now it was up to young Cooper Willoughby to find him before the Cherokees hit the warpath!

THE WESTERING   (2559, $3.95)
There were laws against settin' a blood bounty on an innocent man, but Frank Kingston did it anyway, and Zack Frost found himself hightailin' it out of Indiana with a price on his head and a pack of bloodthirsty bounty hunters hot on his trail!

Available wherever paperbacks are sold, or order direct from the Publisher. Send cover price plus 50¢ per copy for mailing and handling to Zebra Books, Dept. 3097, 475 Park Avenue South, New York, N.Y. 10016. Residents of New York, New Jersey and Pennsylvania must include sales tax. DO NOT SEND CASH.

THE TEXIANS

DAN PARKINSON
AND DAVID HICKS

ZEBRA BOOKS
KENSINGTON PUBLISHING CORP.

ZEBRA BOOKS

are published by

Kensington Publishing Corp.
475 Park Avenue South
New York, NY 10016

First Zebra Books printing: August, 1990

Printed in the United States of America

Part One

BRAZORIA'S TEXIANS

During a brief period in the history of Texas—beginning with the enactment of the so-called Acts of 1830 by the Republic of Mexico, and culminating in those events that occurred in 1836 at the Alamo, at Goliad and at San Jacinto where Texas won its independence—the English-speaking settlers in and around the Austin colonies established for themselves a heritage unique in history. Prior to 1830, those settlers considered themselves simply Mexicans—citizens of Mexico. Following the revolution of 1836, they were Texans—citizens of the Republic of Texas. But for those few years, they were something else—a fiery, determined people whose freely given loyalties had been dishonored, who had experienced all the oppression they could tolerate. In that brief era they gave themselves a new name: *Texians*.

In 1832, Mexico first learned what the word could mean. Led by the Brazoria Militia, the Texians bared their teeth and Mexico learned that a Texian is to a Texan as a wolf is to a dog.

This book is dedicated to those Texians who fought at Anahuac and Velasco four years before the Alamo. It is dedicated also to those parts of the Texas character which were molded in that bloody year. And it is dedicated particularly to the Texians for Brazoria, who are doing what they can to recapture and restore that heritage, to the advantage of their community . . . and, in a way, of all of us.

Texas

On a mantel in the great house of President Anastasio Bustamente in Mexico City rested a machine tendered to the president some years before by one Antonio Luis Santallo, fellow of the academy of sciences and mathematics of Spain, lately head of the institute of mathematic arts of the Republic of Mexico—now, unfortunately, deceased.

The object was a toy, a curiosity, but one which delighted the man who had ruthlessly hacked out his place in the world as el primero, el supremo, the final and ultimate authority of a nation larger than the Empire of Rome in the days of Trajan. It was a clock, but such a clock as one had never seen before. Beautifully worked and embellished, the machined portions were of Austrian design, the tensions and balance were of Prussian steel. And it had no face, no hands, no numerals

It was rather a clock of many pendulums. Suspended from the works, in a case of ornate bronze, were numerous rod-hung pendulums of varying lengths and weights, each swinging to its own tempo, each oblivious to the others whose many paths it paralleled. At the front was a very short, very light pendulum consisting of nothing more than a brass wire with a button at the end, shivering back and forth in its constrained arc almost faster than the eye could follow. At the back was a grand shaft of bronze sweeping sedately to the right, to the left, and to the right again, a prince among pendulums, imperturbable in its slow, regal rhythm. In between were many more of varying sizes, shapes, and weights, some swinging fast, some slowly, some on wide sweeps, and some vibrating in shallow arcs.

The clock seemed a totally random piece of spring-motion machinery, confusing to the eye and hypnotic to the sustained gaze. It marked no minutes, it displayed no hours. Yet so cunningly adjusted were its mechanisms, so deliberate had been the reckoning of Professor Santallo, that each hour, precisely on the hour, the many pendulums approached, and achieved, perfect synchronization in a single swing. And when this occurred the clock rewarded itself with a single, beautiful chime.

President Bustamente had never been a philosophical man. His fascination with the clock was that of a ruthless and practical man with a beautiful toy. He enjoyed looking at it. That was all.

And that, for El Presidente, was regrettable. He might have learned something from that clock, and that knowledge might have saved him his throne—for a few extra years. Had he possessed a philosophic curiosity, he might have looked for human qualities which those pendulums could represent. He might have pondered those qualities and come up with a theory on the cycles of behavior of human cultures.

He might have supposed that one pendulum could be the rhythm of tendencies toward violent action at one end of the swing, toward complaisance and docility at the other. Following that, the next pendulum might have been a measure of public temper, content in one swing, frustrated in the other. Yet another might have measured the rise and fall of leaders and another the ebb and flow of foreign ambitions toward the soil of another domain. And that stately, implacable, grand pendulum at the rear might well have marked the inexorable rhythm with which domain succeeds domain in the history of mankind, by which kings defeat kings and in turn are defeated by new kings.

Bustamente might have seen all this, but had he been of such a mind he probably would never have become ruler of all Mexico. Instead, he had taken, with great practicality and brutal determination, all the correct steps that led to his goal. He had advanced from the shrewd and ambitious politician, to the single-minded leader of discontented peons, to the ruthless revolutionary, to the clever statesman welding a nation together and healing its economic wounds, and finally to the ultimate step, the complete and capable tyrant.

Bustamente had few weaknesses, but he had one. He was unable to see, until too late, that there was one step more in the natural course of events. It simply never occurred to him that all the forces of human destiny must ultimately, periodically, swing into a phase of perfect synchronization, like the many pendulums of Professor Santallo's clever clock.

Bustamente was paying scant heed to his clock on this day, the sixteenth of May, the year 1832. It was a day of many tensions for him, of ominous pressures that seeped even into the cloistered shelter of the grand office of the western world's prime autocrat.

Day by day, the feeling increased in him that his throne was insecure, and always there were the ambitions of that flashy upstart, Antonio López de Santa Anna. Daily the reports on his desk grew, reports from his spies in Santa Anna's corps. The man had power and a loyal following, both among his own soldiers and, ominously, among the peons and smallholders in many parts of the Republic. Santa Anna was not overt in his exercise of that power, but day by day it was growing more obvious that Santa Anna was a rising star in Mexico.

Most recently, Bustamente had directed correspondence to General Santa Anna containing a very blunt, straightforward inquiry. Where did his loyalties lie? How did it happen that with each day his eminence in Mexico became more evident? And, a specific question, how did he explain the buildup of troops at Vera Cruz? Certainly his practice maneuvers at that port city did not require so large a force.

On this day his answer came back—a finely worded, carefully couched response. Santa Anna reaffirmed his undying loyalty to the Republic of Mexico and to its rightful leader. To Mexico and its leader, but not, he noted, to Bustamente specifically. No mention was made of the troops at Vera Cruz.

11

Cursing, Bustamente put the letter aside for a time and set about the day's agenda of trivia. He received the ambassador of the King of France and assured that worthy of his everlasting friendship. He signed papers setting aside lands for the containment of Indians in the State of Oaxaca. He recorded commendations for Colonel Tantanillo of San Ildefonso, Colonel Bradburn of Anahuac, and Colonel Piedras of Nacogdoches.

He read reports on the troop strength of the command of General Manuel Mier y Teran in northern Mexico and denied an application for the promotion of Colonel Jose Antonio Mexia to the rank of general officer. Mexico had too many generals already.

He denied clemency to a convicted friend of the late Vicente Guerrero, Bustamente's predecessor.

He read, slapped down upon the desk and thereafter ignored the latest request for audience from one Stephen F. Austin, Alcalde of Colony San Felipe de Austin on the Rio Brazos in Texas.

He levied a special tax on animals owned by peons and a second shipment tax on grain exported by padrones through Mexican ports. As an afterthought, and with a glance at the Alcalde Austin's letter, he appended a special tax on all bulk exports from ports in the colonies of Texas.

A little later in the day he ordered the ambassador of the King of France confined to quarters.

Finally, with the day's papers cleared away, he returned to the Santa Anna file. He read and reread it for an hour or more, trying to infer meaning from the intuitive unrest that bothered him as he compared the reports. Finally he directed the placement of additional informants in the headquarters of the general's command.

The clock on the mantel ticked steadily away, the pendulums swaying closer and closer to their single, ultimate moment of synchronization.

At his spotless, spartan headquarters in Vera Cruz, General Santa Anna was likewise very busy, but he considered none of his work trivia. Santa Anna had a plan and a sense

12

of destiny, and he followed both with the relentless passion of a crusader.

A steady stream of messengers, spies, and subordinate officers passed through his doorway on this day. Again and again he returned, with various persons, to a large, carefully drawn map of the Republic of Mexico, tacked to the top of a huge oak table, which dominated the office.

At points along various roads fanning out from Mexico City and the interior provinces he marked neat X's, indicating troop concentrations—his troops—of various strengths. The pattern of X marks was becoming distinct. There was an unobtrusive but quite effective cordon of his forces entirely around the perimeters of Bustamente's main concentrations in the area of Mexico City, and a separate and moving cordon of much stronger forces in a semicircle around Vera Cruz. This arc was diminishing inward upon itself. At his command, Vera Cruz could be isolated from Mexico and Mexico City could be isolated from the world.

He smiled slightly as he read a fresh report, and referred to the map again. Several days ago he had moved two battalions swiftly and without notice into the region of Saltillo and then had waited for a reaction. He had it now. His little move had brought a counter-move. Several units of Bustamente troops were being withdrawn from Texas southwestward into Coahuila. He dictated orders to his unit commanders in the Saltillo region to withdraw again, back to Vera Cruz.

Then he directed messengers be sent to Texas in the northeast and to Tabasco in the south to let it be known that he, General Santa Anna, supported the provisions of the Constitution of 1824 that had been suspended two years earlier. He, General Santa Anna, was to be considered a friend and confidant of the oppressed people of the colonial areas of the Republic.

It would have pleased him, too, to have been compared to a pendulum on President Bustamente's elaborate clock.

Far to the northeast on this same day, around the coastal bend and at the upper end of Trinity Bay, which flanks

13

Galveston Bay on the upper Texas coast, Colonel Juan Davis Bradburn buckled on his sword belt and went onto the parade ground to see what the noise was all about. As he appeared, several Mexican soldiers snapped to attention.

Four Negro slaves, property of an Anglo settler somewhere up the Trinity River, had come pounding on the main gate, their eyes wide with terror, seeking protection. They were runaways. Bradburn's eyes narrowed with distaste as he surveyed the cringing blacks. One of the soldiers came forward with a dipper of water and started to offer it. With a curse Bradburn strode forward and knocked it aside. Then he turned to a lieutenant who had hastened forward.

"These"—he waved a chunky hand—"are now under the protection of the Republic of Mexico. They are not to be returned to their owner, nor allowed to leave the fort premises. Put them in irons and put them to work in that new boat slip."

The lieutenant, his face carefully neutral, saluted and turned away to issue orders.

"Niggers!" Bradburn breathed as the slaves were led away. The interruption was an irritant to him. He had bigger decisions to make.

Back in his office the commander of Anahuac returned to his desk and his maps. With a thumb he traced an arc on a chart of the Mexican coastal bend, impressing in his mind the distance between Anahuac and Mexico City—or Vera Cruz—or Saltillo. To the northeast, also a long way off, lay Nacogdoches. From a point midway to Nacogdoches he spanned another radius, then drew a circumference at that distance around Anahuac. The brooding, close-set eyes lit slightly as Bradburn realized again that this, an area larger than some European nations, could be his alone if he made the right choices.

Santa Anna would challenge Bustamente; there was no doubt about that. There would be civil war in Mexico. Bustamente was already pulling field troops south out of Texas. The generals would be choosing sides. Then the garrison commanders. Each would cast his lot with Bustamente or Santa Anna, and each would join the fight.

Bradburn had already made his choice. He was for Bradburn. He then turned his attention to the only real problem he could foresee: The Texians.

He spat. Mexico had made a fearful mistake when it had opened Texas to immigration from the United States. The Americans had come in droves. Unencumbered and unmanageable, they had colonized and produced, farmed and profited, until finally Mexico had realized, belatedly, that there was a difference between a Mexican peon and an American immigrant.

The peon was a docile brute, and could generally be kept that way. Americans were ambitious, self-assured and industrious. And each one of them, aristocrat or rabble, considered himself to be his own law. Every scum who crossed the border into Texas, whether he declared allegiance to Mexico or not, knew in his own mind that he came first, and authority came a poor second.

Bradburn knew the Americans very well. He had been one. The indignities heaped upon him years before in Mississippi were fresh in his mind today. But he would prevail. The Law of 1830 had given him the power to punish these so-called Texians around him, and Bustamente's recent declaration of martial law had given him the instrument.

Bradburn needed an incident. He needed the Texians to make the first unlawful move.

He was about to get his wish. Half a mile away, in the Plazuela de Maliche at the Town of Anahuac, an Anglo ne'er-do-well and three off-duty soldiers sat in the shade and got drunk.

One

All day the white South Texas sun had bleached the streets of Anahuac, pounding relentlessly against the hard gray earth. By midday most of the inhabitants were driven off the streets, into the dubious protection of the little town's variety of buildings. Only a few were abroad as the afternoon burned on, hugging the shaded places and exerting themselves as little as possible.

In the shade in front of a small house off the Plazuela de Maliche four men lounged, sharing the last of a bottle of tequila. Another bottle, empty, lay on the ground. Three were dark-eyed, dark-skinned men wearing tunics and breeches of the Mexican army uniform. The fourth was a spare, languid man with thick blond hair and watery eyes. He wore faded blue pants and moccasins of tanned hide. A tattered shirt covered portions of his upper body, and his lean jowls were streaked and matted with unkempt whiskers. He and one of the off-duty soldiers were tossing knives into the ground between them and wagering indifferently on the killing of a large beetle that labored across the rutted earth.

One of the soldiers was young, almost a boy, with the high cheekbones and slanted black eyes of Indio ancestors. Another was a short, hard-jawed man of about thirty. The third, the one with the knife, had a dark whip-mark across his face, sullen, cautious eyes, and nervous hands. In the past hour or two the conversation had ranged from women to horses to Indians, officers, latrine stories, food, and back to women, and had finally trailed off into a lingering silence as each thought his own thoughts and drank tequila.

Women were scarce in this distant, desolate outpost of the Mexican empire, and those available were seldom desirable.

17

There were a few half-breed harlots living in shacks near the fort. There were the skinny and work-worn women of the Anglo settlers who inhabited the town and surrounding area. And there were the occasional Indian women who came to the fort on their own or as prizes brought in by patrols. But in all they were only a few and, for a common soldier, virtually inaccessible.

Most of the women were the settlers' women. A few of these, the younger and plumper ones, might now and then excite the wary interest of the soldiers and the drifters who lingered around the town, but for the most part the women were not worth noting—unless you were hundreds of miles from home, discouraged, lonely and drunk. In these circumstances a man might reduce his values. He might disregard for a time his memories of soft dark eyes and warm tan skin of the mestizo women of his home village and let himself think thoughts about these skinny Anglos.

Such thoughts now quieted the talk and shadowed the eyes of the three soldiers, and the man with them knew it. He was drunk but they were drunker, and his crafty mind was searching for a way to capitalize on that fact.

The soldiers were important to him. Their tolerant—if somewhat patronizing—acceptance kept him in business and out of trouble in Anahuac. A drifter by experience and opportunist by nature, he had found he could eke out a living among the settlers through the bartering of favors and by petty extortion. Sometimes he could arrange for a house not to be searched or for a trivial infraction to go unnoticed, for a price. And sometimes he could arrange that a house be searched and contraband found, or a trivial infraction noticed and acted upon, if he did not receive his price.

This ability depended on his acquaintance with some of the soldiers at the fort, and he worked hard to keep these acquaintances thriving. He was aware of the icy dislike of many of the townspeople, and he knew what some of them might do to him if they could. In a way, he enjoyed most of the persecution of those who most hated him. In one way or another, however, he could usually make them need him whether they liked him or not. And his favors always had a price.

18

He took a sip from the tequila bottle and handed it back to one of the soldiers. He almost made a disparaging remark about the stuff but decided against it. To these men, who could rarely afford pulque, much less tequila, this was a treat and he, having provided it, was treating. He said instead, " 'At's good stuff. Best I could find."

The one with the bottle nodded appreciatively. He sipped and passed it along.

Gazing around, the Anglo saw a settler's woman approaching on the far side of the narrow street, walking slowly in the heat. She was carrying a basket of clothes, coming from the direction of the wash houses on the riverbank. He recognized her after a moment, and his eyes narrowed.

She was on the warm side of middle age by a few years, not tall but fairly well formed. She had light hair, stringing her forehead under the short sunbonnet, framing a weary, pleasant face, flushed with the heat. He knew her as the imported wife of one of the earlier settlers, and he had a score to settle with her husband. A few months earlier the man had assailed him on the street as a "cheap, worthless drifter." It had done his standing no good among the people who witnessed the incident.

He watched the woman speculatively for a moment, then turned to the nearest soldier, the one with the knife.

"Hey, Gonzales, look over there. That one's got a little meat on her, eh? Not too young, but what the hell. A woman is a woman, eh, hombre?"

Gonzales's eyes took a moment to focus, then cleared slightly. "Sí," he said slowly. "But she is Americana. But, at that, not too bad."

Another soldier, the hard-jaw, was also watching the woman now. "I have seen this one before. She has a man."

"That really don't make any difference, amigo," the Anglo said with a sly smile." I know her man, and he ain't near man enough for that one. Just look, hombres! Look at her."

"Sí, it could be so," the second soldier admitted, watching her now more closely. "But she is Americana."

"Don't matter at all, amigo." Now he put a serious note into his voice. "I'm an American, and I think you boys oughta en-

19

joy yourselves a little, even if it's with an American woman." He let the sense of it sink in, then smiled and winked. "Shoot, hombres, it's all right with me."

The first soldier took a long pull from the bottle.

"I might give her something she would like," he said, alcohol slurring his words. "But look around. Too many people. Too many houses."

The Anglo thought a moment. "Not a great problem, hombres. See, over there she must pass that empty shack. There is a good, solid door and shutters on the windows. If someone were to go around behind those buildings . . . there . . . someone could be at that shack when she passes. Might be nice in there, eh?"

The youngest of the soldiers was staring at the approaching woman now, his eyes wide, intent and thoroughly drunken. "I don't know," he said at length. "She might not like us. Raping a woman is a bad crime, even here."

The soldier next to him laughed. "I know what is wrong with Felipe. He has never had a woman." He laughed again at his joke, and the youngster flushed dark. "Ol' Felipe, he won't even know what to do."

The young man scowled and, with an effort, focused again on the woman. She was almost opposite them now, walking with her head averted, ignoring their stares and the sound of their voices. Her steps had quickened slightly.

"*Ai, compadre,*" the youngster said with bravado, "I am no *niño*. I know what to do."

The American said quietly, not looking at him, "Now might be the time to prove it, Felipe."

"I think I show you," Felipe said, trying to get to his feet. "I show her too, maybe."

Gonzales had put his knife away and now he rose smoothly, cat-like quickness belying the drunken sheen of his eyes. "Maybe," he said, licking his dry lips, "and maybe not. But maybe we find out." He glanced at the others and looked back at the woman. "Anglo."

The other soldiers were up and following him. The American stayed where he was, a grin twisting his face. He watched as they crossed the street, Felipe staggering slightly, and disappeared between buildings. Gonzales was in the lead, un-buttoning his tunic as he went. The others were right behind him.

The woman had not looked back. She walked on, nearing the empty building. In the distance, beyond the end of the street, heat waves danced and played with the sun-bleached horizon. Over on the Plazuela de Maliche a few people were beginning to stir outside their houses.

Two settler boys of about ten came racing around the cor-ner from the Plazuela, and one almost tripped over the An-glo's outstretched leg. The boys glared at the man, then followed his intent gaze.

A little distance away, the woman had come to the empty building. She passed the open door, shifting her load of cloth-ing slightly as she walked. She came even with the corner of the building.

A green-clad form appeared suddenly from behind the cor-ner and grabbed her roughly, pulling her arm back, one hand across her mouth. Another was on her, seizing the other arm. She struggled, and was bent backward and dragged toward the door. The laundry basket lay in the street, clothing scat-tered from its top. They dragged her to the door and through it, two of them holding her with firm, rough hands. Gonzales followed, reaching for the front of her dress. The door slammed, muffling the screams that followed.

The two boys backed away, turned and ran, their eyes huge and frightened. The man sitting in the shade watched the building for a long time, a smile on his lips and satisfaction in his eyes. Finally he reached for the bottle of tequila, finished it, got to his feet and walked away.

Two

Two days' ride west of Anahuac, heavy upstream rains had swollen the placid Brazos de Dios to a roiling red monster a hundred yards wide, churning with the eddies of opposing currents, fretting at its confinement between high clay banks. Debris from a thousand miles of wild valley rode the turbulent water toward the Gulf of Mexico.

At a wide bend, where the torrent had sheared new faces into the banks, a struggle for life was unfolding observed by three pairs of human eyes. A young raccoon, barely half-grown, clung desperately to a drift log which swung momentarily in the backwash a few yards from the east bank. The animal was half-drowned, stunned, and exhausted, clinging with its final strength to a bit of stub root.

Approaching from upstream was a man waist-deep in the swirling water, fighting to stay upright, lunging through the water to reach the log before it turned again and was swept away. His arms ploughed the water, thrusting him forward with each step, straining to keep him upright. His eyes were slitted against the glare of late afternoon sun across the whipping surface of the river.

Thirty feet away, screened by brush on the river's cut bank, another man watched silently. A savage grin spread across a face dark with the scars of ritual mutilation. He was a huge man. Standing he would have towered, seven feet of dark copper skin and lean muscle. Crouching in the brush, resting on his heels, he was still a giant. Black hair hung in braids almost to his waist. His only garments were tattered breeches reaching barely past his knees, crude moccasins, and a wide leather belt with a silver buckle. Suspended from the belt were a short axe and a pouch of drawn hide. In his hand he held a long, carefully wrought bow and several arrows with fire-hardened wood points.

The third pair of eyes was barely visible in a face that, at first glance, might have been all hair. Alert and amused, these eyes watched from a few yards above and behind the Indian, taking in the entire scene at a glance and then fixing on the naked back of the savage.

This third man was small in stature, homespun breeches and buckskin shirt covering a narrow, wiry body. His right leg was shriveled and drawn up behind him, and he stood on a stout wooden peg strapped to his knee. He carried a long, slim rifle of the Kentucky style. His eyes never leaving the Indian below him on the bank, he raised the rifle, drew back the hammer, and rested the long muzzle across a branch.

In the river, a cross current caught the log. It moved sluggishly, beginning to turn toward the main drift. The man in the water lunged toward it, grabbed a protruding stump of root, and thrust his other hand under the body of the little raccoon. Bracing himself against the current, he wrested the animal free of its grasp on the log, pulled it to him and pushed away from the log.

Suddenly the man's feet slipped on the clay bottom and he went under for a moment, then caught his balance and shoved back, fighting the current. The log veered away toward midstream and turned in the grip of the water, sliding downstream.

Holding the raccoon above his head, the man fought his way back to the bank and clambered out of the water. There was a movement to his right, up the bank, and he looked and froze. A few yards away a huge, grinning Indian had risen from the brush and was fitting an arrow to his bow. The man took stock in an instant. He was helpless, caught in the open with no weapons at hand. His rifle lay on a drift pile a dozen yards away, hopelessly out of reach. His knife was there with the belt he had dropped before wading into the water. He had only a small, wet raccoon, and, as the Indian raised his bow, he drew back his arm to throw it.

A crack like a breaking limb echoed above the river's tumult, and the tall savage jerked upright, the bow half-drawn,

23

the grin fading. Then his legs crumpled and he pitched sideways into the tall brush. The arrow, released by dead fingers, arched high in the air and down into the river.

With the sound of the gunshot the man at the water's edge threw himself down against the cut bank, got his legs under him, and raced, bent over, toward his rifle, the raccoon forgotten and beginning to struggle in his grasp. With a leap he reached the pile, dropped the animal, rolled across a mat of tangled driftwood, and came up crouched against the five-foot bank, his rifle cocked and at his shoulder.

Above him, hidden in the foliage, someone whooped and applauded loudly. The voice that followed was choked with laughter.

"Whenever yer ready to put that thing down, I'd like to step up and meet a fella that throws coons at Injuns!"

For long seconds the first man remained where he was, pressing against the bank, straining for a glimpse of the unseen rifleman above him. A few feet away the Indian lay still, half over the bank. A dark hole was visible high in his back, centered between the shoulder blades. The raccoon was stirring now. It made small coughing sounds and struggled to get to its feet. Then the man relaxed slightly, willing the hard tension from his muscles. He stood up slowly, lowering the rifle.

"I can't see you, sir, but I surely thank you. You can come out if you want. I won't shoot."

"Couldn't if you wanted to," the voice said. The underbrush whispered above him and a figure appeared through the foliage. "You thumbed the primer cap clean off your gun when you did that fancy roll."

It was true. The first man glanced at the empty nipple of the rifle, under the poised hammer, and stepped quickly to his pile of belongings to secure another cap from the pouch at his belt. He heard the other come up behind him walking oddly. Turning, he saw a whiskered face with alert blue eyes, regarding him coolly.

"Reckon you ain't been in this country long," the newcomer said after a moment. "Green from the States most likely. Name's Williamson. What's yourn?" The tone of voice and posture, weight resting easily on his one good leg, long rifle across his arm, suggested neither friendliness nor hostility, but a degree of humorous reserve, a caution natural to a man who didn't take much for granted.

The taller man hesitated, then held out his hand. "Matthew Langley," he said. He thought he recognized his benefactor now. Settlers had spoken of "Three-legged Willie," a farmer and hunter from the Brazoria region, a colorful character in a land full of colorful characters.

Williamson regarded him thoughtfully for a moment, then lowered the rifle and took his hand in a perfunctory shake. He gestured at Langley's gun. "Sorta got caught without your protection, didn't ye?" He turned to regard the young raccoon. It had regained some of its composure and retreated to the foot of the bank, where it was crouched, watching the men warily. "If you're fixin' to eat that thing, I believe that's the damnedest way I ever saw a man go about fetchin' a meal."

Williamson walked to the dead Indian and, dragging the great body off the bank, removed the belt and hatchet from it and peered curiously into the pouch. His nose curled with disgust. He threw the pouch into the river and, leaning his rifle against a drift log, stooped and rolled the Indian in after it. Despite his small size and the huge bulk of the Indian, he handled the body easily.

Langley put on his boots and belt and rechecked his rifle. Then he approached the raccoon. He grabbed quickly to avoid being bitten, hoisted the animal by the scruff of its neck and set it gently on top of the clay riverbank. It threatened him with snapping teeth, then scurried off into the brush. That one could tell its grandchildren how it had outsmarted both a river and a man.

When he looked around, Williamson was again regarding him with that quizzical gaze. "Reckon you ain't hungry after all," he chuckled, and picked up his rifle. "Warn't nobody else in shootin' distance little bit ago," he said, "but that shot might bring company. We be better off someplace else. I'm going south—down to Bell's."

Despite the crippled leg and the wooden device that supplemented it, Williamson moved easily as he climbed the bank and disappeared into the forest. Langley picked up his hat and followed him. Within feet of the riverbank the forest foliage formed a virtually solid wall of green. In the woods beyond this wall, however, the view was one of thickly spaced tree trunks, deep blue-green shade, and knee-high vegetation.

Langley's horse, a spunky Morgan, was still where he had tied it, and next to it was Williamson's horse, a fine gray. Both men mounted and headed into the forest. Within minutes Langley's clothing had dried from the soaking in the river to the comfortable slight damp common to this humid region in the spring.

Williamson led the way, riding silently and easily through the forest. They moved south, angling away from the river's long sweep, following a path that was no more than a game trail through the somber woods. West of the river, there was a cleared road all the way from Brazoria up to San Felipe, but there was no crossing the torrent in this area, and the nearest road here was south from Bell's Landing.

They covered several miles before pulling up in a small clearing partially shielded by blackberry thickets. The sun was down, and it was getting dark on the forest floor. Before unsaddling they circled the thicket at a distance, looking for recent sign, and found none.

"This'll do," Williamson judged. "You got any coffee in that there pack? I'm clean out."

The horses were tethered nearby, and a small fire was crackling in the clearing by the time full dark had settled in. Each man ate his own staples, jerked meat and hardtack from the packs, and they shared a quart of early blackberries Williamson collected from the thickets alongside. Langley produced coffee and a pot, and tobacco.

They ate in silence, giving their full attention to the meal, the firelight, and the small creature noises of the woods around them. Night birds vied with frogs in a marsh somewhere nearby, and an owl questioned them from a perch out in the darkness. Somewhere far off a big cat screamed a challenge. Closer by, a bull alligator thrummed his spine-tingling mating call. The symphony of the south Texas wilderness was in full nocturnal sway.

A sudden crashing sound in the nearby brush brought

Langley's rifle up, thumb on the hammer, before he realized it was only a clumsy possum thrashing its way through the thicket, going about its own sluggish business. Lowering the gun, he noted Williamson's rifle had also come to hand at the sound. They grinned, relaxed, and poured more coffee.

"Reckon I'll go on into Bell's tomorrow," Williamson said. "Cross there and light out for Brazoria."

"That's where I was going. Bell's. Got some questions I need to ask around."

Williamson eyed him speculatively. "You lookin' for something?"

"Somebody." He eyed the smaller man narrowly. "You know a man name of Chavez?"

Williamson leaned back and eyed the younger man thoughtfully for a moment. Hesitantly at first, then in some detail, Langley proceeded to relate to his new acquaintance what had befallen him on his way to Texas.

Matthew Langley had been having a run of bad luck, and he was getting fairly tired of it. A boy raised barefoot and cautious in the Illinois hills east of St. Louis, growing up with little to his name but a reading education, a good name, and an old rifle, gets used to streaks of luck, both good and bad, and eventually doesn't think too much about them.

But it's different when the man is full grown and scratching out a lonely subsistence in a few acres of Illinois upland. Then luck is a freeze that comes too early or a wind that blows too hard or a downpour that leaches off the topsoil and leaves rocks where there were growing things, or a plow that breaks on a stump. Luck like that leaves scars, some that show and some that don't.

Then there is the good luck, like losing a cousin you hardly knew and winding up in possession of a carefully folded sheet of foolscap representing ownership of land—quite a bit of it by Illinois standards—in the wild Mexican province of Texas. And the luck is tempered by uncertainty. The deed is Spanish, not Mexican. The grant was made by Spain, and Spain doesn't own Mexico anymore.

So he makes inquiries. Plats are studied, reports read, both good and bad. Some folks, it seems, do know what's going on in Texas.

He learns that in 1824 Mexico's new and benevolent regime enacted a very favorable constitution and passed laws under it to recognize the Spanish grants and convey Mexican deeds for them. The Mexican government also decided that its wild lands to the north might best be tamed by imported colonists, and opened immigration to Texas under the "empresario" acts. It was assisted in this by a stubborn and persuasive Connecticut yankee named Moses Austin, who dreamed of a rich new colony on Texas soil.

Like his Biblical namesake, Moses Austin never lived to see his people receive the promised land. But his son, Stephen F. Austin, carried on for him, and a colony was born. The younger Austin led his hand-picked community, three hundred families of them, to Texas, up the Brazos River and into their wide and fair holding of raw land.

Austin's colony had been the first. Then others came, and pretty soon Texas was filling up with ex-Americans, thousands of them, bringing American sweat and American ingenuity to the task of building colonies. These colonists became citizens of Mexico. They swore allegiance to the Mexican flag and by and large they meant it. They swore allegiance to the Holy Roman Catholic Church and by and large they didn't mean it. They worked at learning Spanish, and they worked at building a new home.

The man with the Spanish deed makes a decision. He has no ties in Illinois, no family left close enough to matter, no wife and no children to hold him, and somewhere down deep a hunger for new country and wild places. He sells out and heads for Texas. And he eventually finds himself sitting in a firelit clearing, telling his life story to a gregarious woodsman with a wooden leg.

The cooking fire had burned low. Williamson added some sticks to it. Langley shared the remaining coffee in the pot into their two cups.

"You know," he said, "I didn't hear about the law of 1830 until I went down to the docks to book passage."

"Looks to me like you're here anyhow," Williamson

reasoned.

"Well, I'd already set my mind to come."

With the advancement of the new Anglo colonies on Texas soil, the cautious elements in Mexico grew more and more nervous about their new neighbors. The Anglos could produce, all right. They hacked out the wilderness and built homes of the pieces. They cleared fields and planted crops and the crops flourished. They stood off Indians and wild animals and cholera, and in a short time the colonists were becoming prosperous.

But they were not amenable.

Mexico's government, with the passage of a few years, had begun to lose its benevolence. Settlers who had been welcomed as fellow countrymen were subsequently looked upon as a resource to be exploited. And then, when they proved difficult to exploit, they were viewed as a threat to the tranquility of those being exploited around them.

Pressure was brought to bear, and the colonists reacted explosively. One hothead at Nacogdoches gathered a band of dour colonists around him and led them in declaring their independence from Mexico. They established a nation of their own, for a very short time—the Republic of Fredonia. Retaliation was prompt. Troops were moved in and the Republic of Fredonia toppled. There were other incidents, too, and the Anglos became less and less welcome on Mexican soil.

Finally in 1830 Mexico admitted that it had made a mistake. A new law was passed which repealed the acts of immigration where Americans were concerned. Restrictions were placed on the existing colonies. The profitable export of harvests to New Orleans and other American ports was prohibited, and enormous tariffs were placed on imports into the Texas colonies. Fortifications were refurbished, new forts were built, and troops were stationed at key points throughout the colonies to enforce the new laws.

Langley's run of bad luck, he explained to Williamson, had begun in earnest at Nacogdoches when a slim, sharp-eyed Hispanic patrolling with some Mexican troops had started eyeing him. It happened at a plat and record office. Langley was at the map desk, his deed in his hand, going over charts

29

with the aid of a clerk. The squad entered, looked around, and the civilian looked him over very thoroughly, taking in the foolscap deed with its Spanish seals. They said nothing, but turned and went back out and down the street. Something about it bothered him.

When the property was located to his satisfaction, far to the west, west of the Brazos above Bear Creek, he handed the clerk a coin and thanked him for his help. Incidentally, he asked who the man was who had come in with the soldiers.

The clerk's eyes narrowed. "Chavez," he said. "*Cuidado, señor.* Be careful."

Being a cautious man, Langley wasted no time restocking his supplies and getting out of Nacogdoches. But coming out of a leather shop he had looked across the street and seen Chavez and the soldiers again, going back into the plat office.

As Langley talked, Williamson was spreading his bedroll at the foot of a huge live oak tree. Langley fed the fire again, then unrolled his own blankets.

"So then what did you do?" the peg-legged man asked finally, not at all satisfied with half a story.

"Why, I headed on west, of course. Went to see my land."

Williamson grunted and eyed him a bit crossly. Langley chuckled.

That's what he had done. Out of Nacogdoches he followed the "trace"—the main road that swept down toward the coast to Liberty and Anahuac. He fell in with a train of wagons hauling hides down to the Trinity and rode along with them. There were two wagons with the train that had carried settlers, their families, and their household goods through Cherokee country. With one family was a boy of about sixteen itching to get into the pine woods off the trail to hunt. Langley chatted with the lad's father, then set off with the boy on a side trail to see if they could bring in a deer for supper.

They had gone about a mile when they heard hoofbeats behind them around a turn. Langley pulled up, thinking someone was coming from the wagons. When he turned, Chavez and four soldiers were galloping around the bend. The Mexican grinned broadly when he saw Langley, and when they reined in, they had him ringed.

30

"To make it brief, Mr. Williamson, they had me cold. Chavez played cat-and-mouse for a while, but the upshot was that I was illegal, I was in the country without authorization, I was carrying contraband property, and while he was about it he liked the looks of my horse, too."

Williamson gazed at him in sympathy, and asked, "What about the boy that was with you?"

The boy had ducked off into the woods, and apparently they hadn't seen him. Or else they didn't care about him. The hoorawing went on for some while, until Chavez finally had his fill and ordered Langley to produce the document he had been seen with in Nacogdoches. Two of them had their muskets trained on him. He handed it over in its oilskin pouch.

The immigration officer looked at it carefully, smiled a thin-lipped smile, refolded it, and put it in his own belt pouch.

"You shall not need this again, señor," he said coldly. "Now drop your rifle and step down from that horse."

That was too much. Langley brought the rifle up level and was drawing the hammer when one of them clubbed him behind the ear. As he slipped sideways, then floated toward the hard ground, he had thought he heard horses coming.

"The rest of it is all muddled up in my head," he told Williamson. "I can remember bits and pieces, but not much.

"There were a lot of people around, and some loud talk, and somebody making threats and somebody else making other threats. Then I guess someone got me into a wagon, because I remember bouncing along a trail, and then there was a campfire. . . ."

That part puzzled him. There had been soft hands at that campfire, caressing his aching head, wrapping bandages, feeding him some sort of soup. There had been a passenger stage standing by the trees. And he vividly remembered the impression of dark hair and soft, concerned eyes. But there was no face to go with them.

He sat silent for a while. Eventually maybe the pieces would all come together.

"I be damned," Williamson said finally. He was thoughtful for a while, puffing again on his pipe. "Chavez . . . wonder if that's Bradburn's bounty agent from down at Anahuac. Understand he's a real busy one. So then what?"

"Well, like I said before, I headed on west. When I finally came around I was stretched out in a hide wagon with a feller riding alongside lookin' after me. Had a hell of a headache, but I wasn't too bad off. My horse was tied on behind and I had this rifle beside me. The kid had brought them after they'd run the patrol off."

The only thing missing was the Spanish deed, and there was little he could do about it. So, having no better plan, Langley had followed the original one. He rode on cross country, two more days, and looked at the area the clerk had pointed out on the chart. It was beautiful land, rich and wild and waiting for the hand of a man to make it yield its treasures. It was his, Chavez or no Chavez, deed or no deed.

"By God, it's mine!" His own explosion shook him out of the reverie. "Pardon."

"That's all right." Williamson was studying him. "Know just how you feel. But what about that woman?"

"What woman?"

"Why, the one that fixed your head for you, of course."

"Oh. Well, I've about decided I must have dreamed that, being out of my head, you know. There never really was one, I imagine."

Williamson shook his head. "Damn shame," he said.

"That there wasn't any woman?"

"That you lost your deed." He considered it, then rolled into his blankets. "Maybe somebody at Bell's would know that Chavez feller."

As Langley rolled into his own bedroll, Williamson said, "You know, if it was me, I think I'd head on over to Anahuac and look that feller up. Take that deed back or print a new one on his hide, one or the other."

Three

Langley and Williamson were up with the dawn and breakfasted. Their mounts saddled and packed, they continued down the trail to Bell's Landing.

Three-legged Willie had accompanied an old friend upriver, from Brazoria to San Felipe, and was riding back alone, caught on the wrong side of the river by a washed-out ferry, when he had come upon Langley's tracks just south of Fort Bend. Some distance farther along he had spotted the footprints of the big Karankawa.

"He was between you and me, followin' you, for about a mile back there," he explained as the two of them rode through magnificent morning forest colors toward Bell's Landing. "And I didn't figger he belonged to you, so I just tailed along to see what was up."

He reckoned that the savage was a lone renegade, far north of the usual "Kronk" habitats, and was probably interested in Langley's rifle, or his horse, or maybe his boots. "You got a fair understandin' there," he allowed, judging the size of Langley's feet. "That Injun mighta thought so, too."

They covered the miles easily and stopped only once, near midmorning, when they came to a narrow, rutted dirt trail coming from the east and veering off to the southwest. It was the Brazoria-Harrisburg road. From a screen of foliage they watched a troop of cavalry moving down the trail, riding fast. There were two officers and about thirty troopers, all mounted, white banderas and green tunics gleaming in the sunlight, tall shakos with plumes bobbing on their heads. A supply wagon with driver and guard followed.

When they had passed, Williamson said, "Them's likely some of Piedras' troops from up the trace. Lot of soldiers

33

movin' south these days, things shakin' like they are down country. Ol' Bustamente, he's gettin' scared."

An hour later they were at Bell's Landing. The soldiers were not in sight, having either crossed the river to the main settlement or—more likely, Williamson speculated—gone right on south toward Velasco. On this side of the Brazos the little settlement was a collection of ramshackle buildings, some in use and some still under construction. Two or three dogs yapped at their heels as they approached. A man and a boy waved to them from a field where several black men, stripped to the waist, were wielding hoes.

Across the river was a somewhat larger settlement. Docks for a raft ferry faced each other across the swollen stream. The ferry was at the other side.

Past several houses and sheds they came to a low building about twenty by forty feet, with a wide double door. By its fittings the place was a combination store, common room and meeting hall. Several men sat around inside, talking and sipping whiskey from tin cups, some eating meat and cornbread from tin plates, and within minutes after their arrival several more came in. Williamson seemed to know them all, and howdied and shook with each in turn. Langley was introduced as "a friend of mine from up above Fort Bend."

Williamson ordered a meal for both of them, and while it was fixing, Langley found the sutler and made some purchases to restock his pack. He bought powder, lead, percussion caps and a crescent of beeswax, flour, sugar, coffee, salt, and a twist of Virginia tobacco, and refilled his water cask. The purchases took a noticeable chunk of his remaining worldly fortune. He shrugged, grinned at the man, and paid the bill.

The settlers were congregated around Williamson across the room, some of them sitting on plank benches, in serious conversation. Langley walked over to join them. The faces were shadowed and solemn. The talk was of Anahuac. Some soldiers had raped a woman there, right on the street, they said, in broad daylight. It was an outrage.

The newcomer leaned against a wall and listened as other

items of news were discussed. Only parts of it made sense to him, but what he heard had the same ominous ring as other statements he had heard since coming to Texas.

"Bradburn caught th' *Sabine* bringin' in an immigrant family. Fined Cap'n Brown fifty dollars and locked up the greeners. Hear tell their littlest young 'un caught the pneumony."

"Hear about the Parish's boy? Shot in the leg trying to get some mules across the crick down to Perry's Landing."

"Likely to lose it, too."

"The Tuttles downriver and Peter Morgan an' his family are leavin'. Fed up to the craw an' over."

"Cap'n John talked to Ugartechea. Says he won't do nothin' about the embargoes. Bradburn's orders, he says. . . ."

"Ugartechea ain't got the guts to buck Bradburn. None of 'em has."

"Lot more troops bein' pulled out, back to Mexico."

"Detachment come through here not more'n a couple hours afore you fellers walked in. Watered up and lit out downriver. . . ."

"Bustamente's afeared of that Santa Anna. Pullin' in a lot of field troops. . . ."

"Last I heard Santa Anna's loyal as any. . . ."

"That wuz last month. Don't mean nothin'.. . ."

"Yessir, you just watch, that there Santa Anna's gonna wind up a'settin' in Bustamente's chair soon's he gits ready. . . ."

"Shame about Parish's boy. Wouldn't never a'thought they'd git hurt. When they say their 'Hail Marys' they mean em. . . ."

". . . embargoes. Nothin' atall from the States 'cept what slips by. We be out of provisions by fall, way it's goin' now. . . ."

"Hear you fellers at Brazoria stowed some cannons away some'ers, Willie. Reckon we might oughta do that up here, too. . . ."

The conversation swept on, around and around the circle of serious-faced men. Two Negro field hands came into the building and picked up a bound parcel, handed the sutler a smudged piece of paper, and departed. A woman in long dress and sunbonnet entered, carrying eggs in her apron. Every man in the room stood. She smiled at them, traded the eggs to the sutler for a sack of flour, and left.

"You think Santa Anna's gonna try to take over, do ye?"

"John Austin says so. Says it's a fact."

"Might be an improvement. . . ."

A shadow came over the room as a great, dark figure entered, silently, and the talk stopped abruptly. The newcomer was a tall, wide-shouldered Negro, gray-haired, heavily muscled and stolid-faced. He wore a sleeveless shirt and tight, ragged breeches that barely reached the calves of his legs. On his feet were soft moccasins with tarred soles. He carried a good percussion gun of large bore and had a big, wicked-looking knife at his belt.

For a moment the room remained totally silent. All eyes turned to the newcomer, and then to the door. The black glanced solemnly around the room, then padded to a far corner and leaned against the wall, reposed and disinterested.

Following the black man through the door was an equally huge white man, the like of whom Langley had seldom seen before. He was a bear of a man, broad and burly, at least sixty years old, who gave the impression of completely filling the doorway as he paused there. Graying dark hair fell to his shoulders from under a coonskin cap, past a face of rough-cut stone and a bull neck. The shoulders sloped and bulged under a weathered buckskin shirt. Fresh buckskin clad his long, slightly bowed legs, and his boots were of stout mule-hide with heavy soles. Two side belts spanned a broad, hard belly, holding a large pistol and a foot-long, wide-bladed knife. He carried a Kentucky rifle. A blacksnake whip was coiled at his shoulder.

Williamson was the first to speak. "How do, Britt? How's the wife?"

The big man was glancing from face to face and his eyes stopped for a moment at Langley, sizing him up, then moved on.

"Dot's fine," he rumbled after a moment. "How's yours?"

"Just on my way home to find out," Williamson said. "Been upriver." He jerked a thumb toward Langley. "Feller here come a ways with me, Britt. Name of Matthew Langley. Quick man with a coon."

Britt eyed him sharply, curious, then extended a massive hand. "The name is Bailey, sir. Do you rassle?"

The casual question was combined with a crushing grip on his hand, catching Langley off guard. But he didn't let it show, and returned the grip more or less equally. "Not unless I have to. Pleasure to meet you, Mr. Bailey."

"Damned if it ain't," Bailey said, releasing his hand. "Bubba, bring me a chair and whiskey."

The black crossed the room to where a single high-backed chair stood near an ornate, French-style hutch. He brought the chair and set it down behind Bailey, who sat without looking. At the plank bar the sutler was already drawing dark whiskey into metal cups, and Bubba carried them, handing one to each of the men. After all the settlers were served, Bubba took the last cup of whiskey for himself and returned to his place in the corner beyond the door.

Bailey downed the whiskey in a gulp, leaned back and crossed his legs. A man Langley knew as Clayton asked, Goin' huntin', Britt?"

"Over 'bout the Colorado," the big man replied.

"Bears?"

"Whatever gits in the way. Willie, you look worse'n sin with them whiskers all over your face. Ever shave 'em off?"

Williamson was lighting a pipe. "I don't dare to," he said. "If Jenny was ever to see my face she'd either shoot me fer a varmint or run off back home a'screamin'." He paused, and asked seriously, "When you reckon to be back his way, Britt?"

"Few days maybe . . . week or so. You want somethin'?"

"Just askin'. Way things goin' around here lately, might get interestin' pretty soon. Just might be a fight."

"With the soldiers, you mean."

"Yeah, or between 'em, or both."

Bailey didn't seem concerned. "Could happen," he said. "Texas was Spanish when I come here after the war. Now it's

Mexican. Has been for—what—about eleven years now. Then first it was Guerrero runnin' the country, now it's Bustamente. Things don't get better, just change. But there's always fightin'."

He added, "There's always fightin' if a man wants to look for it, or start it, and sometimes if he don't. But let me know if somethin' starts. I'd hate to miss it. What was that about this feller and coons?"

"Oh," Williamson said, "I done Mr. Langley a disservice when I run onto him upriver. He was fixin' to dispatch a Kronk by thrown' a coon at him an' I spoilt his aim."

Not satisfied with the riddled answer, Bailey turned to Langley. "You probably ain't gonna tell me about it neither, I suppose?"

A young boy ran into the room, said "Soldiers comin'," and hurried back out the door. Bailey and several others were on their feet in an instant.

"Bubba . . ."

The Negro swung to the door and out, returning in a moment to report, "Four an' that white man, Mistah Whitlet. Comin' over on the ferry. They 'bout here."

Williamson moved to Langley. "Patrol out of Velasco," he said. "Feller with 'em's another bounty agent, name of Whitlet, watches ships for 'em.

"Whitlet's prob'ly scoutin' for illegals. He draws a bounty on 'em. Favors the ones as ain't landed yet, and you ain't got a title. Gonna let him take you in if he spots you?"

"No," Langley said.

"Thought not." He turned and nodded to some of the men near the door. One of them made a circling motion with his hand. The soldiers were coming here.

Williamson spoke quietly and rapidly.

"May be just checkin', but if they spot you, Whitlet's your worry. Them soldiers might get occupied for a few minutes. Kill Whitlet an' they'll have you to a firin' squad. He's gover'ment. But if he cain't haul his own bounty, they don't care too much. And long as he don't leave dead . . ."

Two uniformed soldiers, bayonets on their rifles, entered and walked straight to the center of the room, glancing at each person in turn. Behind them came a tall, lean man, then two more soldiers who stopped inside the door, one at either side.

The Anglo, Whitlet, was a dandy—slim and manicured, wide-brimmed hat, white broadcloth suit, and blacked boots. Belted pistols rode low on both hips. He had a sharp face, calculating and arrogant eyes, and a habitual sneer. He strode well into the room, hooked thumbs in the double belts carrying his pistols, and turned slowly, studying the people there with the look of a man counting cattle.

Langley noticed that the settlers had altered their positions in the room. The big black was where he had been before, leaning easily against the wall on the far side of the door, but Bailey was now in the same position on the near side. The two soldiers there were neatly and expertly flanked.

Williamson was standing a step or so from the soldier nearest Langley, a light-skinned man with black eyes and short epaulets on his green-clad shoulders. Williamson was again lighting his pipe, and taking his time about it. His rifle dangled carelessly across his arm.

A couple of the men, Clayton and George McKinstry, postmaster from Brazoria, were seated on a bench across the room, beyond the remaining soldier. McKinstry was whittling on a piece of wood.

Langley eased back to the shadowed corner by the plank counter and leaned there. He stood at ease but with his hands braced firmly on the counter top, rifle at his side.

In the dimly lighted room the green-and-white-clad soldiers and Whitlet's spotless white suit looked crisp and colorful—and somewhat out of place—among the drab and plain-garbed settlers. Whitlet especially. He was a caricature, a type that Langley had seen often before. New Orleans, for instance, was full of Whitlets—quick to insult, high-handed toward inferiors, groveling with superiors, handy with knife and pistol, useless in a fair fight. He was a jarring note in the surroundings here in Texas.

His gaze inspected each of the people around him as he turned, coattails back to reveal the pistols. He seemed to make a few mental notes about each one—except possibly Bailey. The man didn't spend much time looking at Bailey. Finally his scrutiny reached Langley and the sneer turned shrewd and contemplative. He hesitated only a moment, judging the unarmed Langley, then moved forward, a pistol now in his hand, his thumb on the hammer.

"Sir"—the voice was a purr—"by orders of His Excellency don Domingo de Ugartechea, commanding at Velasco Fort, I place you under . . ."

He was close enough now, and Langley's boot caught him square on the chin. The man hauled backward a short yard and toppled, hitting the floor spread-eagle and flat on his back.

The soldiers hadn't moved. They were looking into the muzzles of rifles on all sides.

For a moment there was no sound in the room. Then Bailey asked, "He ain't dead, is he?"

McKinstry walked to the unconscious man and peered at his ruined face. "Don't believe so, 'cause he wouldn't be bleedin' thataway if he was." He looked up at Langley. "Admire how you did that, mister."

Williamson's soldier was staring unhappily into the muzzle of the three-legged man's Kentucky rifle a foot from his face. Williamson said softly, "Your friend there ain't in too good a shape, Manuel. Oughta take him on back home an' get him looked at."

The soldier's epaulets sagged slightly and his features relaxed. Sí," he said quietly. He signaled and the other three advanced, carefully lifted the inert Whitlet, and carried him out. The sergeant started to follow, then turned again to Williamson. "Thank you for understanding my position, Señor Williamson. My men leave with honor." He shot one searching glance at Langley and marched out, ramrod-straight.

When they were gone, Williamson said, "Well, that done it, Mr. Langley. If yer goin' up to Anahuac, you might oughta leave early . . . maybe right now."

He went with Langley to help saddle his horse, and when the job was done Langley turned and found several of the others standing around him. The black, Bubba, brought out his pack and helped him secure it to the saddle.

"By the way," Williamson asked those around them, "any of you know another bounty agent by the name of Chavez? Mr. Langley needs to talk to him, too."

Several heads shook, but one grinned.

"I know him, sure enough," Clayton said. "Worse'n that there Whitlet by a mile, and mean as a snake. Bunks over at Anahuac, but he's been out ridin' circuit for Bradburn last couple weeks." He shot Langley a happy grin. "You gonna mash his face, too, mister?"

"Need to see him about some personal property."

"Might be if you headed right on out, you'd be at Anahuac ahead of him."

Britt Bailey was standing near. "Need anything, feller?" he asked.

Langley found the stirrup and stepped up into the saddle. "Thank you, Mr. Bailey, but I'm well outfitted. Hope you have a good hunt."

"Same to you." Bailey grinned.

"Thank you, Mr. Williamson," Langley said as he shook hands with the three-legged woodsman.

The sun was still high when he flicked the rein and turned the Morgan's head back up the track toward the Anahuac road. Behind him he heard Bailey's voice, "Saddle up, Bubba, an' holler that ferry boat over here. Let's go huntin'."

Four

The Morgan was a good mount. The animal covered miles with an easy, constant pace, readily responding to its rider but conserving strength with each movement—an excellent horse for a long trail.

As he rode east from Bell's Landing, Langley noted the changes in the land around him. Upriver a few miles he had been in the wilderness. Here was farmland, scattered fields among the forests, checkerboard pieces of open ground carved from the wood with fire and axe, black virgin earth uncovered to the eyes of man. Here, he thought, was the soul of the frontier, the gentle rape of the lush, untouched soil. The settler took his land as he took his bride, with savage lust and burning love, to take and keep and use and pamper, to plant with his seed and to guard with his rifle and his life.

The settlers came to the towns to barter and buy, to talk and listen, to stock their powder flasks and fill their bellies with liquor and touch minds with those around them—exchanging news and views, plans and ambitions. They gathered because people need to gather—to converse and cuss, to laugh and dance and drink, to fight, to bleed, and to draw blood.

But then, their energies spent and their gregarious instincts appeased, they always went home again—home to the hewn cabin and the soil. To the woodsman it was the deep gray-green hush of the forest. To the planter it was the young crop greening the earth. To the fugitive it was a secret glen where his fire would not be seen and his horses could browse. To a man with troubles it was a poultice to soak up stinging memories and heal an angry soul.

This, then, was the true worth of Texas. Here was sweet land for the taking, if a man was big enough to take it, and a chance to settle that question in the only really satisfactory way—to win or to die trying. It was a man's birthright to have a portion of this land, and it was worth dying to keep it. If he didn't have it, it was worth dying to get it.

This fact was what the tyrants and the bullies seemed always to fail to understand. Their security depended on the existence of common people, and these were uncommon people. With their land beneath their feet and their families at their sides, these were peaceful, amenable people. Threaten that way of life and they would fight. God, how they would fight.

Langley had seen it in their eyes at the sutler's, as the bits of news and gossip revealed a picture of increasing suppression. He had heard it in their voices when the name of Bradburn was mentioned. He had felt it well up in him a few days ago when an arrogant Mexican soldier had taken from him the paper that represented his land, and he had felt it again when the dandy, Whitlet, had drawn his pistol. Britt Bailey had said it—there's always fightin' if a man wants to look for it . . . and sometimes if he don't.

Long shadows preceded him and he rode on to the east. The road was a wide trail of pounded earth, winding through forests and thickets, then opening suddenly onto another cleared field. Cabins were built in some of them, usually well back off the road and well out in the open. They were for the most part small houses of hewn log, some more elaborate than others, but all with a look of determined permanence—and all carefully defensible. Then more forest—wild as though man had never viewed it.

And in the forest it was suddenly becoming dark. Langley judged that he had traveled twenty miles or more from Bell's Landing. He judged also that he was hungry. He made camp in the woods, leading his animal through the tangled thickets until he found a suitable spot far back off the road. He ate a skimpy meal from his pack, boiled coffee, and, as

43

the last evening light faded, smoked and stared into the fire.

As dusk turned to full dark his horse, haltered and grazing in the tall grass of a clearing nearby, worked its way closer to him until it was well within the firelight. A pack of wolves had passed this way during the day, leaving their scent, and it pleased Langley, in a wry fashion, that the horse preferred his company to that of the wolves.

Matthew Langley was used to being alone. It seemed to him sometimes, in this, his twenty-eighth year, that he had always been so. Unlike many of their peers in Mason, Illinois, Prentis and Ida Langley had not managed to produce a large crop of children. Three were born to them and two lived. Matthew, the first-born, was just eighteen when fever swept the mound country. After the plague receded he was alone.

There were neighbors, here and there, and for a time he found comfort in them, but they too had their dead to bury and their lives to rebuild. Some, mingling sympathy with the need of a strong back, offered to take him in, but he refused. The grief that burdened him, he found, could be submerged in plain hard work. He dug into his father's acres — now his alone — to bury his sorrow and confusion in the tilled soil. At an age when young men seek company, frequenting the haunts of their peers to strut, and the homes of young ladies to court, Matthew Langley worked each day to exhaustion in a struggle against the unforgiving land, and generally kept to himself.

There had been one friend. The cabin of Moses Kraft was less than a mile away, and on occasion that fierce old man and some of his kin would visit to help him clear a field or repair a fence row, and for a while take his mind off solitude. At other times Langley would walk to the Kraft farm to share a meal or to help with the tending of stock. He came to enjoy listening to old Moses Kraft and learning from him.

Kraft could retrace every step of that outlandish expedition so long ago when Clark led a handful of American militia through the Shawnee wilderness all the way to the big river to reduce the British hold on a young nation's backside. He had met Boone and Branson, had shared a cold meal once with Clark himself in the Five-Day Swamp, had been held hostage by savages, and had killed two of them in making his escape.

And when the day came that Moses Kraft, now snow-haired and feeble, fell and broke his hip, it was Langley who carried the old man home across snow-dusted fields to his final bed. Moses Kraft had helped the boy past his bad times. The man Langley became would never forget.

That was a long time ago, however. With the passing of years Langley had continued to cling to those lonely acres, putting more and more of himself into producing crops, tending stock, and accumulating, now and then, a little bit of money.

By the time he felt able to raise his head and consider an occasional social outing, the proper time for learning to maneuver in the circles of his counterparts had passed. He felt awkward and removed among his neighbors on his infrequent trips into Mason. It was easier to return to his fields and his books. A natural, quiet openness often attracted people to him briefly, but close relationships failed to materialize. In a country rapidly becoming gentled, there was about this tall, reserved young man an air of lonely distance that most people found uncomfortable. He met a kindred spirit now and then among the dwindling few frontiersmen who happened by, but these were people who sought the far places. The mound country no longer attracted or held their kind.

For a time, his efforts on his farm produced marginal prosperity. But the elements did not favor him. Little by little, between storm and drought, the farm began to fail. Even before he left for Texas he knew he would not return to the States. And a senseless brawl in New Orleans had simply confirmed it.

His brow seamed at the memory of that brief, bitter, pointless struggle on a New Orleans back street—a pretty girl with many petticoats and a flashing young gamecock of an escort, half drunk and spoiling for trouble. A tip of the hat and a smile thoughtlessly given, then harsh words and shrill threats. These were followed by a knife across his face

45

and blood streaming into his eyes. A blind scuffle, drunken cursing and the feel of wrist bones giving way in the twisting crush of his hand. A thrust and a scream, his knife buried to the hilt. . . . A pale young man, very young and sober now in the last moments, bleeding away his life in a pebbled dooryard while a pretty girl in yellow crinoline gasped and stared, hands to her breast and savage excitement sparkling in her eyes.

Now, deep in this somber Texas forest, the memory seemed very distant. It represented no guilt, no emotional stirring, simply a fact. Like any wilderness, Texas had a cleansing effect upon the soul. In the face of raw nature only the present is important—and maybe the immediate future.

Reflecting, he had drawn the big Arkansas knife from his belt and was turning it over in his fingers, catching the reflected firelight on its steel. It was a good knife, a fine knife in fact, forged by a craftsman on the pattern of the Sheffield knives of England. Some had told him the half-legendary James Bowie carried one very much like it. So, in fact, did half the settlers in Texas at the time.

With a shrug, he found his whetstone and strop and fined the knife's edge to razor sharpness. Then he heated a little water in a pan and shaved off five or six days' growth of beard. Refreshed, he smoked a pipe while he again got used to the idea of being, irreversibly, a Texian.

Later he crawled under a heavy blanket and slept with his rifle at his hand. He was on the road again before daylight.

If Texas was a troubled land in 1832, it was also a beautiful land. The cool light of dawn crept over towering oaks and thick undergrowth crowding both sides of the road, seeping into the hidden path of the roadway through festooned boughs overhead and touching the dew-heavy grass with silver.

It had rained lightly just before morning and the moist sod muffled the sound of the horse's hooves. Gray-white tree boles stood like pillars supporting the dark green forest roof, and a million birds discovered they were still alive and began to sing about it. A white-tail buck with velvet prongs darted into the path ahead and turned to challenge Langley before disappearing, ghost-like, into the brush. It was the kind of morning an enthusiastic Texian might call "a passel o' purty an' feisty as sin."

The Morgan was full of vinegar and raring to run, and Langley let him out. He stretched his legs and hit his stride, and in a moment the forest was flicking past like images on the wind. A mile went by and the forest thinned to a meadow of knee-high grass, thickly dotted with groves of trees. A family of deer and a couple of mustang ponies, grazing together, bolted and ran as he raced by. Across the meadow a black bear rose to its hind legs, sniffed the air, looked around in nearsighted puzzlement and then ambled off into the woods.

Into the trees again, another half mile passed and suddenly there were no woods on Langley's left. The forest ceased abruptly, and cleared, plowed fields spread wide. A house stood there, this one at the side of the road, and he was at it before he could slow the Morgan. A gnarled, stoop-shouldered man lounged against a lone tree a few feet away as he hauled on the reins and halted the horse, half-turned in the road, facing the stranger.

"Proud you made it in time for breakfast," the man said in a easy drawl.

He turned his head to spit tobacco juice and remained leaning against the tree. Langley noticed that he had a rifle tilted across his arm.

"Mornin'," he said. "Didn't mean to run up on you like that. Just letting this knothead stretch his legs."

"Thought ye might a'been hungry," the man said, letting the rifle sag a few inches as a sign of welcome. He had a wrinkled face and quick, dark eyes shadowed by the wide brim of his hat.

Langley could smell meat frying and coffee in the pot. He decided he was hungry, at that.

"Git down and come in if ye've a mind to," the man said. "We can jaw around back as good as here. Some corn in the barn there if yer horse ain't been fed."

There were several; people behind the house, where a long plank table was being spread. Several horses were in and around the barn, two of them saddled.

"Throw on some more pork, Lottie," the man said. "Got another hungry belly to feed."

Breakfast was fried ham, cornbread, and coffee, which seemed to be the steady diet of Texians, along with occasional beef and such wild game as came to hand. The company ate sitting around the long table under a spreading live oak tree while two women, the host's wife and niece, did the cooking and a couple of Negro women, on in years, served. Langley was, he learned, the guest of Jeremiah Blanchard, a small-holder with two labors of land—or about 350 acres—whose place served as way-station for the mail coach and stage route linking Liberty and Anahuac on the Trinity with San Felipe and Brazoria on the Brazos.

The niece was Charlotte Blanchard, a young woman with brown hair and dark eyes—soft eyes, he thought, oddly—who tended her cookstove and ignored the people and conversations around her. Langley found himself watching her off and on. She reminded him of someone, but he couldn't think who it was. In addition, he was fascinated by her attire. She wore no bonnet, and her long, brushed hair hung free, caught at the back with a silver comb. A blue homespun shirt like a boy's barely hinted at feminine contours beneath, and the sleeves were rolled up to free her hands for cooking.

But mostly, it was the skirt. He had seen short skirts before; they were the latest craze in New Orleans for day wear, skirts that revealed sleekly booted ankles. Some came barely past the knees, in fact. They were popular in Texas, as very practical attire. But he hadn't paid much mind to them before.

He noticed this one, and the slimness of the form it attired. He hoped Miss Blanchard might join the group at the table, but she remained aloof and uninterested, tending the food at a wood-burning grill by the back of the house. Once, when she turned, she caught his eyes upon her and returned the gaze—quizzically, he thought—then looked away.

There were three other men and one woman. Mr. and Mrs. Barrett Stanger were traveling from Liberty to Brazoria and had stopped for the night at Blanchard's. The other men were drifters from up the Trinity, heading westward, maybe to Goliad or Seguin. They, like Langley, had just stopped for breakfast. Blanchard, it seemed, was a very hospitable man.

The food was good, the coffee plentiful, and the conversation serious. In Anahuac, the men who had violated a settler woman had been identified. Three soldiers from the fort there. A delegation was being put together to go to the fort to demand that the men be punished. There was talk, too, that an Anglo had been involved, a local character of bad reputation in the town. There was going to be trouble in Anahuac.

There were also comments about the number of troops moving west and south through the country, troops withdrawn from several garrisons along the eastern border. Something was definitely afoot in Mexico.

The two drifters ate hurriedly, anxious to be on their way. Blanchard walked around to the front with them, then returned after they had ridden out.

Langley stayed long enough to help Stanger hitch up a team to his wagon, and to wish Mrs. Stanger a pleasant journey. Then he retrieved his horse and led the animal around front where Blanchard, smilingly, presented him with a bill for one dollar for the breakfast, the feed, and the hospitality. He paid it without argument. Though he spoke gravely when he said goodbye to Blanchard, and though it had cost him a dollar, he was more than a little amused. That, he decided, was one way to live off the land.

He waved to Mrs. Blanchard and rode off. Charlotte was not in sight. Some way down the road he turned and looked back.

A hungry bear, drawn by the smell of food, had ambled into the field behind the little house, and the shy and timid Charlotte Blanchard was after it with a musket. He could hear her voice, high, clear, and angry as she leaned back to get the heavy weapon to her shoulder. Its kick when she fired it almost knocked her down, and a gout of dirt erupted in front of the bear's nose.

"Git!" she yelled. The bear was already hightailing for the nearest woods.

Part Two

ANAHUAC

May 23, 1832

Texas was a huge, formidable, and majestic raw country buttressing Mexico's northern civilized provinces and slashing northward like a tremendous spearhead into the mountain heart of the continent of North America. Its northern mountains extended into the general territory that Lewis and Clark had charted. Its western perimeter was a river, the Rio Grande, which sluiced hard and cold from the granite of the Sangre de Cristo mountains and cascaded down the long stretch of the southern Rockies to become a wide, sometimes benevolent stream bordering Chihuahua and Coahuila, flowing finally past Matamoros and into the Gulf of Mexico. On the east was the unpredictable Sabine River. And slicing downward, through the heart of this sprawling province from the windy plains high in Comanche country, through the land of the Kiowa and Tonkawa, through the vast Caddo realm and finally the deep forests and seaside plains of the giant, primitive Karankawa, was the central highway of Texas, the Rio Brazos.

A hundred stories are told about the name of a river that the earliest Spanish called Brazos de Dios — Arms of God. But it is now, simply, the Rio Brazos. Shorter than the Rio Grande by a hundred miles or more, the Brazos still is the legendary river of Texas.

In its final hundred miles toward the coast, the Brazos was a regal stream, haughty and imperious, majestic and sometimes violent. It was the warrior prince of rivers, and its retinue included two beautiful streams that flanked it, one on either side, as it coursed through the colony of San

Felipe de Austin. Paralleling the Brazos a short way to the west lay the idyllic little San Bernard, a tame and pleasant stream. To the east of the Brazos, also parallel, was a stream that in many lands would be named a river. In Texas it was Oyster Creek. These three streams and a few minor ones occupied the wide Brazos valley.

East of the valley lay the final two hundred miles or so of Texas, butted up against the United States at the Sabine. There was pressure here, the pressure of myriads of land-hungry people swarming into the Louisiana Purchase lands, filling them up and eyeing Texas, across the river, with hunger.

This eastern slice of Texas was cloven at its base by a great system of bays into which other rivers flowed. The Brazos, in fact, was the only river in Texas to meet the Gulf of Mexico head-on without spending its vitality first on estuaries. Galveston Bay sprawled across south central Texas like an inland sea, and at the top of it, a turreted crown, lay Trinity Bay, outlet for the Trinity River.

Where the Trinity met the bay stood a fortress, one of many established at Texas ports following the Law of 1830. This fort commanded the entries to central east Texas, and its purpose was to tame the turbulent trade of the enthusiastic Texians.

When Colonel Juan Davis Bradburn, renegade from Kentucky, fugitive from Mississippi, and a hero of the revolution of President Bustamente, was assigned this region, he was given three garrisons to command. He commanded Fort Anahuac at the center and headquartered there. He commanded Fort Velasco at the mouth of the Brazos and Fort Bolivar overlooking Galveston Island through lieutenant colonels subordinate to him. Through circuit patrols he policed the inland area up to San Felipe on the Brazos and Liberty on the Trinity—and, in fact, as far beyond them as he cared to send his soldiers. The man who had once been a thief and slave trader in the United States had found a new life and a glorious dream in Mexico, and now saw his dream beginning to come true. He dreamed of empire.

For more than a year he had been building up pressure on the Texians who peopled his domain. When the government said inhibit trade to foreign ports, he had cracked down, hard. He had slapped embargoes on all ships trading in his region. When the government had said levy taxes on imports, he had complied with enthusiasm — and with cannon to back him up. When the government had given him the power of sanctuary, he had used it to encourage the slaves of the Texians to run away, then had locked up the slaves and used them on his own projects.

He had harassed the settlers brutally and maliciously. He had frustrated them at every turn. He had added a new dimension to the immigration act by employing civilian bounty agents with the power to seize and arrest. He had imposed arbitrary penalties and capricious obstacles for the colonists, and had done so intentionally. It was Bradburn's aim that the settlers should rise in revolt, should commit acts so obviously treasonable that he would be unquestioned in the retaliation that would follow. And he would retaliate. When he was through there would be few Americans left in Texas.

Now the government had given him the ultimate tool, martial law. And as if his destiny were written in a script, the incident he needed to spark the flames of revolt had occurred. A settler's woman had been molested by soldiers, and the citizens of Anahuac demanded punishment. A delegation had come to him about it.

He grinned in delight as he recalled their faces when he threw them out. Now, he thought, let them fume and orate among themselves, and see what happens next. They will react, and it won't be long in coming.

And when they reacted he, in turn, would react. Bradburn was well enough acquainted with revolution to recognize the roots of it, and he knew exactly how to nourish those roots to full flower.

Down the hall, in his own office, Lieutenant Colonel Suverano, nominal commander of the garrison, drummed his fingers on his tabletop and pursed his lips as he tried to understand the actions of his superior. Surely the man

55

must be mad; there was going to be serious trouble here, and he seemed determined to urge it on rather than head it off.

An orderly brought him a directive from Bradburn. He was to place troops around the town tonight, to move in should any disturbance begin. And if there was a disturbance, the troops were to arrest those responsible and present them for incarceration at the fort.

My God, he thought, now we are enforcing civil ordinances. How much would the Texians stand?

Five

The town of Anahuac was in a turmoil. Drunken soldiers had assaulted a good woman, on a street in broad daylight, and nothing was being done about it. The citizens of Anahuac had long been angry with the military rule from Anahuac Fort, and now they were in a frenzy. Women stayed in their homes, shutters barred. Men walked the streets with a lust to kill, looking for an appropriate target.

Nearing the town, Langley avoided several Mexican patrols and occasional traffic on the road. He kept to himself as he rode in, noting the peculiar silence of the place. Texians were normally exuberant, boisterous, and talkative people. But these, by and large, were not. Their talk was in brief, quiet comments among themselves, and reverted to tight-lipped silence in the presence of soldiers. For their part, the soldiers seemed alert and worried, going about always in groups of three or four or more, weapons ready.

The town was a village similar to what he had seen of Bell's Landing but less settled, more ramshackle in its buildings, more random in its spread. Some of the buildings were of brick, more were of hewn logs, and most were just shacks, thrown together by passing transients conserving their best efforts for elsewhere.

For all practical purposes this was the seat of military rule for a huge area of Texas, extending through the valleys of the Trinity, San Jacinto, Brazos, and San Bernard rivers, and, in the coastal area, as far as the Colorado River. The center of this rule was the walled fort less than half a mile south of Anahuac on Trinity Bay.

Langley entered by a side road, looked around for a few

minutes, then went to find a stable for his horse. The lurid rays of the setting sun across Trinity Bay bathed the town in red and amber, and the streets were beginning to fill with people. He found a well-appointed livery barn to care for his horse and his gear. He had noted few arms being carried in the streets, so he strapped his rifle to the pack and left it, too. He did, however, retain the broad-bladed knife at his belt. The long buckskin shirt he now wore hung well down over the sheath but was split at the sides for easy access to the weapon.

The liverer gave him a word of advice as he turned to leave the stable. "Might be some doin's in town tonight, mister. Stranger oughta watch hisself."

Past the livery he turned left and came to the central square. There was a crowd there, listening to a young man with reddish hair who was making a speech in high-pitched, angry torrents of words.

". . . roaming the streets of our city right this minute," he was saying. "Free of any censure for what has been done, with no threat of punishment hanging over them, no fear that the justice of civilized men can touch them. Justice must pass them by, I say, because there is no justice. . . ."

Curiosity getting the better of him, Langley edged toward a worried-looking man in the back of the crowd and asked what was going on. The man studied him for a moment, then spread his hands.

"That's Pat Jack up there talkin'," he said. "Bunch of soldiers molested a woman here the other day, and him and some others found out who they was and went out to the fort to press charges against 'em. They didn't get no place. Bradburn, he skinned 'em down for wastin' the army's time and run 'em out."

The young man was holding the crowd's attention masterfully. He was invoking heaven and promising hell if accounts were not set straight. He proposed that the townspeople set an example by dealing with their own in stern retribution and hope the army might follow suit.

"Who's he talking about?" Langley asked.

58

"Fellow they got locked up over at the old armory. Real scoundrel he is, too. It was him that likkered up them soldiers and put 'em onto that woman."

Langley listened for a while, then decided it was none of his business and went looking for something to eat. A man directed him to a building across the square. He edged around the square, staying back from the crowd. He noticed a few soldiers here and there, staying well back out of the way. All of them were in company and armed.

Dusk was settling and a few lanterns were being lit at intervals around the square and more toward the center, where Pat Jack was speaking. Arriving at the eatery, Langley entered and found three or four people eating, while a woman cooked and served from a wood stove in the corner. The menu was pork and cornbread.

The ruckus out in the square was still going strong. Through the open door he had a constant view of milling people, torchlight and swinging oil lanterns. Someone else was making a speech, and the crowd was becoming noisy.

At a table near him sat a small, bent Mexican in soiled work clothes and his equally small, bent wife. The man's sad eyes had sought him out several times during the meal, then furtively turned away. They had finished their meal some time before and now just sat, staring out the door.

Finally the little man spoke to him, hesitantly, *"Perdoneme, señor . . ."* He turned and the man blinked, then got his nerve up and continued, *"Por favor, señor . . .* you are not of this pueblo?"

"No, I'm just visiting."

Again the man hesitated to speak, and the diminutive woman tugged at his sleeve and whispered something to him in sibilant, rapid Spanish. The man considered, then turned to Langley.

"Señor, I am Miguel Jesús Almirante y Medoya, *a sus ordenes.*"

With this pronouncement he stopped, waiting while Langley completed the formalities. Then he asked, *"Señor, mi casa . . . perdone . . .* my home is beyond the plaza, a few streets over, and we desire to go there. But"—he patted the old woman's hand—"there is much unfriendliness in the town tonight and Maria is afraid. I must ask you a favor, for which I would be eternally at your service. Would you escort us to our house?"

Langley said he would be honored to oblige, as soon as he finished his coffee. Outside the noises of the crowd built to a crescendo, and torchlight wove a crazy, erratic pattern through the square. Above the turmoil could be heard a series of angry shouts, beginning at the far side and moving toward the middle of the square. The crowd surged inward, then back. He couldn't see what was happening.

"Maybe we better go now," he said. "Sounds like it's gettin' rough out there."

The man's head came barely to the middle of Langley's chest, and the woman was even smaller. He shepherded them out into the street and along the building fronts, moving around the confusion in the open square. He guessed there must be a hundred men out there, maybe twice that many, and they were all shouting.

Midway along the next side, after they had turned the corner, the crowd opened momentarily and he could see the center of the riot. There, by the light of many torches, a man had been stripped naked and tied hand and foot to a long upright rail. Several men on a wagon bed were holding the rail upright. The tied man lunged frantically as several others began splashing him with globs of smoking tar, which they dipped from a bucket with shingles. He screamed shrilly, cursed and screamed again. The shouting went up another notch in volume. The little Mexicans had seen it too, and the woman's eyes went wide, her hands to her mouth.

"Come on," Langley said urgently. "Let's get out of here."

As he whisked them away he heard the wretch at the rail scream again, and someone shouted in a hoarse, hysterical voice, "Feathers, Joe Boy! Now feather 'im!"

Langley half carried the little Mexican couple clear of the crowd and down a side street where the man pointed out their house. He took them to the door, waited until a candle was lit and looked around inside.

"All right, now, Señor Almirante, I suggest that you lock this door and bolt that window and then get to bed. I don't think anyone is going to bother you."

"*Muchas gracias, señor.* We are very much in your debt," the man said. The woman again tugged at his sleeve and whispered to him. His eyes lighted. "Señor, Maria begs me to ask whether you have a place to sleep while you are in Anahuac. If not, we would be honored to have you stay here."

And protected too, Langley thought. Bravo, Maria. "No," he said, "matter of fact, I don't. Are you sure I wouldn't be a bother?"

Almirante assured him it would be an honor and no problem, and the matter was settled with the promise, "*Mi casa es su casa.*"

There were only two rooms—one small and the other tiny—and one bed. "You will sleep there," Almirante said, with a grand flourish. Langley looked at him questioningly. "I will sleep there," the little man said, pointing at the middle of the bed, "and Maria, there, by the wall."

It was a place to sleep. Langley thanked him gravely, said he would return later and would knock in a certain way, and left. He heard the bolt close. Back at the plaza he stayed in the shadows and watched, grimly fascinated. The tarring and feathering was complete. The form that hung from the rail, now being carried high by strong arms around the square, was unrecognizable as a man. It was covered from head to toe with chicken feathers, black tar showing in bare spots here and there. An upthrust torch revealed blood oozing from the tar near the waist, and on one leg.

The crowd was in a turmoil of ecstasy, shouting and singing, hurling jibes and curses at the punished offender, though many others were hanging back in the shadows, not taking part. Someone was erecting a high pole in the center of the square. Someone else was calling for rope.

Suddenly from a quiet corner there were shouts and scuffling. A lantern flared and Langley could see a sepa-

61

rate riot there. The crowd had extruded toward that corner and two Mexican soldiers were being pummeled by several men. Loud, drunken, cursing voices were raised, rivaling the revelry of the main crowd. One of the soldiers pulled away from the brawl and ran. The other got up, was knocked down and jumped on by several men.

The one in the clear veered past a knot of spectators and ran directly toward the narrow alley where Langley was standing. As he passed a lantern Langley could see that he was just a frightened boy in uniform. His eyes were wide and blood streamed from a broad cut on his cheek. As he hurtled into the alley the crowd surged past the nearby lantern, and for a moment it was dark. On impulse Langley caught the young soldier by an arm, jerked him around and thrust him back against the wall. "Stand still," he ordered in a harsh, low voice, then turned again and leaned against the building, languid and unconcerned, blocking the crevice with his body. The light flared again and several people looked around, then ran past him down the row of building fronts. Back the other way, the second soldier had gotten up again and was backed to the wall, a long knife now flickering in his hand, holding several angry townsmen at bay.

Several men separated themselves from the main crowd and got between the soldier and his attackers, pushing the civilians back, cursing and upbraiding them. One of the newcomers was a fancy-dressed young man with a tall hat and an ornamented walking stick. "Are you damned ruffians trying to get us all jailed?" he shouted, his voice carrying strong and stern above the crowd. With his stick he pushed one of the men back a step and announced, "By God, sir, these proceedings will be by law."

The soldier with the knife took advantage of the interruption to melt into the shadows and disappear. In the center of the square a temporary gallows was now taking shape, and the man who had been tarred and feathered was being carried toward it through the mob. Someone had boosted him onto the rail so that, instead of hanging from it, he sat upright, gripping with hands and thighs, his unrecognizable head twisting here and there for some sign of rescue, finding none. He almost fell from the rail several times, but was pushed back up each time by rough hands. As this specter was carried toward the gallows, the mob's tumult took on a new note, beginning at the fringes and working inward.

Suddenly there were soldiers everywhere. They emerged from the corner streets in solid, disciplined ranks, bayonets leveled. They materialized from the alleyways between buildings and out of the doorways of several buildings. Within a moment the square was ringed by troops and the mob in the center was condensing, crowding in on itself before the advancing wall of bayonets.

Langley felt a sharp jab in his back and spun around, then backed out into the open, his hands up before him. Three soldiers had come up behind him and more were entering the far end of the passageway. The man nearest him said something he couldn't hear and flicked the blade forward savagely, scratching his chest. He backed again, farther into the square.

A dark shape appeared from the gap he had left, passed the farther soldiers and spoke rapidly to the one challenging him. It was the young soldier he had covered for. After a moment of hesitation the trooper lowered his weapon, and the young soldier turned to him. "You are free to go, señor, but please to depart now . . . ¡despacio, por favor!"

He complied. The soldiers moved aside for him as he moved back into the narrow gap, through it and into an alley, beyond which was a vacant tract of land. The youngster followed him, looked around, shouted something again in Spanish to some soldiers coming toward them, and pointed across the field. "Vaya usted," he said to Langley, "y muchas gracias."

There was no argument. Langley went across the field, walking fast but afraid to run. There had been no gunshots, but the soldiers were armed and nervous.

On a deserted back street some distance away he paused to listen. There was still some mob noise from the square, but it was dying to a mumble. Several voices were shouting commands in Spanish, clear and businesslike in the night air. Far off, in the direction of the fort, he could hear a bugle.

Feeling suddenly tired, Langley turned and wandered back to the house of Miguel Jesús Almirante y Medoya, knocked and entered, and shared a bed with that gentleman and his wife.

Six

The little town of Anahuac was hushed and tense under the early morning sun. In the plaza the litter of last night's events lay strewn over the hard-packed earth, a broken lantern here, the butt of a burned-out torch there, a few broken jugs, some tatters of clothing, the toppled timbers of a makeshift gallows, a wagon with its tongue hauled up, a tar bucket. Nervous people went about their morning errands and gathered in knots and clusters to exchange information.

A dozen men or more had been arrested; no one was sure yet just how many. Pat Jack was among them, and Monroe Edwards—wouldn't Bradburn be delighted to get his hands on that one!—and Samuel Allen. The charge was unlawful assembly. Jack, in addition, was charged with organizing a civilian militia without authority. Riders had left in the night to carry the news to a dozen other settlements, and a delegation was being formed to go to the fort and petition for the men's release.

The man who had been tarred and feathered was still alive, but was critically ill. He would die soon.

Langley went to the livery to assure himself that his horse was being properly tended, then went for his breakfast at the house where he had eaten his evening meal. The breakfast menu was pork and cornbread.

Several other people were there when Langley came in, and he heard more of the morning news. A young lawyer, William Barrett Travis, green from the states and full of wrath and righteousness, had taken it upon himself to free Bradburn's prisoners. He was even now on his way to the fort in full eastern finery. There were varying opinions of

Travis and his quest.

"He ain't smart but he's hell for brave," said one.

"Bradburn'll have him strung up to the flagpole with that fancy walkin' stick of his tied around his head," another said.

"The man's an ass, sir, a complete ass," declared another.

"Said he was goin' anyhow to get Bill Logan's slaves back for him," another explained. "Might's well git them fellers destockaded whilst he's at it."

"They're goin' ahead an' gettin' up a delegation over to Brownerd's. Travis ain't gonna do no good."

Langley inquired about Chavez. The answers ranged from "Never heerd of him" to "Ain't seen him around lately."

Later he spent an hour or two walking and thinking down by the bay, watching mullet jump out in the water while seabirds of a dozen varieties wheeled overhead. Down the shore toward the fort a ship was anchored in mid-channel, its twin masts and furled sails mirrored in the quiet water. It was a small schooner of the type that plied this coast, carrying cargoes of all kinds. Farther down the bay a sloop was hauling anchor and dropping sail, small boats moving back and forth between it and the near docks. Miles to the south, across open water and hidden below the horizon, lay Bolivar Peninsula and Galveston Island. With no more wind than it had now, the sloop would take a day or more to reach the pass into the open Gulf.

When Langley returned up the slope and into town there was fresh news on the streets. Travis had been locked up with the rest. Bradburn, it seemed, had jailed the young lawyer on two charges, practicing law without a license and abetting slavery. One grizzled and phlegmatic woodsman summed it up nicely: "That Travis rapped his walkin' stick on Bradburn's desk and Bradburn rapped his knuckles on Travis's head; then he hauled him out an' throwed him in."

Travis, he learned, was also a "greener," an illegal immigrant, and as such had no rights in Mexico. Certainly no right to practice law. In thinking about the situation, it seemed to Langley as though fully half the people around were illegal immigrants, like himself.

Further demoralizing word came some time later, when the delegation to the fort came straggling back. They had been thrown out without an audience.

As the day wore on, Langley became more and more caught up in the troubles of the people around him. It was depressing and degrading to watch these high-spirited Texians becoming more and more frustrated. At the same time, he was developing an odd, tantalizing perspective on this place and this time. Texas was something a little more than just large-scale land and random humanity. The mix produced a strange product—a spirit that pervaded many of those who found themselves here. Subtle factors were blending here, mixing and remixing under the hot Texas sun. The flavors of the diverse backgrounds the settlers brought here with them were cleaned and honed by the circumstances under which they arrived. The common problems and common goals they found here melded these flavors into a complex, elusive whole.

The shape of the mix was the shape of current affairs—a dash of tyranny and a pinch of determination not to be tyrannized, a large dose of uncertainty and an equal measure of realization that this, for most of them, might be the last frontier. There might be no fresh starts. The texture was in their memories. There were a few who remembered the bitter struggle of thirteen outmatched colonies to win the right to determine their destiny for themselves. There were many who bore the scars of the war of 1812, who had fought on the Canadian border or in the streets of Washington, or in the swamps outside New Orleans. Of the men on the streets in Anahuac this day, several had followed Andy Jackson's broad back in the Creek campaigns and most, at one time or another, for one cause or another, had known fighting.

And at the base of it all was the land. The fertile, waiting land. The wild, hostile, beautiful land. The promised land. The land of Stephen F. Austin's promise—for each family a league and a labor. Enough land for a man to walk on, to spit on, to ride and hunt on, to grow crops on, to work and cherish and die on.

Langley's goal was not a league and a labor. It was only about a third of a league, and it wasn't Austin land. The Spanish grant preceded that empresario and even preceded Mexico itself. But the principle was the same, and he could understand the sentiments of those around him. These free necks were not accustomed to the yoke of martial law.

In all, it was not a good day in Anahuac.

Unlike the towns of the eastern and the midwest United States in 1832, Anahuac—in common with most Texas colonial settlements—was a "town" only in that it was a collection of buildings and people. There was only a small permanent population. For the most part, the people in town at any given time were a mixture of settlers from up the Trinity, off-duty soldiers from the fort, transients and drifters down from Nacogdoches and the Trace, and men from other Texas settlements visiting or doing business. People came and went constantly. But the intrinsic population of the town itself was only a few hundred people, who sustained themselves by selling to and serving the surrounding settlers, the travelers, and each other.

Of these inhabitants a handful, by virtue of concern, holdings or persuasion, ambition or intellect, had become an informal elite influencing most of what transpired here at the civilian level. By common consent the little town's people and many of the area's settlers looked to this group to provide the sense of direction and the element of purpose that the town—as a town—required. Particularly since martial law had eliminated the official functions of the alcalde and the vestige of formal hierarchy behind his office, civilian "authority" had reverted to this group.

But this same group, most of them, at any rate, were now incarcerated in a "stockade" that was really the remains of an old brick kiln, inside the fort. It was a stunning psychological blow to the town. People sensed impending chaos. There was an immediate drift toward reorganization. Groups of people met spontaneously on the streets and debated courses of action and mingled with other groups. Within hours new, informal, interim leaders had begun to surface and one of them, much to his amazement, was the little harness-maker, Miguel Jesús Almirante y Medoya. In several years as a resident of Anahuac, the timid little man had rarely opened his mouth in public and then only to voice a greeting or console a bereaved neighbor. On this day his role changed.

It came in the afternoon, when Colonel Bradburn dropped the second boot. A squad of soldiers came from the fort and posted a notice in the Plazuela de Maliche. Almirante dutifully walked across the square to read it.

Straining to see over the shoulders of some of his larger fellow townsmen, he learned that the men arrested during the night were charged with serious offenses against the government of Mexico and would be held in custody, at the dispensation of the commanding officers, pending transportation to Vera Cruz for trial before a military court. Further, the people of Anahuac town, each and all, and such transients as were presently within its confines, were to consider themselves under technical arrest and subject to questioning in the matter. Also, the roads were closed to travel, civilian access to the docks was suspended, and a special tax was levied against all property in the town as a restitution for injuries and indignities suffered by one Federico Gonzales, corporal, during the illegal assembly of the preceding night.

"By God, sir, this is too much," a man said, and another declared, "This can be settled with powder and ball!"

All the years of sustained humility faded from Almirante as he read the notice a second time. His back straightened and his eyes narrowed with outrage. The notice was a thrown gauntlet, a direct, intended insult to everyone in the town. A crowd was gathering around and talk of revolt was abundant. Men with fire in their eyes were fingering their knives and looking around for an enemy to attack.

"It is too much," Almirante said to no one in particular, "but there is a right and a wrong way to fight."

He didn't realize he had spoken aloud until, in the silence that followed, he saw people looking at him. Abashed, he started to turn away, but a huge Anglo, towering over him, caught his arm. "Go on," the man said. "What is the right way to fight, Mr. Almirante?"

Glancing around nervously, Almirante's eyes fell on another Anglo, his house guest, Matthew Langley. And suddenly, inexplicably, the man nodded to him and smiled. The gesture reassured him. In the faces around and above him he now saw no hostility toward him, only curiosity. *Por Dios*, they were interested in what he had to say.

He took it slowly, finding the words. "One does not oppose authority if that authority is honorable . . . and leaves a man's pride intact. Maybe one does not even fight oppression if it offends only his living but not his pride.

"A man must respect his country as he respects his neighbors, but if the day comes when the two . . . his country and his neighbors . . . are not in accord, then he has a decision to make. I, Miguel Jesús Almirante y Medoya"—he looked around, seeking understanding—"I love my México. Twelve years ago, when she was being birthed from Spain, I fought to help her because there was oppression under Spain. Now there is oppression under México. Again I must oppose. But revolution is not the answer this time."

It was probably the longest speech the little man had ever made, and he paused, unsure of himself. The crowd remained silent.

"To be punished like men is one thing," he said. "To be men and be punished like children is intolerable, and I think El Comandante knows this. I believe he wishes the people of Anahuac . . . maybe all of Colony de Austin . . . to revolt. Like *el tigre* he waits along the cleared path to spring upon the hunter. But the hunter who would hunt again does what *el tigre* does not expect." He shuffled his feet and looked down at them, then back up.

"This order says the docks are closed," Almirante said. "I have a bale of leather at the docks. I think I will go to the docks and get my leather."

They mulled it over. Then wiry William Scates, a carpenter with sunburnt features, said, "I believe there's some kegs of nails down there for me. If you don't mind, I'll just walk along."

The Reverend Thomas Pilgrim, tall and lean, wide hat shadowing his somber eyes, nodded as Scates moved through the crowd to stand next to Almirante. "I will go, too," he said, the twang of Connecticut in his voice. "James, I'd ask you to send your boy to my house to tell them there will be no school today. The children should go to their homes and stay there."

James Morgan's young son raced away on the errand, and Morgan moved closer to the preacher and the small Mexican, who were in the center of the crowd now. Several others moved with him. On the fringes of the group a heavy-shouldered, black-mustached settler regarded the assembly for a moment and then turned away. "Idiocy," he muttered.

A few others withdrew from the crowd. John Manley Smith and a man named Hayden walked back to the shade of Smith's cabin porch and watched from there, taking no part in what was happening. One or two others drifted away. But more came to take their places.

Thirty-eight men—townsmen, settlers, traders and miscellaneous individuals—divested themselves of all arms and marched empty-handed toward the guarded docks. A full platoon of baffled soldiers fell back to let them pass. At the docks, sentries looked to their officers for orders, received none, and stood aside.

From the docks they went back through town to the main road, some of them mounted now and others joining them, and marched past the sentries stationed there, ignoring their challenges. The uniformed men blockading the road were good troops, crack soldiers, and some of Bradburn's best. But they had not been ordered to fire on unarmed civilians. They fell back, and the motley parade of settlers passed them by, then turned at the Reverend Mr. Pilgrim's command and passed through again. In the lead were Pilgrim, Almirante, Morgan, Scates, and a blunt-nosed little priest, Padre Michael Muldoon. Langley

71

trailed along with the rest, fascinated.

As they came back through the sentries, an officer with drawn sword declared them under arrest and a brawny woodsman back in the crowd replied, "Somebody done beat ye to the mark, sonny. We're already arrested, ever' last one of us. Says so on that paper in the square."

There was no room in the fort to confine any additional prisoners, let alone nearly fifty of them. The only available jail was already packed. And the set of the men's jaws made it clear there would be bloodshed if the soldiers tried to break up the crowd. This was probably the determining consideration. These soldiers were well aware that un-armed Texians aren't necessarily docile Texians, and that they were outnumbered by the mob by about five to one. There is no dignity in defeating unarmed opposition by force of arms. There is even less dignity if the unarmed opposition wins.

Catching a glimpse of the wrinkled, determined face of Señor Almirante as the settlers recrossed the blockade line, Langley was impressed by the position this little man and the others had put Colonel Bradburn in. Now he had a hard choice—enforce the orders and shame his command, or withdraw his orders.

Messages went to the fort and back, the couriers riding hard. The troops were withdrawn from the roads and moved back through town toward the fort, the platoon at the docks joining them. The notices in the plaza were taken down.

There were few soldiers on the streets by sundown, but the crowds in town, on the streets and in the square, had increased. Groups of settlers from up the Trinity were coming in, drawn by news of the imprisonment of a group of settlers at the fort and the possibility of a confrontation in the offing.

At Brownerd's there was to be an informal meeting, a group of concerned townsmen drifting together to assess the situation. Almirante was invited, and decided he would go. Langley's curiosity was aroused. He might stop by there later, just to see what was going on.

First, though, he went to a smithy near the livery barn, borrowed a pot, and melted some lead. Using a mold with applewood grips, he cast rifle balls and added these to the pouch in his pack. Returning to the barn, he stowed his pack again, checked his rifle and re-strapped it to the pack, and talked for a few minutes with the liverer, James Morgan. In the space of a day he had become acquainted with a number of the citizens of Anahuac, and had walked along with Morgan in the unarmed uprising earlier in the afternoon. Morgan was relating how Patrick Jack's brother, William, had arrived in town an hour earlier, talked with a few people about Bradburn's arrest of the colonists, and then had ridden straight on out to the fort.

"Messenger found him 'bout noon on the Harrisburg road, already on his way here," Morgan said. "He rid in rarin' to take on the whole Mexican army, then said he was gonna set matters straight and headed out. I 'spect the soldiers prob'ly got him locked in the kiln with the rest of 'em by now."

Morgan described the man as "a sorta dragged-out copy of his little brother, all full of fuss an' feathers an' near blind as a buffaler. Got a real high, squeaky voice on him, too."

Another man who had come in with Jack had mentioned a patrol of soldiers heading in from Harrisburg, probably coming in tonight or in the morning. Morgan said, "I figured you might be interested to hear that, seein' as you been askin' about Chavez. It's his patrol that's comin' in."

He advised that the patrol would likely come through town and go straight on out to the fort when it arrived. Later, he thought, a few of them might get leave and come back into town. Looking back at the day's events, Morgan was uncertain what might happen next.

"One thing sure," he said, "We throwed Bradburn off his stride when we all marched down to the docks, and nary a one of us carryin' a weapon. Most of us figure Bradburn's tryin' to rile us up to start somethin' . . . been comin' on for a while now. Some of the boys like to oblige him, too, when the time's right. You know Bill Scates?"

Langley remembered the wiry carpenter from earlier in the day.

"Well, ol' Bill, he's one of 'em would like to see some shootin' start, but he's got his own reasons. He built them cannon mounts out to the fort and he says he can't rightly remember whether he ever studded them things down or not. Says he hates to do a bad job, but he's afeared them cannon might come plumb loose from their battens if they was to try shootin' 'em."

Morgan's curiosity finally got the best of him. "You plannin' somethin' unkindly for Chavez, Matthew?"

"He has something of mine," Langley said. "If I get a chance, I'll take it back."

Morgan thought that over. "Well," he said, "you best watch yourself with that 'un. He's a quick one with a knife. Kilt a fair knife-fighter right out there on the street, front of Reverend Pilgrim's schoolhouse, a while back. You ever use a knife?"

Langley admitted, quietly, that he had.

Morgan glanced to the big blade at the visitor's belt, then back to his narrowed eyes. "Yessir," he said. "I reckon you probably have."

Langley thanked Morgan for his information, then settled up for boarding his horse. "I'll pay you for yesterday, today, and tomorrow," he said. "That way, in case I have to leave in a hurry for any reason, I can just take my stuff and go."

"Reckon a dollar'd be about right," Morgan said. "And if ye need me any time I'll be here, and yer horse an' possibles be ready to go."

Seven

William H. Jack was an angry young man. Fury and outrage flashed from his myopic eyes and quavered in his high, rasping voice as he regaled the group at Brownerd's with the details of his audience with "that abusive, degenerate son of a spurious canine, Bradburn."

"He threw me out!" he shouted, and the rafters echoed it back. "He threw *me* out! That misbegotten scion of an aeon of dubious ancestry bade me leave without a fare-thee-well and shut the door in my face when I did."

For a full twenty minutes those assembled at the sutler's had listened in rapt admiration as the young lawyer gave vent to his rage by weaving a vast skein of resplendently descriptive oratory out of the tattered threads of Bradburn's honor. He didn't speak. He declaimed. He didn't describe. He orated. And the high, nasal rasp of his voice gave the performance a quality that even a heathen Comanche might have admired. Naturally, the assembled Texians loved every minute of it. When the young man finally ran down and collapsed for a moment on a plank bench, his profoundest applause came from a grizzled oldster in the shadowed corner of the room.

"Gee-Horsey-Fat!" the elder rasped in total admiration. "I never knowed they was so many words could all string together and mean somethin'."

Langley had arrived with Morgan in time to hear most of it. Young Mr. Jack, it seemed, had swathed his spindly form in righteousness and gone calling on Colonel Bradburn. With all the tact and diplomacy his eighteen months of legal training had provided, he had requested an audience and had begun a delineation of his credentials when Bradburn looked up from behind his desk and said, bluntly, "Get to the point, greener."

The lack of civility stopped Jack only for a moment. He decided to meet bluntness with bluntness and asked by what right Bradburn was holding civilians in jail, rather than turning them over to civilian authorities.

Bradburn's smile was calculating. "If you are a lawyer sir, are you here representing the prisoners?"

But Jack was aware of the trap Travis had fallen into and was ready for that one. "No, sir," he answered. "I am here as a private individual in the interest of my brother, Patrick Jack, and certain of his friends."

"I am very pleased that you don't break the law," Bradburn said. "Your brother and the others are under military arrest by order of General Teran. The matter is not subject to further discussion."

This was a challenge Jack couldn't refuse. He pointed out that General Teran was in Matamoros and couldn't possibly have known about nor ordered action regarding the affairs of the previous night. Bradburn's smile faded.

"Are you questioning my word," he asked coldly, "or my authority?"

"I am simply asking what justification a military officer has in holding civilians for an alleged civilian offense," Jack hedged.

Bradburn stared at him for a moment, then reminded him shortly that he had been studying the United States Constitution too long, and that this was Mexico.

"But, sir, I am referring to the rights granted in the Mexican Constitution," Jack said.

Bradburn's patience had come to an end at that point. "Mr. Jack," he said, "you have one minute to leave my office and this military base, or be arrested for illegal immigration. Take your choice."

In relating it, now, Jack's anger was almost hysterical.

76

Never in his life had he been so abused by so common a ruffian.

Hearing the account, Langley suspected that if Jack had seemed dangerous to Bradburn in any way, he would never have left the fort. There was a general murmur of comment after Jack's oratory ceased, the settlers' sympathy for Jack—and their amusement at his exploit—mingling with their exasperation at the whole state of military affairs in Anahuac. Some of them were ready to take up arms and attack the fort, the consequences be damned. They were certainly not going to set their neighbors free by talking. Others maintained calmer heads and tried to find a reasonable way of dealing with the belligerent colonel, without success.

Finally William Jack caught his breath and rose again. Stepping forward across a hastily withdrawn foot, the nearsighted young man swept his arms in a dramatic gesture, knocking a pipe spinning from the teeth of a settler next to him.

"I will ride forth from this place," he declared, "and arouse the people of Austin's colonies all the way to Brazoria and San Felipe. We will fall upon Bradburn like the wrath of God and show him the evil of his ways."

"Hang on, there young'un." Frank W. Johnson was not much older than Jack, but his stature, his bearing, and his calm authority gave him the vantage point of an elder. "Now, before you go rampagin' off into the night runnin' into trees and Injuns and such, let's have a little thought on this subject." With a firm hand he returned Jack to his plank seat, and turned to the rest of the group in the room.

"Now, it is likely," he said, "that we are going to need some help here before many more days have passed. And as you know, we already have sent messengers to the other settlements, and can expect some reinforcements soon.

"Under the law, we cannot form a civilian militia, but without organized force we have no hope of negotiating with Colonel Bradburn. Let's have each of your thoughts on the subject, and then consider it. I, for one, am in favor of forming a militia here and now and of asking the other settlements to do likewise."

"John Austin's already got a militia," a man said. "Don't call it one, but that's what it is. He'll come if we need him."

"Ol' Steve Austin ain't gonna like it," someone else said.

"We oughta get the Trinity bunch down here and surround the fort," William Scates said, "and start shootin' at sunup. We could hold 'em in there for a while."

"Hesh up, Bill," a settler admonished. "Ye just wanta see them cannons floppin' off their carriages, is all."

Señor Almirante stood up in the back of the room.

"My neighbors," he said, "Señor Johnson's words were well taken when he said 'negotiate.' He did not say fight. Were all men in Anahuac to take up arms at this moment, we could not stand for an hour against the soldiers in the fort. You know that. We are too few.

"On the other hand, even if we were a multitude and could overpower the garrison here, we would have gained nothing. Yes, we would set the prisoners free, but we would have raised our hands in revolution against our government. They, and we, would be fugitives with every man against us.

"We must not stand against our government. We must, instead, stand for our rights under that government. That we can do with honor."

"Hear, hear," someone said, and several nodded.

"That," Johnson said, "must be our point. Rights, under law, with honor. Negotiate, with the strength to debate our issue."

"Austin'll come," Morgan said. "And he'll bring men. So will the Trinity bunch if we ask 'em."

"You can't organize a militia in Anahuac," the Reverend Thomas Pilgrim said flatly. "As we all saw last night, we are too close to the fort to move freely."

"The preacher's right. We oughta get the word around quiet-like, and move on up the Trinity to get things squared away."

"Frank Johnson can lead us," Scates said. "I'd answer to him."

A man bustled in through the open door, one of several stationed outside to keep the meeting private. "Soldiers comin'," he said. "Patrol ridin' in from the north."

Langley and Morgan exchanged glances. Morgan stepped into the center of the room. "All of ye listen a minute," he said. "This feller here, he's got some private business to do with that bounty agent comin' in. Now if he goes an' does it, it might stir things up even more. He might get hisself killed, or might get us all blamed for killin' Chavez.

"Now I reckon it's his business what he does, but it's for you to say. If you want things quiet, you can hold him here. If not, then say so."

Several of them looked Langley up and down. Some of them knew, or had guessed, about his "private business."

"He's a Texian, ain't he?" Scates said. "I say if he's got something' to do he oughta get to it. Ain't our business to stop him."

Almirante was studying Langley. "You will have to fight, no?"

"I hope not," Langley said. "I don't know what I'm going to do yet."

"You'll have to call him out," Scates said.

A number of them had turned to Johnson for advice.

"You got business to do, mister," he said, "you go do it. It won't bother us any."

It was full dark outside, and only a couple of fitful lanterns lit the square, casting small islands of light on the dark ground. Clouds covered the moon and stars completely, and there was a heavy smell of rain in the still air. Few people were on the streets at this hour, and few lights showed in windows and doors.

Langley walked from Brownerd's diagonally across the square, stopping short of the far side to listen. Hoofbeats came indistinctly a block or so away, walking. He backed a few steps to where a lantern hung on a post and stood with his back to the glare, watching the street to the north. A sudden gust of cool, damp air whipped his hat brim up and chilled the sweat on his shirt. He freed the hasp of his big knife and waited. The horses were coming into the square, still invisible in the darkness.

Then he saw them, a string of mounted men and extra horses, plodding along toward him with tired steps. He squinted into the night, trying to make out features. The first soldier passed him, a few yards to the left, taking no note of him, and then the second, followed by two pack horses. The third tall shape loomed out of the darkness, and Langley saw the dark civilian coat. He took one step forward and called, low and chilling, "Chavez."

The mounted man jerked upright in his saddle, his horse wheeling partway around at the movement. The face below the wide hat leaned forward, trying to identify him.

"Chavez," Langley said, hissing it through his teeth, "you are a thief, a scoundrel, and a sniveling coward."

The man recoiled at the insult, his hand going to a pistol on his saddle. "Who are you, señor?"

"You've met me," Langley said. "I am Matthew Langley. You have my deed of land hidden in that pouch of yours."

The pistol came partway up, but didn't level. The soldiers had halted, holding back, puzzled. Langley hadn't moved. The knife was still in his belt.

Chavez recognized him now, and his voice went low, insinuating. "Señor," he said silkily, "you have made a grave mistake, and I am most sorry that you have insulted me. A dog that bites must be shot, even if it bites in error."

The pistol came level and a lantern flared, then another and another. The sudden light revealed a dozen or more men standing a few feet away, previously hidden in darkness.

"Señor Chavez," Frank Johnson said, "I don't really believe an honorable official of Mexico would shoot down a man in cold blood."

Chavez's pistol didn't drop, but he turned and scrutinized the men, whom he hadn't seen before now. Then he turned back to Langley.

"He is right, señor. It is a shame a man must be bothered showing honor to a peasant, but it is so. You have insulted me, señor. You will apologize."

"I will not apologize, sir," Langley said. "I do not apologize to thieves."

Chavez's face darkened and his eyes burned in the lanternlight. For a moment he seemed tongue-tied, and then the pistol wavered.

"Well, Chavez," Langley taunted. "Will you turn over my property, or will you honor my challenge . . . or will you raise that gun and shoot me where I stand?"

The man sat mute for along moment, his eyes blazing hatred. Then he forced words through frozen lips. "You will regret, señor. You will regret." He kneed his mount savagely and rode past Langley, almost bowling him over, and waved angrily to the troops. *"¡Vengamos!"*

The soldiers followed him at a gallop through the square and on out of town, toward the fort.

"Well, I be damned," William Scates breathed. "Thought we was gonna see a killin' sure enough."

"Didn't reckon he'd ignore that challenge," another said.

Johnson thought about it for a moment. "I'm not sure he will," he said.

Dejectedly, Langley followed them back across the square to Brownerd's, feeling foolish and let down. It had been waste of time and nerve. He had found his man and played his hand—and nothing had come of it.

The anticlimax was bitter. Morgan walked alongside him. "Well," the liverer said finally, "I guess you didn't get what you was after, but if it's any consolation, Chavez is gonna be ashamed to raise his head around here or the fort for a long time."

It was no consolation. He wanted his deed.

After a few sympathetic words to Langley, the meeting at Brownerd's took up where it had left off. He sat and listened dully. It was agreed finally that some forceful action was necessary. They would gather what men they could and go to Liberty, up the Trinity River, for reinforcements. Couriers would ride immediately for Brazoria and Bell's Landing to call for assistance from the Brazos men. And young William Jack would do what he had decided to do—ride to San Felipe and then down the Brazos to stir up as many armed men as possible to join them. They would confront Bradburn with a show of force, and negotiate for the release of his prisoners.

When the meeting broke up, several went to arrange for the messages to go out, north and west. Others divided the town and set out to round up men. The messengers would leave tonight, with no delay. The fledgling militia would leave at first light, upriver toward Liberty. Word was sent to John Austin at Brazoria that they would rendezvous at Minchey's, just below Liberty, in five days.

At Johnson's suggestion two additional groups of three men each were dispatched, one down Trinity Bay to Bolivar Point and the other around the bay to Point Hope, to watch for incoming ships, and to signal them down. The captain of the schooner *San Juan,* the only ship presently in port, went out to find a crew to withdraw his vessel quietly down to the mouth of the San Jacinto River. Without a ship, Bradburn could not send his prisoners to Vera Cruz.

A late storm was rolling in from the north; flares of lightning crisscrossed the clouded sky, and gusts of cool wind whipped through the town. Occasional large drops of rain were spattering the clay ground when Langley, Almirante, and William Scates went across to Mary Sullivan's place for a late dinner. The widow Sullivan had closed her door, but opened it again for them and fired up the still-hot stove.

The men found a change in the menu this time. Someone had brought in some flounder, and she fried the fish and served it with fresh-baked brown wheat bread. After several days of pork and cornbread, the fish tasted almost good. As always, the coffee was black and plentiful.

Rain was falling in earnest when they left again, not

heavily yet but steadily. Scates and Almirante hurried away toward their houses, the little harness-maker repeating his invitation to Langley again to share his bed. Langley said he wanted to walk and think a while, and maybe go by the livery, and would be there a bit later.

Standing alone in the darkness, rain beginning to drip from his hat, he looked around him. A few yards away, in the square, was a lantern sputtering on a post. Across the way was another one. A window down the street glowed with fitful candlelight. Brownerd's door was closed and the building dark. After Almirante and Scates were gone, he was alone in the square. He draped a poncho, which he had gotten earlier, across his shoulders and pulled his hat down low over his eyes. In the shelter of a porch he lit his pipe, then strolled out across the square. He was feeling defeated. He didn't know what to do next. Maybe go to the fort . . .

The poncho whipped across his chest viciously and jerked at his neck, and a gunshot cracked loud in the empty square. Langley spun around, trying to find the source. Another shot, this one the sharp thump of a heavy pistol, and he felt a sudden ache in his side as he saw the muzzle blast, beyond the corner of a building. His knife was in his hand. Blue lightning blazed across the sky, and for an instant the square stood out in bold relief. There was a man, thirty yards or so away, a smoking pistol in his extended hand. The lightning flash left a void of utter darkness behind it, and Langley ran, crouched, for the near side of the building. Reaching it, he sprinted along the wall, rounded the corner, and ran blind to the next corner, pausing there.

With the next flash of lightning he whirled around the corner and stopped, his arms spread and knees flexed. Chavez stood there, crouched low and forward, and a knife flashed in his hand. For an instant he stood, then pivoted on his right foot, putting his full weight into an upward thrust. Langley jerked aside, felt the blade rip into his poncho, and twisted to bring his right hand down hard

83

on the man's arm. The hilt of his heavy knife struck muscle and Chavez cursed as he drew back. Darkness descended again and Langley's reflexes took control. He dodged to the left and felt the whisk of air as Chavez's knife slashed past his shoulder. He thrust hard, straight ahead, and felt his knife enter flesh and slip to the side, deflecting against bone. A stinging cut flashed across his forearm as he withdrew and ducked again.

Another slash grazed his cheek as he reversed himself and dodged to the right. He backed a step, crouched low, left arm up and knife arm flared out at his side, his eyes searching in the darkness. He heard quick breathing and lashed out at it, a slash across and another back, and ducked again. He had grazed the man somewhere.

Backing to the left, Langley pulled off the wide-brimmed hat and held it by the crown, waiting. Lightning flared again. In the instant of its light he found Chavez and shoved the hat full against his face, blinding him. With the same motion he lunged forward, low, under the man's guard, and slashed the Arkansas knife deep across his exposed abdomen. It cost him another cut, this one on his left shoulder, but as he withdrew the blade he heard Chavez gasp as he realized the belly wound. The lightning's glare died and again there was only blackness. Rain was pouring down his face, the sound of it a roar to his ears, muffling all other sounds. He dodged to the right, circled wide, and sensed a thrust from Chavez. He dodged again and the man's blade went into his leg, just missing his groin. He lashed out with the other foot and felt his toe strike a hard place. Again Chavez grunted and Langley went in toward the sound, his left hand finding and clutching the man's shoulder. He thrust with all his power, starting low and coming up. His knife entered, ground on bone and stuck, as Chavez's blade ripped across his back at the shoulders. He yanked on his hilt and rain-wet fingers lost their grip. The knife slid from him, lost. He threw himself to the side and back, landing on his knees and sliding away, coming up hard against a wall. He grappled at the hewn log surface, lurched upright and backed again into the darkness. Again there was lightning. Low and brilliant, the blue fire flared jaggedly across the sky, blinding light flooding the narrow alleyway.

Chavez was down. Ten feet away the man lay propped against the wall, one knee in the mud, with both hands at his throat where the hilt and three inches of blade of Langley's knife protruded downward from his jaws. As the lightning flared out and jarring thunder rolled in to replace it, he slipped against the wall and fell, facedown.

Langley's knees went weak and he sat down hard in the mud, and stayed there for a time while the storm cracked and thundered above him and rain soaked him to the skin. Finally he brought his nerves and his breath under control and stood, staggering slightly. Shock was setting in, making the sequential panorama of storm light around him seem distant and unreal. Carefully, slowly, he walked to the body of Chavez and knelt there, finally rolling the man over. It took several tries before he could pull his knife free of the lower skull where it had imbedded after piercing the throat. Mechanically, he wiped the blade and returned it to its sheath.

Fumbling inside Chavez's sodden coat, he found a packet of papers folded into an oilskin, withdrew them and slipped them under his belt. The man's knife lay where it had fallen, a long, slim dagger with razor edges. He looked at it and then left it where it was. With dull eyes he gazed around, spotted his hat in the mud as lightning blazed again, recognized it dimly, and retrieved it.

There was a horse tethered to a tree behind the building. Langley stumbled to it and managed to mount, feeling cold and weak. Slumped in the saddle, he urged the beast out and across the square.

Eventually he realized that he was at the doorway of the livery barn. He pounded on the wall, and in the process lost his balance and fell from the saddle, landing limp, half into the barn. The horse shied away, then stood. A door opened and yellow light flooded him.

"Good God Almighty," a voice erupted. Then, "Beth! Beth, put on a slicker and run for Dr. Labadie! Hurry, woman!"

Part Three

Turtle Bayou

June 3, 1832

Moses Austin's comparison to the Biblical Moses is, with several broad exceptions, a fairly good one. The elder Austin was the original "empresario" of Texas colonial days. With vast determination and tenacity, he sought land in the Spanish province. With the assistance of a shrewd nobleman, the Baron de Bastrop, he acquired it. And with a coldly objective selectivity, he began naming his chosen people. Unlike the followers of the first Moses, these were not homeless wanderers, but people of power and position in their own areas of the United States. But, like that first Moses, Moses Austin did not live to see the conquest of the promised land. He passed the dream on to his son, who renewed the agreement with the new nation of Mexico and pressed on.

If Moses Austin paralleled Moses, then Stephen F. Austin was his Aaron, and still another Austin, a tough, dour adventurer from New England by the name of John Austin, was his Joshua.

John Austin was a warrior, a leader of men, a careful and precise molder of destiny. Despite the name, John Austin was no relation to Moses and his son Stephen. But the match of Stephen F. Austin and John Austin was fated. What each was not, the other was. Stephen was the diplomat, the negotiator, the careful, patient mender of torn fences. John was the fighter, the war chief, the military backbone of a civilian force.

John Austin was not new to Texas. He and several others in the Brazoria settlement were veterans of the ill-fated Texas expedition of Dr. James Long, the filibuster who had attempted years before to carve a private empire out of the raw Texas mainland—and had almost succeeded. John Austin and other survivors of that expedition spent some time in a Mexican prison following the defeat of their forces. When they were finally released, Stephen F. Austin was waiting for them. He needed them for his new colony.

The two Austins, Stephen at San Felipe and John at Brazoria, anchored the two ends of the Brazos River settlements. Stephen F. Austin was chosen "alcalde," or civilian political leader, of his colony. At his urging, the colonists elected John Austin as second alcalde.

On this day in the early summer of 1832, the two men were a long way apart. Stephen Austin was in Saltillo, trying with all his wit to hold together a shaking legislature in the face of revolution. General Santa Anna's move against President Bustamente, as yet unannounced, was becoming common knowledge, and Bustamente's first reaction was martial law. John Austin, meanwhile, was riding hard toward the Trinity at the head of a small troop of Brazoria militia, in answer to a call from Frank Johnson of Anahuac and his brother Hugh Johnson, alcalde of Liberty.

Behind them, at Brazoria, Captain John Rowland saw to the unloading of his little schooner, also named *Brazoria*. There was milled lumber for the building of a great house at William Wharton's Eagle Island plantation, furniture for the widow Jane Long's tavern and boarding house, and some farm implements, whiskey, brandy, and flour. With the offloading completed, Captain Rowland put his first mate in charge of the schooner, hired a wagon, and set off upriver to visit friends.

At the mouth of the Brazos another schooner, the *Sabine*, was outbound from Brazoria. At Fort Velasco, Lieutenant Colonel Domingo de Ugartechea accepted Captain Jerry Brown's report of cargo and relayed an order from Colonel Bradburn in Anahuac that the next ship outbound was to call immediately at Anahuac, to pick up prisoners for return to Matamoros. Formally, Captain Brown assured the colonel that he would head straight for Anahuac. After clearing the Brazos Port Captain Brown grinned and set sail for New Orleans.

And at Minchey's plantation on the middle Trinity River Robert Williamson, known as "Three-legged Willie," swung down from his lathered horse and stamped to a nearby lean-to where he bent to extend a hand to an injured friend.

"Howdy, Coonslinger," he said.

Eight

At an encampment in the piney woods, Three-legged Willie leaned his Kentucky rifle carefully against the bole of a cypress tree, pulled up a wooden box, and sat down, his peg leg jutting out in front of him. He studied the set, determined expression on the face of the young man before him. Frank Johnson had done some real soul-searching before deciding to take up arms against Bradburn, but once he had made up his mind there was no further question. Johnson and his older brother, Hugh, the alcalde of Liberty, were Virginians by origin and Texians by decision. They were both, Williamson felt, excellent men.

The little Brazorian wrapped his face around a pipe and lit it with a coal from Johnson's fire. "Austin oughta be here any time now," he said. "I left 'em this mornin' just a few hours out. Heard anythin'?"

"They should be crossing now, or soon. If he's ready, I expect we'll pull out for Anahuac this afternoon. You know, Bob," he said thoughtfully, "we maybe should have stood up to Bradburn a year ago. Maybe it wouldn't ever have come to this, if we had."

"Wouldn't of made no difference. Then or now, there's certain critters don't understand any kind of reason 'cept power. I know what's botherin' you, Frank. Been thinkin' on it some myself. We're makin' our play, an' if Bradburn don't back down, we're committed."

"We're already committed, Bob. I guess I'm hoping that one showdown will be all it takes. But I've got my doubts. How's your friend?"

93

"Langley? That young'un is rarin' to go, but he ain't movin' so good. Cut up a fair bit, ain't he?"

"The way he looked when Morgan found him, it's a wonder he made it at all. But he hung on, all right. Lordamighty, Bob, you should have seen that bounty agent. Slit clean across the belly and his throat laid open clear up into his head."

"Like to a' seen that fight," Williamson said. "Looks like he got what he come after, though. An' a extra horse, too."

"What I don't figure is why he's set on going back to Anahuac with us. He don't even know those fellas in the stockade."

"That don't matter, Frank. I know most of 'em and I'm goin' anyhow, ain't I? Point is, he's a Texian now, like the rest of us."

Johnson chuckled. "Don't jibe me, Bob. You're here because it looks like a good fight. And maybe that's reason enough. Mornin' Jawbone . . . Wylie. Come pull up a stump and sit down."

Wylie Martin and Ritson "Jawbone" Morris were an unlikely pair, but firm friends. Martin, a brawny, raw-boned man in his fifties, was a quiet individual with perennially sad eyes, a pepper-gray beard and a reputation for being lethal when riled. He carried a well-worn and well-kept old flintlock rifle with an elaborate brass patch-box inlet into the stock. Legend had it that he and his "Bess" had yet to miss an intended target.

Jawbone Morris was a peeled onion of a man. Prematurely bald and close-shaven except for a bristling mustache, Morris had been likened in appearance to a cannon swab—but never to his face. The nickname was a natural one. In a land of great talkers, Jawbone Morris was one of the greatest.

The two joined Johnson and Williamson. "If them Brazos boys ain't here soon," Morris said without preamble, "I'm for headin' on out without 'em. We got enough men right here to either get them fellers loose or bring that

94

snuffbox fort down around Bradburn's ears."

"You know better than that, Jawbone," Johnson said. "I know you and Wylie can lick your weight in cougars, but those aren't cougars down there, those are soldiers, and mighty good ones. We need Austin's boys. He'll be here any time."

"Ain't no such thing as a good Mex'can soldier," Morris retorted. "I been aimin' for some while now to see what kind of targets them pretty white crossbelts 'ud make."

"I hope it doesn't come to that," Johnson said. He noticed Martin was patting the stock of his long gun. He was well aware that a lot of these men were hoping for a fight at Anahuac. Turning to Williamson, he said, "Bob, you know Bradburn pretty well. What do you expect he'll do when we stand up to him?"

Williamson thought for a moment before answering. "Some of the boys know him better than I do," he said. "A couple of them knew him back in Mississippi. But I'd say we better watch oursel's real close. That colonel is mean as a snake, and he's tricky. And what may be most important, like him or not, he's got a powerful lot of guts. You know, a man don't get to be a colonel without somethin', and he's got more'n his share of that somethin', or he wouldn't be where he is right now.

"Now, what he'll do depends on what we do. I figger so far we're doin' just what he was hopin' we would—armed resistance—only we got one up on him by gittin' organized first. There's gonna be more of us there than he counted on."

He relit the pipe, glancing at all three of them.

"Way I figger is, you fellers at Anahuac was supposed to get so riled up you'd just up and attack the fort and Devil take the hindmost . . . like Jawbone here's wantin' to do. In that case, I expect you'd have woke up all of a sudden an' found yerselves outmanned, outgunned, an' outthunk. An' I believe he'd a' had them soldiers shoot ye down to the last man.

"So instead of that, ye pulled back here an' got reinforcements comin' in from Brazoria. That," he said, with a grin at Morris, "makes it a different kind of shootin' match. We cain't take Anahuac Fort with rifles and muskets, but neither can they just come marchin' out and take us.

"I reckon he'll deal with us," he said to Johnson. "He'll have to. But I don't expect I'd put much coin on what he says bein' what he means."

"Ye could say that about any of 'em," Jawbone Morris spat. "They ain't a honest officer or soldier or politician in all Mexico. And that's a fact, sir, by God."

"Why do you think he's stirred all this up?" Johnson asked seriously. "And why do you say he'd have us wiped out if he could?"

"Partly matter of principle," Williamson said. "Sorta the same reason we're all here right now. I don't b'lieve there's a man in the bunch here that'd risk his drawers for ol' Monroe Edwards, that thievin' snip . . . nor for Travis and a couple of them others, either. But they're Texians and so are we, so we got to go help 'em.

"Same way with Bradburn. He's got hisself a little empire goin' here, if he can keep it, but what he's got in mind don't set well with Texians, and he knows it. If we wuz Mexican peones like down aroun' Saltillo, we'd kowtow to him an' he'd order us around an' ever'body be happy. But we just ain't built that way. So he wants to run us out of this territory, any way he can."

"Some of them peones gets a mite mean when they gets riled, too," Martin said. "I seen some of 'em in the war with Spain. Damn good fellers not to be in front of."

"Shore, but maybe they don't rile so easy," Williamson said. "And as for shootin' you out of hand," he added, "Bradburn's got to be in a hurry to trim down this here area. They's a war comin' in Mexico, an' ever'body knows it. Most of the big soldiers is choosin' up sides right now, an' Bradburn's caught in the middle. He cain't guess how things gonna come out no more'n we can. Maybe Santa Anna's gonna take over. Maybe Bustamente'll have his head.

"But ye see, if Bradburn can come up with a real power base here . . . if he can call all the shots his way . . . then he'll be in position to dicker with whosoever in hell happens to be runnin' Mexico on the next go-'round.

"That," he said with finality, "is how I calculate it."

Johnson thought it over for a moment. "And that," he said, "might just be how it is. The way you see things, Bob, if you come out of this scrape with your skin still wrapped around you, you oughta go into politics."

"Hell," Williamson spat. "I'd sooner steal hosses."

"Politics is the best way to steal anythin'," Jawbone said. "I ain't sure but what runnin' fer office beats hell outa' makin' a honest livin'."

There was a stir at the far side of the camp, and Morris let out a whoop. "That's them, shore as shootin'. Austin's here and he brung half of Texas with him."

The four rose and walked toward the center of the sprawling camp. All around them, men who had been sprawled in the shade now were on their feet and moving in to meet the newcomers. The party riding in had about fifty men in all, and the man in the lead stood out among them like an oak tree in a pine grove. John Austin was a solid man, bull-shouldered in his buckskin shirt and sharp-eyed beneath the brim of his wide hat. One of several present survivors of the Long Expedition into Spanish Texas, Austin had returned to the country as a settler at the insistence of his friend and namesake, Stephen F. Austin. He had quickly become a man of note among the settlements and, ultimately, a leader of these frontier people. This big New Englander was, Williamson thought, cut from the same cloth as those around him, but maybe with a finer pair of shears.

The party rode in at ease, greeting friends among the Trinity crowd, shouting back and forth, laughing, exchanging jokes and renewing acquaintances. Some of them led pack animals loaded with supplies. Austin walked his horse to where Johnson and the others stood, and raised a hand in greeting. "Howdy, Frank . . . Wylie . . . mornin', Jawbone. See ye made it all right, Willie." He looked around the camp, taking in each detail. "Seems you men are loaded for bear. How are things?"

"Hotter'n two kinds of hell, Cap'n." Johnson stepped up to take the reins. "Glad you boys could make it."

Austin stepped down. "Wouldn't miss it. You all know the men with me?"

"Shore do," Johnson said, stepping forward to shake hands with some of them. There was Henry Brown, steady and careful, Kentucky-bred, second in command to Austin in the Brazoria militia. Tough, scrappy young William J. Russell was there, too, his ever-present half-cocked smile spreading across his freckled face. George McKinstry, Brazoria's postmaster, stepped down from his mount and tied his rifle across the saddle. In a slow Georgia drawl he howdied Morris and Martin and nodded at Williamson. He was introduced to Johnson and shook hands. "John," he said, turning to his chief, "I'll see to gettin' the men fed. We got time to break open a keg of whiskey?"

"Might as well," Austin replied. "Way I remember it, these Trinity hooraws are usually thirsty." Austin turned back to Johnson.

"Looks like it, for a fact. We've got to get those fellas out of there, John. If Bradburn gets a chance to ship them off, he'll see to it they never make it back. We figured with you and your boys here we can raise the ante on him."

Morris glanced around toward the edge of camp, where the Brazorians had come in, and now stared hard, a look of disbelief on his face. The others looked, too, and Austin chuckled, then laughed. A short distance away a ruckus was going on at a campfire where a small banty-rooster of a man was backing away from several irate woodsmen. There was a spilled beanpot by the fire, and one of the little man's boots was dripping beans and juice.

Morris starred, aghast, then sputtered, "I be damned. I be double-damned if that li'l hootinjay ain't gone and high-stepped square in the middle of them fellers' cookin' pot."

"Ain't that Pat Jack's brother?" Martin asked.

"Yep," Austin laughed, "that's William. Bill, why don't you go bring him in before those Trinity boys take his scalp for a watchfob."

As Russell strode toward the trouble spot, Williamson said, "Funny little feller, blind as a bat he is, but don't never underrate him. You know, Jawbone, a feller challenged young Jack there to a duel one time, back in the States, and you know what he done?"

"Come to Texas right then, most likely," Morris said blandly.

"Not by a durn sight. It was his choice of weapons, so he chose shotguns . . ." he paused for effect, "across a dining table."

Morris squinted at him a moment, then decided he wasn't joking. "So what happened? They kilt each other, I imagine."

"The other fella changed his mind," Williamson said.

Russell returned with William Jack in tow. Jack was fussing in a high voice about "the dang places to put a fire, right in—" but he brightened when he saw Johnson "I told you I'd bring in a bunch from the Brazos," he said. "When I set out to do something, I do it, Mr. Johnson."

"Well, now, William, I admit you helped spread the word," John Austin said bluntly, "but that isn't exactly why we're all here. We came because these fellas needed some help."

"He's right, Mr. Jack," Morris said. "A Texian's a neighbor, like him or not. An' when one's in trouble we're all involved. Mighty good thing to remember in these parts."

Jack's neck was turning red. "Well, damn it, my brother's in that brick kiln," he said.

"Don't worry, William." Austin softened his voice. "There's more than a hundred men here now and more at Anahuac. I expect Bradburn will listen to reason when we get there."

99

"I don't think he will." Jack's anger wasn't going to die quickly. "I don't think that overbearing excuse for a baboon will ever change his mind till someone shoots him through the head."

Wylie Martin was cradling his old rifle across his arms. "Amen," he said. Young Bill Russell's smile changed to a grin of anticipation.

George McKinstry returned at that moment, munching on a tortilla filled with beans. "The men all been fed," he told them, "and a cup of whiskey each. You all want some, you'd better get it now."

They ate standing, quickly and hungrily, while Austin and Frank Johnson made plans. Austin would lead the expedition, direct the march and take charge of encampments. In case of a fight, he would command. Johnson would direct scouting and would be in charge of negotiations at the fort. They then surveyed the camp briefly as packing and harnessing got under way.

Adjacent to the camp in the north clearing was a band of wagons, immigrants passing through to the west. They were also packing to move out. The travelers had kept to themselves, except for a few young bucks who had got wind of an adventure and come over to join the Texians' little army. Johnson had sent the younger ones back to their families. A few of the older ones he had allowed to remain, with the promise that when negotiations at Anahuac were done they would leave as a group, catch up with the wagons, and be a little more obedient to their parents in the future.

"You have any sick or injured here?" Austin asked him.

"Three in all. One old feller down with chest pains, a youngster with a copperhead bite on his foot, and a man cut up in a knife fight with a bounty agent. They're not any of 'em fit to ride or run."

Austin considered it. "Best we leave them," he decided. "But away from here. If things go wrong, the army will be backtracking for stragglers."

Walking to the wagon caravan, Austin found the

trailmaster and arranged passage for the three men, with their goods and gear, west to Blanchard's way station on the road to Bell's Landing. They could be tended there until they were fit to travel again.

"They're not going to like it," Johnson mused. "All three of them are aiming to go to Anahuac with us."

"Tell them this is a direct order," Austin said. "Tell them if they intend to join this militia they'll obey the captain. And if not, they'd better go someplace else."

Johnson chose his scouts for the march, picking Three-legged Willie and a Trinity militiaman, O.D. Brenan, to ride forward point.

"Work out ahead of us a ways, Mr. Williamson," he said. "I don't expect any trouble, but Bradburn's reassigned the patrols and the road will be guarded at some point. Brenan, you know the road better, but Williamson's been scouting longer. You follow his lead."

Some of the men around them gave way to banter as the peg-legged woodsman and the Trinity man rode out.

"Hoo, boy! I tell you, any so'jer point a musket at Brenan's liable to get it bent around so's it'll shoot back at him!"

"That's nothin'. Just imagine bein' stomped on with that stick Willie wears!"

Williamson regarded Brenan soberly as they rode out, and Brenan grinned back at him. Beyond earshot of the camp Williamson said, "I'm wonderin', Mr. Brenan, whether we oughta stand for that kind of hoorawin' or whether we oughta do somethin' about it."

"I believe we should do somethin' about it, Mr. Williamson, sure enough. Got any ideas?"

"Nope. Not right now, but somethin' might turn up. We'll think on it."

They let their horses stretch into a lope as they entered the forest at the edge of camp. A mile or so out, Williamson took a long lead while Brenan held back, out of sight but within hearing. It was an Indian maneuver—two scouts at an interval, the first to see anything visible, the second to see what might have been hidden when the first went by. In this manner they covered miles steadily, pacing themselves, occasionally looking down side trails and exploring for sign.

The sun was halfway down the sky when Williamson, nearing a bend in the trail, reined in and sat silent for a moment, listening. Dismounting, his rifle at the ready, he advanced on foot around the bend, moving like a forest shadow. Past the bend he left the trail, faded into the underbrush and came in sight of a clearing. There was a Mexican patrol there, the soldiers lounging around, many of them asleep. Taking his time he counted them, placed them in his mind, located their horses nearby and squinted to determine how far vision could penetrate the dense forest all around. Satisfied, he slipped back to the trail and to his mount. A hundred yards or less up the trail he met Brenan and gestured for silence.

Sidling up close, Williamson spoke in a low voice. "Mr. Brenan, you still recollect that hoorawin' some of our friends gave us back there?"

"Yes sir, Mr. Williamson, I do for a fact."

"Well, sir," said Three-legged Willie, "now I got an idea."

Several miles north of Anahuac, at a bend where the trail from Liberty neared upper Trinity Bay, the midafternoon shadows were lengthening in the pine and sweetgum forest when Three-legged Willie Williamson and Bull Brenan turned east off the trail. They circled south and west several hundred yards and then separated, moving silently back toward the Mexican army patrol taking its siesta in a grove of tall pines.

There were no sentries about the camp, and no real attempt at watchfulness. If the soldiers were aware of the stirrings at Anahuac or the gathering of armed men north of them, they were not worried. No one was close to their position yet.

102

Teniente Miguel Nieto, officer in the Army of the Republic of Mexico, sat with his back to a pine bole, his hat, pistol, and sword at his side. Around him some of his men slept, others dozed in the shade. But Teniente Miguel Nieto was not asleep. At the moment, he was feeling disgusted with his lot in life.

Educated in Spain, the second son of a family of wealth and position, he took fierce pride in his commission as an officer and felt demeaned to have been ordered out into this dismal jungle on a fool's errand. Here he sat, a direct descendant of the Conquistadores, waiting in the wilderness for an imaginary threat from a pathetic bunch of Yankee farmers. What kind of an army was this, anyway? Farther into Mexico, troops were moving into position for serious warfare. General Santa Anna had broken with El Presidente and there would be war. There would be honor and glory for a young officer on the right side — he wasn't certain which side he considered "right" yet — and careers would be built on the decisions made in the field.

But the field was far away. Here in Texas, the only conflict was a squalid civil disturbance that could come to nothing. Nieto could see the days slipping past him, lost opportunities sliding into oblivion. That Yankee dog Bradburn was at fault, he thought. Such a man should not command a garrison of Mexico. Even here in this wilderness it was a loss of honor for Mexico to be represented by such. Now, Colonel Suverano — there was an officer and a gentleman. But he was only second in command. The Yankee Bradburn ruled in Texas.

The peaceful afternoon was shattered by a rustling of brush and a badly accented voice. *"Alto, hombres, por favor."*

The command was not loud, but distinct and authoritative. Robert Williamson, astride a sleek gray, rode out of a clump of brush and boldly into the encampment. "Raise your hands, gentlemen. You are surrounded."

Before Nieto or his men could get to their feet there was a rustling in the brush on the other side of the clearing and a gruff voice called in English, "Hold your fire, men. Don't shoot unless you have to."

Again there was movement and a slightly different voice said, "One of you men get out there with Mr. Williamson and secure their weapons." A moment later the brush parted and a large, pleasant looking man on a palfrey rode into the clearing.

Williamson, meanwhile, had ridden directly up to the lieutenant, who had risen and was holding his sword and pistol in his hands. The Texian reached down and took the pistol from the officer, who seemed to awaken suddenly and grasped his sword protectively with both hands. "I will surrender my sword only to your superiors," he said, drawing himself up tall. Brenan, meanwhile, was quickly and carefully collecting the firearms and blades of the eight soldiers in Nieto's command.

"By all means, Lieutenant. By all means," Williamson said with a smile.

Methodically and with no wasted time, Williamson and Brenan got the stunned soldiers assembled, mounted, and moving north along the trail. They had gone several hundred yards before Nieto suddenly realized that no more Texians had joined them. In a moment the humiliating truth hit him with appalling force. His patrol had been captured—without resistance—by two civilians. His hand jerked to his sword and he saw Williamson's musket come up to cover him.

"No need for that," the Texian said. "You just keep that thing 'til we get back to our 'superiors,' like you said."

Brenan and Williamson exchanged wry grins as they herded their charges north along the trail. It was occurring to both of them that they had just won the first military engagement between Texas and Mexico. Both of them knew it would not be the last.

Two miles up the trail Williamson and Brenan, with their captives, came upon Austin's party. The man leading the main body of the Texian volunteers stopped his horse in its tracks, gawked at the group coming toward him, then turned and spurred back along the trail, shouting as he went. "Hey, everybody! Hey! Williamson and Brenan . . . they're comin' with about half the damn Mexican army!" Minutes later the scouts were herding their captives into the admiring ranks of Texians and recounting their conquest to Johnson and John Austin.

"Their arms and supplies and some extra horses are still where we found 'em," Williamson said. "Couple miles on down the trail."

Austin nodded appreciatively and exchanged glances with Johnson. This was good, they both realized. This was excellent, in fact. A refinement of plan was already taking shape in the minds of the two captains. The capture of a patrol of regulars, caught completely off guard, signified several things of importance. First, they were ahead of the game by at least one move. This patrol had not been on the alert, expecting trouble. They had been at ease and careless. This meant Bradburn either didn't expect them to march on Anahuac, or at least didn't expect them so soon. Further, this was not a defensive unit, just a periphery patrol. It just might be that Bradburn didn't realize yet that they were here at all.

"Is this all of them?" he asked.

"Yes, sir," Williamson said. "Every one. None of them got away."

They would be seen and reported before they reached Anahuac, of course, but maybe not by much. The captured lieutenant was brought forward. He glared at them, waiting.

"I'll take that sword, Lieutenant," Johnson said. "You won't be needing it for a while."

The officer regarded the mounted man before him, a civilian dressed in pinstripe pants, a blue cotton shirt, mulehide boots, and a buckskin jacket. "You are an officer?" he asked. "You are the leader of these"—he gestured with blazing contempt—"these soldados?"

"That I am," Johnson said. He moved forward and unceremoniously relieved the man of his sword. What is your name, Lieutenant?"

"Nieto. Miguel Nieto, Teniente, Army of the Republic of Mexico."

Johnson could see the indignation and the humiliation in the man, and for a moment felt sympathy. Those, however, were the fortunes of war.

Nine

Austin's men camped that night at Turtle Bayou just above its junction with the Trinity River. They stopped early to take advantage of the heavy cover and isolated region only a short ride now from Anahuac. Johnson was worried, too, about the troop. The command he shared with Austin was growing larger and larger as they marched. Men were joining up along the way, and some of them were not known to him. Some of them were old settlers, but some were newcomers and drifters—a very mixed lot. There would be trouble keeping this little army in line, he knew. He found John Austin in agreement.

If Stephen F. Austin had one outstanding talent, above all others, it was his genius in selecting and combining people. Selecting them for special skills, abilities, and talents beyond the ordinary, then combining his selections into a working team. Austin had used this genius to fulfill his father's dream of a colony on Texas soil. And among those he had hand-picked was John Austin.

A veteran Indian fighter and soldier, the commander of the Brazoria militia was one of the finest border captains of his time. He knew military tactis, and he knew men. And he knew how to use them both together.

"The differences between a militia and an army are two," he had told Frank Johnson. "One can work for you, and one can work against you.

"In a regular army all the determination is at the top. The officers make the decisions and meet the challenges; the soldiers just follow orders. A soldier is a tool to be used. In a militia, however, the determination runs the full depth. Every man in the company is working toward the same goals, or else they aren't there at all. This makes a good irregular, volunteer militia, man for man the equal of any army that's ever been fielded. A militiaman wants to win, for reasons that are his own. A soldier just wants to be fed and to stay alive.

"On the other hand, what an army has is discipline. When a soldier is given an order he obeys it. When a thousand soldiers are given an order they obey it—all without hesitation and all at once. Only one man—the man at the top—has to decide.

"This," he continued, "is what the army has that we don't. Discipline. It runs deep in those soldiers while we"—he indicated the chaos around him where men were building fires, tethering stock, cutting meat, joking, arguing, and milling around—"we hardly have it at all."

The big Brazorian lighted his pipe and accepted coffee from a fresh-faced youngster making the rounds with a huge steaming pot. "Make no mistake, Frank," he said at last. "If we should have to line up on a field with Bradburn's men, man for man, we would be lost. Our best bet is the chance that he won't realize our weakness. Bradburn's most likely to think in terms of numbers. And," he added with a chuckle, "we certainly seem to have numbers."

Near sundown two or three groups of stragglers from Anahuac came up the trail to join them. The men at the fort had learned that they were coming. Guards were subsequently placed around the encampment to make sure the little army would not be taken by surprise.

Austin, Johnson, and several others stood on a shoulder of ground at the south edge of the ring of cooking fires. Across the way someone had broken out a keg of brandy, and the camp was becoming raucous. In the center of camp the Reverend Thomas Pilgrim and Father Michael Muldoon were shooing revelers away from the guarded prisoners. The little priest and the tall pastor conferred for a moment with Benjamin Tennel; then the three of them walked across to where the captains were gathered.

Austin turned toward them, and a gunshot split the sound of the camp. A youth standing between Austin and Frank Johnson, just in front of Wylie Martin, gasped and fell. Fifty yards away a man with a smoking rifle dodged around a campfire and ran for a saddle horse. In the momentary confusion, the man reached his saddle and spurred for deep woods—just as William Russell strode out of those same woods, buckling his belt. The nervous horse shied and the man fell. In an instant Russell had him pinned to the ground.

The gang who dragged the man back to the captains was not a sympathetic group. He was roughed and tumbled when they shoved him forward, stripped of weapons and whimpering. He stumbled and went to one knee. Old Wylie Martin was bending over the dead boy in the midst of the group, and when he looked up his eyes were slitted and cold. The shooter regained his feet and Wylie stepped forward and hit him in the mouth. The man toppled.

The dead volunteer, a bullet through his heart, was a youngster of barely seventeen, the son of one of Martin's closest friends.

The man on the ground was struggling to get up again. Jawbone Morris pulled him to his feet and braced him firmly in front of Austin and Frank Johnson. "You jest stand here real quiet, now," he hissed, "or I might break your damned neck."

Long seconds passed while Austin inspected the man, coldly and without emotion. He then pulled out a pipe, filled it, lighted it, and puffed several times before speaking.

"Now, then," he said finally, "we'll talk. Who are you?"

The man slouched and looked away. Jawbone Morris jerked him upright and hissed, "You ever seen a man's ear notched with a sharp knife, sonny?"

Benjamin Tennel had been studying the culprit. Now he turned to Austin. "I know who he is. His name is Hayden. He's a drifter. Came into Anahuac just a few days ago."

Austin hadn't taken his eyes off the man in Morris's grasp. "Why did you kill that boy?" he asked. The man remained silent, his eyes downcast.

"The boy was standing between you and Frank, John," Father Muldoon said. Austin nodded. "You might be right, Padre.

"All right, Hayden." He put a fist under the man's chin and raised his startled eyes level with his own. "Do you tell us what that was all about, or do I turn Wylie and Jawbone loose on you?"

Hayden swallowed hard, searching the faces around him for a sign of sympathy and finding none. The sun was going down. A shaft of red light through the trees hit the man's face, lighting eyes glazed with fear. He looked at Muldoon and gasped, "Can't you help me? You're a priest." The padre met his eyes and shook his head. Hayden lurched from Morris's grasp and fell to his knees in front of Pilgrim. "For God's sake, brother, help me," he pleaded.

"God's business is your soul, Brother," Pilgram said sadly. "Not your neck."

"Talk, Hayden," Austin said.

"I can't, Captain. I can't."

"Then none of us can help you."

"If I talk, will you save me?" The man was trying hard to keep from shaking.

"If you talk, you'll die easier."

Hayden had made his best deal. "It was Smith," he said finally. "He paid me. I was after you."

Austin considered this. "There are about a dozen Smiths in the colony," he said finally. "Which one paid you?"

"John . . . John M. Smith . . . of Anahuac."

"John M. Smith? I don't believe it," Bill Pettus interrupted.

"Well, I believe it," Morris said. "Smith is a right good friend of Bradburn. Keeps him informed on what's goin' on in town."

110

"That's pretty strong," Pettus said. "We don' know that for sure."

"I remember this man," Tennel said. "He has been around with Smith. 'Course that doesn't prove he's workin' for him now."

"I don't know," Wylie Martin rubbed his jaw. He was kneeling again by the dead youth. "A man can get pretty honest when he's about to be carved up."

"Yes, but is he honest or just trying to keep from getting carved?" Pettus said. "God, sir, let's be sure we go after the right man. We've already got this one."

"I'm with Wylie," Morris said. "I think he's tellin' the truth. Smith musta been behind this."

"But Smith's an American, like most of us here," Pettus said. "Would he have had a fellow American murdered?"

Jawbone Morris turned on him in a rage. "What the hell do you think that black-hearted Bradburn is, sir, an African? Dammit, man, Americans are just like anybody else. They's bad ones, and Smith's one."

"Like Bradburn," Martin agreed.

Through it all, Austin had stood at ease, studying the cringing Hayden. Now he asked Father Muldoon, "Is he telling the truth, Padre?"

"I think he is," Muldoon said quietly.

"Mr. Pilgrim?"

"I agree."

"All right. Hayden, you will not be tortured." He turned to Hugh Johnson. "Hugh, this is in your jurisdiction as alcalde, and as this man's intended victim I'd rather not judge him. What do you say?"

The alcalde was silent for a moment, then looked at the men around him. Most of the camp's company was present now. "We have put ourselves under the command of a militia," he said finally, "with my brother and Captain Austin in charge. This is not a legal militia, under martial law, but I believe . . . we must all believe . . . we are morally right to do so. What we are doing is right, and necessary, but only so long as we conduct ourselves as a

111

proper militia. We must not function as a mob.

"A mob might tear this man apart, or it might let him go. We can do neither. Right here, in this place, we must determine how we are to mete justice, and how to keep order among ourselves." He paused, and looked around in the silence. Justice must be dispassionate, and it must be prompt. And it must be gauged according to the crime."

"For God's sake," Hayden screamed, "You're sentencing me to death. You can't do this!" He looked wildly around him and his voice trailed off in silence. "You can't . . ."

"You killed a man with your rifle. You will die by the rifle. Is this satisfactory to the military authority here present?"

Both Frank Johnson and John Austin nodded.

"Then as executive officer of this militia command I hereby pass this sentence, and as civilian alcalde of Liberty I uphold it. There is no further appeal." Johnson turned and walked away.

Four men grabbed Hayden and dragged him to the bank of the bayou. They stood him there, hands tied behind his back and a blindfold on his eyes. Father Muldoon crossed himself and the Reverend Thomas Pilgrim mumbled a prayer.

Jawbone Morris watched his friend Wylie Martin cross the young murder victim's hands across his chest. "Wylie," he said, "you and me been around some, and I reckon we seen some men die, good and bad. We might as well do the honors."

The old frontiersman nodded and picked up his flintlock rifle. The two men loaded carefully, placed themselves twenty-five yards from the bound man, and raised their rifles. They cocked them and the man holding Hayden stepped aside. Martin took sight. "Jawbone, you shoot him between the eyes. I'll aim for the heart." Morris nodded.

Frank Johnson stepped forward. "Ready?" The two nodded. "Aim. Fire." The rifles cracked as one. Hayden swayed and fell.

* * *

By lanternlight they dug two graves and buried the murdered man and his murderer side by side, on a knoll near Turtle Bayou. After it was done, a man asked Jawbone Morris, "What's wrong with ol' Wylie? He's been sittin' on that log over there since dark, just scowlin' and starin' at that old rifle."

Morris glanced across at his old friend. "Did you look close at that feller we had to shoot? Wylie set out to hit the heart, but it was my shot that kilt him. Wylie didn't more'n graze his ribs. Tell ye another thing, too. I was you I wouldn't grin about that, nor even let on I'd noticed. Old Wylie never was one for makin' things out funny, and right now he's as like to skin anybody that upset him as not."

The man's face lost its humor as he realized Morris was serious. "You mean because that was his friend's boy that got shot?"

"Maybe, partly. Mostly I reckon it's because that probably's the first time Wylie ever missed a clear shot."

A little later, when a keg of New Orleans whiskey had been opened and cups passed around, John Austin took a cup to where Martin was sitting, handed it to the old frontiersman and sat beside him. For a while they sipped the fiery liquid in silence and gazed into the shadows of the dark woods.

Martin was the first to speak. "Don't fret yourself about me, John. The boy gettin' killed like that jest got me rattled." He was silent for a bit, musing. "You know, John, I remember my pap when he was my age. He was an old man then. But most of the time I don't reckon I'm old at all. But I wonder a bit now." He got out a pipe and filled it. Austin waited, knowing there was something the old man needed to say.

"Me and this rifle here, we've seen a lot of folks die. Fact is we've helped a few along. Never thought more'n was needful about it. But a while ago, when I seen that boy standin' there with a bullet hole in him and his eyes goin' dead, then seen him drop, well, it felt like I was dyin' right along with him. I swear, I would trade me for him if I could. He still had a long ways to go, but me, I been there . . . at least most of the ways."

He turned the old rifle across his knees and looked at it. "Did you know I was borned in '76, John? That's a fact. Year the United States declared against King George. I carried this here same rifle against the British in 1812, right down to New Orleans with Andy Jackson. I fought Indians with this rifle, and I fed myself and some others with it, more'n once.

"Been tellin' folks I ain't never missed a shot in my whole life. Well, that ain't true. I shot the feller that crippled my kid brother, few years back. But you know, I just nicked him up on the first shot? Had to run him down and brain him with this stock, so I could reload and shoot him proper. You know, John, I was rememberin' that when me and Jawbone lined up on that feller while ago."

The rambling tone of reminiscence trailed off and Martin drew himself around to face the captain. Austin waited.

"John, I carried this old rifle when we pushed the British out of New Orleans, and I carried it when we pushed the Kioway back from the Sabine valley. I'm hopin' to carry it that way one more time, to help push the Mexicans out of Texas. Is that what we're doin' here, John? How do you stand?"

So that was it. Austin let it sift for a moment before answering.

"I guess I know how you feel, Wylie, and maybe someday it will come. But, no. That isn't what we're here for. This isn't a revolution, Wylie. This is just an unfortunate but necessary action by a civil militia. There's no question here of loyalty to Mexico, just a question of simple justice between us and one garrison. We're here to free some Texians, Wylie. Don't try to make more of it than that."

The old man let it soak in. It was a gentle rebuff, delivered by a competent officer, but Martin had his hackles up now. "You know as well as I do, John Austin, that war is in the air. Independence is startin' to be the natural talk of the colony, and I'm for it, now."

Jawbone Morris and two or three others had drifted up and heard the last comments. "Amen," the bald Texian breathed, and gulped the last of his whiskey. Voices across the camp interrupted them.

"Hey, look who's here. Luke Lesassier . . . Glad you could make it, Luke . . . Luke, you look a sight. Let me take your hoss."

"Sure thing." The Frenchman dismounted. "I come. Where is John Austin?"

"Right yonder, past them fires. Good havin' you here, Luke."

As the man came toward him, wide-shouldered and lithe in the dancing firelight, John Austin sighed. Only two things could bring Luke Lesassier out of his beloved deep woods. One of them was the promise of a good fight.

Later that night, when most of the fires had died to coals, Austin sought out Frank Johnson and Three-legged Willie Williamson.

"I'm not real sure," he said, "which is our biggest problem . . . to back down Bradburn or to keep from starting a premature war."

"You want a war, John?" It was Williamson, his eyes searching and thoughtful.

"Right along with everybody else, Willie. But not now. Not yet. We're a long way from being ready."

115

Ten

The temper of Colonel Juan Davis Bradburn was well known in the garrison at Anahuac and was considered best not aroused. The outlander colonel was viewed by other senior officers and by the aristocratic scions of noble families in his command as an upstart and a barbarian, but a very dangerous man. By the lesser bloods around him he was considered a devil. Bradburn was well aware of the feelings he aroused in his command and, in his cooler moments, he played upon these emotions shrewdly for maximum advantage. He was also aware of his own explosive temper, but considered it an asset.

At this moment, he was seething. Bunched muscles rippled hard in his hunched shoulders, and he gripped his hands behind him to keep them from shaking. Booted legs spread wide on the woven straw carpet of his office, he towered, six feet four inches of blazing wrath, over the three paling juniors who stood at trembling attention before him.

In a corner of the room a lean, aristocratic man wearing the epaulets of a colonel sat straight in a wicker chair, arms crossed and troubled eyes on the floor.

Bradburn tried for a moment to control his rage as he felt his neck swelling, bulging above the tight collar, then gave it up. The veins stood out under his ears, and his face darkened to furious purple.

"Idiots!" The intended shout came out choked, as though he were strangling on his own venom. "Imbeciles! Stupid, bastard whelps of a village whore!" The junior officers paled even more, and the colonel across

116

the room winced and tightened his lips.

"You are not fit to be officers in my command!" Bradburn shouted. "You are not fit to clean the stables. My powder . . . all my powder! Left behind in a craven retreat from a bunch of ragtailed farmers! By God, I'll have your hides for this!" He whirled suddenly and paced the length of the room, then back, and squared off before them again. His arm shot out, and his palm rang against the cheek of the nearest lieutenant, then swung toward the window, pointing. "Do you know what is in those two kegs in that shed? Look, you cravens! That is one and one half kegs of powder. And that box there . . . one dismal roll of fuse!"

He drew himself up, regaining control with an effort, turned to the wall again and then back. His voice now was hardly more than a whisper. "I promise each of you this. If those traitors open fire on this garrison we will return their fire. But the last three charges of powder will be for you, and I will personally deliver them. You are dismissed!"

When they had filed out Bradburn resumed his pacing, heavy boots ringing dully on the muffled floor. Colonel Suverano remained seated and quiet, shamed by the display.

One half mile away, armed settlers occupied the town of Anahuac. There, in a small cellar hidden beneath one of the buildings, was virtually the entire powder and fuse supply of the Anahuac fort, overlooked when troops stationed within the town were withdrawn to the fort. Suverano knew very well that Bradburn himself had supervised the withdrawal.

Bradburn's angry pacing was interrupted by a hesitant knock. A frightened guard reported a delegation of settlers at the fort gate, petitioning audience with the commandant. Bradburn started to shout again, then caught himself. The fit of temper was past. His pale blue eyes shifted past the door to the barred main gate.

"Let them in," he said. "Without arms. Then let them

117

stand in the sun there in the compound. Under escort guard. I will see them when I'm ready." The guard backed out. Bradburn closed the door and began composing himself. Suverano stood to leave. "Stay, Colonel," Bradburn suggested. "You might learn something about handling provincials."

Through the window, he studied the group being escorted through the gate. There were five of them, an ill-assorted lot and visibly ill at ease. Soldiers accompanied them into the compound and halted them on the small parade ground, where they stood waiting in the hot sun. Bradburn knew Hugh Johnson well, and had given some thought to humbling him when the opportunity presented itself. Thin and straight in the afternoon sun, Johnson was one who took his civilian authority far too seriously for Bradburn's taste. He recognized Johnson's brother, Frank, and mentally chalked up a mark against his name, too. The third was that ridiculous cockerel with the alley-cat voice, William Jack. The other two, a short, blocky man in town clothes and a wiry, aging woodsman with long silver hair and the face of an Indian, he remembered having seen but didn't know.

Bradburn straightened his tunic, seated himself behind his desk, leaned back and lit a cigar. "We will wait a while," he said pleasantly. "Wine, Colonel?"

Bradburn's cigar was half gone when the Texians, hot and angry, were escorted into the office. The big colonel leaned back in his chair and surveyed them blandly, twirling the wine in his glass. "I would like to know just one thing," he said. "Why do you people insist on asking for interviews at siesta time?"

Frank Johnson was acting as spokesman for the delegation. "We believe our business is too serious to wait upon the formalities, Colonel," he said, wiping sweat from his hatband.

"Serious? I know of nothing you might discuss that is serious to me. It must be serious only to you." He was a cat with mice.

118

Johnson kept his voice even with an effort. "Colonel Bradburn, we are here to discuss a very serious matter. I must insist that you give us an honest audience."

"An honest audience! I always give an honest audience, sir, to anyone permitted through my door . . . even to those who would commit rebellion and treason against my government." He came forward in the chair, his brow lowering, the game over. "We of the Republic of Mexico do not take kindly to you Americans coming into our country and ignoring our laws, upsetting our customs. In case I have not previously made it clear, you are not welcome here. Not any of you."

Frank Johnson sensed Wylie Martin tensing beside him and answered quickly, "Colonel Bradburn, every man in this room is as much a citizen of Mexico as you are. Your attitude . . ."

"Not all," Bradburn's smile was cold. He looked directly toward William Jack.

Wylie Martin was bristling. He pushed past Johnson. "Mister, I come to Mexico in '24, and been here ever since. Bill Jack may be new here, but I ain't, and by God, no popinjay is gonna call me an outsider."

"Wylie," Frank said softly, and Bradburn recognized the woodsman. One of the executioners of Smith's man at Turtle Bayou. "You see how it is, Colonel," Johnson was saying. "Even a good citizen can be belligerent if he feels he's been insulted, or treated badly by those in authority."

"Treated badly? I have never before laid eyes on Mr. Wylie Martin, yet he comes here to my post with a bunch of armed rabble at his back."

Wylie started forward again, but Frank Johnson motioned him to silence. It was going to be no use. "Colonel Bradburn, we demand, I repeat, demand, that the prisoners you are holding illegally be released to the constitutional alcalde of this district, here present."

Bradburn came upright in the chair, his eyes narrowing. His fist hit the desk, knocking over the wine bottle.

An orderly hurried forward to pick it up and clear away the spill. "You demand, sir?" The colonel rose to his feet. He was taller by several inches than those facing him. "How dare you come into my office and demand?"

"As to my prisoners, sir, they are no concern of yours, or of this . . . your brother. The men in stockade here are held by my order as military commander of this district."

"But those men are civilians, not military, sir. And we request they be turned over to the legal civil authority, the alcalde of Liberty." Frank Johnson indicated Hugh.

"Now you request." Bradburn's laugh was short and cool. "Make up your mind, sir. Do you demand or request?"

Frank Johnson had had enough. "Bradburn," he said through tight jaws, "I will say it politely just once more. The men you are holding here are held illegally. The only possible charges against them are for civil offenses. You are far beyond your authority."

Hugh Johnson cut in. "Colonel, I too am a citizen of Mexico, and an official of the Mexican government, and I agree. You have exceeded your authority. It is my right, and my duty, to demand civil justice for civilians in accordance with our Constitution."

Bradburn ignored him, directing his attention to Frank Johnson. "I understand that your outlaws are holding some of my men."

"We are not outlaws, Colonel. And yes, we do have some soldiers with us, who may be from this garrison. They are our guests for the time being."

"Ah! They are guests, I see." Bradburn turned challenging eyes on William Jack, who seemed to be biting his tongue. He had been allowed to come along only upon his guarantee that he would remain silent. "Well, let me be clear. I am entertaining no guests here. The men in my stockade are prisoners. Military prisoners. And I don't like threats of force. There must be a hundred and fifty of your armed riffraff in Anahuac."

Frank Johnson was tired of it. "More than that, Colonel. And we aren't threatening. But we do intend to see justice done in a legal manner, if possible."

Bradburn also was wearying of the game. He turned to the fifth man in the delegation. "Your name, sir?"

"Lewis. H.K. Lewis of Liberty."

"Very well, now I know all of you. You have wasted my time, gentlemen, and I have other business to attend to. I cannot release your friends. They are prisoners of Colonel Suverano." He indicated the officer still sitting quietly in the corner. "And he refuses to release them."

William Jack blurted, "You can't do that. You're in command here, not him."

Bradburn glared at the little lawyer. "I know who is in command here," he said. "Sergeant, show these men the door and the gate."

As they turned to leave, Frank Johnson said, "If you change your mind, Colonel Bradburn, we are staying for a while in Anahuac. All of us. We are headquartered in the Plazuela de Maliche in town, but you can find us most of the time in those woods just beyond your wall." He grabbed Wylie's arm, leading him out of the office and herding the others before anyone could say anything more. As they left the fort they all looked toward the old brick kiln that served as a stockade. None of the prisoners were visible.

On returning to town they learned of news from Velasco, through Brazoria. "General Santa Anna has declared against Bustamente," John Austin told them quietly. "There's going to be war now, beyond any doubt. A lot of the military are throwing in with Santa Anna, and a lot of the peones, but Bustamente has his forces in good order around Mexico City."

"I knowed it," Margin said. "That's why all the troop movements of late." He looked back toward the fort. "What about them, though? Where they gonna stand?"

"Well, Suverano's a friend of Teran, and Teran appears to be going with Santa Anna. But Suverano has no

121

power here."

"And Bradburn?"

"You've been in there. You tell me."

"I reckon he knows what's happening," Frank Johnson said. "And if he was with Santa Anna he wouldn't want to upset the colonies. The general is going to need all the help he can get out here. And he isn't with Bustamente, or Suverano'd have had his scalp by now, with Teran's help."

"You sayin' what I'm thinkin'?" Martin's glance was sharp, his eyes speculating.

"He is," Austin said. "Looks as though Colonel Bradburn's planning to go it alone."

"How can he do that?" Lewis asked. "If there's going to be civil war, he has to pick a side."

"Not," said John Austin, "if he has another game in mind. Not if he wants Texas."

Someone whistled. For a long moment no one spoke. Finally Hugh Johnson looked around at the group. "Then maybe our problem here is different than we thought. Maybe now it's just him and us, to settle this thing here."

"But whose side are we on, then?" Martin asked.

Austin's answer was slow, but firm. "Our own, for the moment. And when the time comes, I believe I will be with Santa Anna."

All around them the camp had been quiet. Then, as if at a signal, several conversations began and Luke Lesassier shouted, "Hey, Jake. Open up couple them kegs there. Me, I want to have a drink for Santa Anna!"

"Frank?"

"Go ahead, Jake. Nothing's going to happen for a while, and the boys could use a drink. John, let's do some thinking about tomorrow."

By the time full dark had settled in, several kegs of whiskey had been broached, and it had developed into

122

what Three-legged Willie would call a "right memorable evenin'." The little Texian army had arrived, and had made camp. Most of the town of Anahuac had joined them, and now there was nothing to do but wait. What happened next depended upon Juan Bradburn, John Austin, Frank Johnson, and God. In the meantime, there was a pleasant evening to pass, Texas style.

Although Austin and the Johnsons, with a few close associates, had found quarters in town, the main camp was outside of town on the fort road, spread over the flats and into the brushed fringes of the woods. Thirty or forty separate campfires were being tended under a clear, starry sky. The areas between fires were lit by the silver of a bright last-quarter moon. Beans were cooking, pork was frying, coffee was boiling, and a substantial amount of whiskey was being passed around. Everywhere people were moving about, grouping and regrouping in conversation. Laughter rang out here and cursing over there. Quiet voices discussed serious thoughts and harsh voices vented serious emotions.

"We got the makin's of a shindig here," observed John Austin. He and Frank Johnson had walked down to survey their troops. "No, that's all right. Let 'em howl. Before this night is old they'll hear the noise real clear over at the fort. Give 'em something to think about."

Between them they selected seventeen level heads, all still sober, from their combined forces and sent them off to stand guard. Five were posted at intervals along the trail and a dozen scattered around the fort. The Mexican army could sleep easily tonight—if they slept at all. Nothing was going into or out of Fort Anahuac.

"Where's Wylie? And Jawbone Morris?"

"They went into town," Johnson said. "Wylie wanted to look around for that fellow Smith, and Jawbone went along to keep him company."

Austin's face clouded slightly. "Wish someone else had gone for him, instead. I wanted him alive."

"If he's got any sense, he won't be around."

123

They walked through the camp, stopping for a moment at each fire, pausing to chat with each group. "You boys relax tonight and enjoy yourselves," Austin said. "The evenin's free. But keep your wits about you. Before daylight, I want men in those woods over there by the fort."

By the time the fourth keg had been opened, the evening's enjoyment was in full swing. Several fistfights had broken out. A dozen tall tales had been told and a hundred more were waiting. Father Muldoon had performed three weddings — two between Trinity drifters and girls of the town, one for an Anahuac couple who had lived together for five years and had four children. And the Reverend Mister Pilgrim had solemnly baptized a Liberty youth with Father Muldoon sanctifying the service to make it legal in Mexico.

Luke Lesassier tried for a while to teach French to three chiding young men from Nacogdoches, then became disgusted and taught them how to fight instead. Bill Logan, whose runaway slaves had started the unpleasantness with Bradburn, came in with one of his slaves, a buck named Mose who had been found wandering up the road from the fort. After escaping from Logan, the slave had found it even more desirable to escape from the protective custody of Bradburn. He was sent home, with the promise that "When I get back, I'm gonna kick your black butt all over East Texas."

"Maybe that's why he ran off in the first place," Williamson suggested, but mildly; a man didn't tell his neighbor how to handle his slaves, his women, or his animals.

Wylie Martin and Jawbone Morris drifted into camp and joined the party at one of the fires, dipping tin cups into the whiskey barrel there. Across the way, at another fire, a ruckus was going on, two men quarreling, their voices carrying clear across the camp. By agreement, the two quarrelers picked up rifles and whiskey cups, paced away from each other several yards, turned, and each

124

placed a whiskey cup on his head and shouldered a rifle.

"Here, now!" Morris rumbled. He and Martin exchanged glances, grabbed their rifles, aimed and fired almost together. At the other fire, the filled cups exploded on the two men's heads, the rifles were lowered, and they gaped around in drunken astonishment.

The old hunter and the bald man reloaded. "Couldn't have them fellers shootin' at each other," Morris remarked passively to those around him. "They're both Brazorians, and the shape they're in, they mighta kilt each other."

Padre Muldoon found himself a cup and filled it.

Nearsighted young William Jack was wandering around the camp, trying to stir up trouble. Restless, angry and frustrated, Jack was convinced that only his own leadership could remove his brother from Bradburn's stockade, and he was for starting a firefight with the fort immediately. He had little faith in the cool, slow maneuvering of Austin and Frank Johnson. Most of the settlers ignored him, humored him, or bluntly sent him packing to other parts of the camp. But as the liquor flowed he found a more and more ready audience in the drifters and border tramps who had joined the group coming down the Trinity. In a fairly short time the high-voiced young lawyer had a sizable band of these rootless souls accepting him as their leader and drunkenly encouraging him in a plan to set out at once and raze the fort.

The end of the venture came at its beginning. Jack got his little band organized into rank and file order, headed them toward the fort and walked headlong into a tree. His army dissolved in howls of laughter. Nearby, George McKinstry watched the episode soberly and then walked across to join Robert Williamson, Bull Brenan, and some others at a quieter fireside.

"I wish that young feller over there would settle down and quit actin' like the Hand of God or somethin'. He's been shootin' off his mouth all afternoon and some of those drifters are listenin' to him."

"I wouldn't worry about him too much, George," Williamson said. "He's just worried about his brother, is all. And if any of that bunch did set out for the fort, they'd be sober enough when they got there to turn around and come back."

"Feller could get killed tryin' to take that fort with just rifles and muskets."

"That's a fact. Nobody's going to do much to Bradburn right now without some cannon."

"But we could give him hell with a couple of field pieces," Bill Russell pointed out. This brought a moment of thoughtful silence.

A tall figure had moved quietly into the firelight, and now came forward and squatted by the glowing coals. Unlike many around the camp that night, John Austin was cold sober. "Just so some of you will know," he said, "if Bradburn doesn't listen to reason pretty soon, Frank and I think we should get a little more serious with our negotiations. There are cannon at Brazoria, and we will go for them if we have to."

The captain sipped scalding coffee at the fire while the conversation his comments had started went on around him. Uppermost in his mind right now was the single objective of getting those prisoners out of the fort, peacefully if possible. Second was the question of what Santa Anna's declaration against President Bustamente held in store for Mexico and, more specifically, for Texas.

General Santa Anna was a hero in Mexico, and a man of great power and greater ambition. Popular with the peons throughout Spanish Mexico, a brilliant military strategist and dedicated scholar of Napoleon's campaigns, he was, all things considered, a formidable man. And now he had begun his move against the president. For all Austin knew, war could already have broken out in the Estados nearer Mexico City.

As of the latest report—Austin had a messenger system relaying word to him from Brazoria—Santa Anna was holding Vera Cruz, the most important seaport in

Mexico, as his base of operations. On John Austin's mind now was how this turn of events affected the situation at Anahuac. More than just here and now, more than just their hatred for Bradburn, the settlers were ready for a fight. Many of them were openly discussing a war for Texas independence.

One thing was sure. If there was ever an ideal time to strike a telling first blow, it was the present. With war or impending war in Mexico, Bradburn's little outpost in Texas might well be left to its own devices for a while. And it was certain that of the combatants in the main conflict, neither would want to confront the citizens of Texas directly at this early stage. Santa Anna, on the contrary, had been wooing the Texas Anglos for months, while Bustamente, at the very least, would probably prefer just to leave them alone for the time being.

But Austin knew the terrible price of open war, and he was a careful judge of competence. The settlers might be ready for a battle, but they weren't equipped for war. John Austin was deeply in love with Texas, and he knew its weaknesses as well as its strengths. These were good men around him, but not an army. They could mount an attack, but not a campaign. They could win a quick battle, but not a sustained engagement. They were recklessly adventurous, hotly optimistic, and terribly vulnerable.

Sipping his coffee and half listening to the sounds of the camp around him, John Austin wished his friend Stephen F. Austin were here to guide him. But the colony's founder was far away in Saltillo, attending a session of the legislature.

The captain stood and stretched his legs. To George McKinstry he said, "It's getting late. Let them go a while longer, then pack in the whiskey. And you might pick a few good men to go out and replace the pickets in an hour or so.

"A little after midnight, let's move some men down through those woods to where we can cover the fort at daybreak. Oh, and if John Williams insists on heading out to the fort in the morning, let him go. He thinks he can talk to Bradburn, maybe soften him up a little. He might as well try."

"I know Williams," Bull Brenan said. "He's nothin' but mouth. Just a politician, is all, lookin' for a feather in his cap."

"Let him go anyway. He'll do no harm."

At dawn young Bill Russell of Brazoria joined Jawbone Morris and some other Trinity men in a small meadow in the forest, some distance back from the perimeter of the cleared plain around the fort. They had a fire going, with a huge coffeepot boiling on it, and looked cold, wet, and uncomfortable. Someone handed Russell a cup of coffee.

"Be a hot day today if it ever gets around to startin'."

"Damn well hope so," someone said. "I'm half froze right now." In the early hours a heavy dew had settled, soaking the men and their gear, and now a cold dawn breeze off Trinity Bay was working on them. The coffee tasted better than usual.

"I guarantee you one thing," Russell said, scratching his arms and neck, "You boys over here on the Trinity have got some mosquitos I'd like to take home to plow fields with."

"Big 'uns, ain't they."

"Want some sweetenin' in that coffee?" Jawbone Morris handed Russell a nearly empty whiskey jug, and he freshened his coffee cup from it.

"Wylie Martin here?"

"Naw," Morris said, "he took off somewheres afore light. Be back after while, I reckon. What's Austin and Johnson want us to do this mornin'?"

"Haven't heard. Just stay around close, I guess. Wait for word. How does that big fort look close up, Jawbone?"

"It's big. Brick walls, thick as hell. Rifles sure aren't gonna penetrate 'em." He set his cup down. "Hiram, that coffee was worth gettin' up for."

"Glad you enjoyed it, Jawbone, but I didn't know you ever went to sleep last night."

"I didn't. But if I had, it would have been worth gettin' up for." He unfolded, stretched, and yawned. "Russell, I been tryin' to promote a expedition here this mornin', but these fellers are tired out from all the hoorawin' last night. So I tell you what. Let's you and me go crawl up close to that fort and take us a look. We might even have us some fun."

"What kind of fun did you have in mind?"

"Well, them Mescan soldiers, they have them a muster every mornin' out in front of the main gate. Don't know what might come up, but I got me a new double-barreled shotgun I ain't shot nobody with yet. Might take it along."

Russell thought it over. John Austin might raise hell. But then again he might not. "Sounds like a right sportin' idea," he said finally.

"All right, you finish your coffee and I'll go get that there Belgian-made fowling piece of mine. It's a right purty thing. Ought to be toted now and then."

In the dawn light they reached the edge of the cleared plain and then, on their stomachs, crawled through the grass to within rifle-shot of the fort itself. Jawbone had lovingly loaded the Belgian shotgun with a double charge of powder and a heavy load of large bird-shot, and Russell tried to stay a little behind him and on the off side in case he decided to shoot it.

The fort was a long, single-story building one hundred and twenty feet in length by thirty feet wide, dominating a small, light-walled compound and commanding the bay shore and a good stretch of prairie to the northeast. At the end facing the bay was a five-sided bastion with walls about twenty feet long, unroofed. Several outbuildings were visible, as was part of the long building housing the old brick kiln, now used as a prison.

"How thick are those walls?" Russell asked, keeping his voice low.

"Four or five feet, I imagine."

"Well, you ain't gonna bust them with no shotgun. Take a cannon to get in there, sure's the world." Russell raised his head carefully to look to the south, where the corrals were located. "Sure would like to get to those horses."

"Never make it on this open prairie," Morris whispered. "Bradburn keeps all the grass burned off. You see? We're lucky to find this little bit of cover this close. Might crawl up there in the dark of night, but it'd be hell gettin' away."

They lay there, slightly hidden in six-inch grass in a small depression, while dawn came full and the sun rose. Within minutes, it was starting to get hot. With the patience of woodsmen, they lay still and waited and watched.

The sun was full up and rising when the main gate opened and a sergeant came out of the fort, glancing around. He was still there, standing by the gate, when a bugle sounded from inside the compound and, a few minutes later, green-uniformed men started emerging from the fort, laughing and talking among themselves. The sergeant shouted orders and the men straightened into ranks. A roll call started. The two men in the grass could hear each name distinctly, and each response. The officers appeared, striding from the gate.

"Damn if that there captain don't make my shotgun itch," Morris said, and brought the piece to his shoulder. Russell shrugged and brought up his rifle. Aim was bad from the prone position. They fired together, and Morris immediately let off the second barrel. The ornate gun bucked viciously in his grip, but held together.

For a moment there was chaos among the troops in front of the fort, but only for a moment. A few fired blindly in the direction the sound had come from; then order was restored and, about the same time, someone spotted the Texians, and a volley ripped the sod around them. Morris slapped Russell on the shoulder and shouted above the roar. "Don't bother reloadin'. We ain't got time." As one, they rolled to the side and back, then scrambled for the protection of the trees. In the forest they paused, listened a moment to the sound of ragged firing still coming from the fort, looked at each other, and grinned. Then they walked back to their camp, ready now for a second cup of coffee. Behind them, the soldiers had retreated into the fort and were maintaining a steady fire, tailing off finally into occasional shots directed at shadows in the woods.

William J. Russell of Brazoria and Ritson Morris of the Trinity settlement had fired the first shots by Texians against Mexican troops. In the sulphur smell of the powder smoke was the first faint scent of revolution.

"Well, did you kill anybody?"

"Can't rightly say. But one thing's sure. They're gonna be a sight more careful about morning muster from now on."

It was, indeed a hot day around Fort Anahuac that day, and a noisy one. Periodic skirmishes occurred all through the day, all at long range and all without effect. The soldiers in the fort had been spooked by the dawn attack, and were shooting at anything that moved.

A self-appointed peacemaker and politician by the name of John Williams complained bitterly to Frank Johnson about letting his men get "so thoroughly out of hand," then saddled a horse and rode determinedly toward, up to, and into the fort, having decided to ignore all the shooting and proceed with the talking. Out at the edge of the prairie, one Texian was injured. Jesse Saunders, a nephew of Doctor B.T. Archer of Brazoria, was wounded by an accidental discharge of one of his twin dueling pistols.

John Austin and Frank Johnson made inquiries and then summoned Jawbone Morris and Bill Russell to base camp. When the two arrived, Austin regarded them coldly for a moment, drew himself up, cleared his throat and then relaxed and grinned.

"Oh, hell," he said. "Go on back to whatever you were doing."

Eleven

On the second day of the siege of Anahuac, Colonel
Suverano rode out from the fort under a white flag, accompanied by John Williams. While the other Texians
had been shooting, harassing, and blockading, Williams
had been talking. He rode now with the self-effacing assurance of one who had single-handedly and through
pure intelligence solved a problem that many others had
failed to alter through brute force. He introduced
Suverano to Austin and several others and made a somewhat pompous little speech about the "easing of tensions"
between military authority and colonial forces, about the
preordination of Santa Anna's coming eminence in Mexico and the need for united effort to support the general
in this critical time of Mexico's history. Through it all,
the aristocratic Suverano remained mounted, waiting patiently for a chance to speak with the Texians' leaders.

When Williams ran down, Suverano addressed himself
to Austin, in crisp Spanish with a Castilian accent.
"Captain Austin, the military command of Anahuac district will be agreeable to sincere efforts to resolve this
unfortunate situation. May I suggest a commission of
our two interests to discuss a settlement."

Austin knew the colonel only by hearsay, but had the
feeling that in matters of honor, Suverano would be a
straightforward and reasonable man. "Do you speak as
commander of Anahuac, Colonel?" he asked.

"No, I do not. I speak for myself only, and as a follower of the movement of General Santa Anna. In date
of rank I am senior to Colonel Juan Bradburn but my

133

status in his command at this moment is that of guest. But"—he paused for a moment—"I carry a special commission from General Santa Anna with the countersignature of General Teran. And by this commission I can assure you that any agreement worked out by a conference of our two principals will be honored."

"It is agreed, then, Colonel. We will negotiate. Your pleasure?"

"One hour from now, before the garrison gate."

Suverano returned to the fort, Williams again accompanying him. Of the Texians in the clearing then, only one, Jawbone Morris, voiced any objection to the idea of negotiations. Morris considered Williams a buffoon and had a deep conviction that all Mexican officials were untrustworthy. He said so.

At the main camp Austin called a general muster and spoke to the Texians.

"We are few here," he began. "And without artillery or extended supplies. With each passing day the suffering of our countrymen in that garrison becomes greater. A treaty is proposed, and both Frank Johnson and I are in agreement with at least attempting to negotiate. We don't know what will come of this, maybe nothing. But we can only gain by trying.

"The conference team will be three. Wylie Martin, because of his experience as a military officer. W.D. Hall, as second alcalde of Liberty, representing the Trinity area. Myself, representing Brazoria and the interests of Stephen F. Austin."

Frank Johnson would command a party spread through the edge of the forest facing the fort clearing. Jawbone Morris would lead as assault force on the road in case of treachery, to reach and defend the Texas negotiators.

"And we're gonna be ready to move in quick," Morris spat. "Don't never trust nothin' wearin' a green uniform, nor nothin' ridin' with 'em."

Halfway out from the garrison wall, uniformed orderlies placed a table and chairs on the grass. Another stood by, holding paper, ink and pens. Williams rode from the fort, accompanied by Lieutenant Colonel Juan Cortina and Captain José Gonzales. The captain's arm was bandaged and carried in a muslin sling.

Williams started to make introductions when the two parties met at the meeting ground. "We all know each other, John," Austin said. "*Salud*, Juan . . . José, are all things well with you?"

"*Buenas tardes*, John Austin." Cortina smiled. "We are well, despite a small accident suffered by my friend the captain yesterday. Are things well on the Rio Brazos?"

"Not too bad," Austin said. "Not near as messed up as things are around here right now." He dismounted and stepped to the table. The others did the same.

"Do you think we can reach an agreement, John Austin?"

"My Texians will honor any agreement we reach here," Austin said. "And will expect the army to do the same. It eases our minds considerably to be dealing with men of honor. . . . Without yourselves and Colonel Suverano, I think we would not have expected honor from Bradburn in this matter."

"Now, gentlemen —" Williams stepped forward hurriedly. "I think we should keep this meeting formal and get right to business."

"Juan and I are old friends, John." Austin's tone was bland, but authoritative. "Would you mind helping those men with the horses while we talk?"

Austin and Cortina seated themselves at the ends of the table. Gonzales, Martin, and Hall took chairs, and Cortina directed the orderly with the writing implements to the sixth chair, near him.

"If we can settle this thing here and now without a fight," Austin said, "I urge that we do so. Neither Mexico nor the settlers need hostility between us."

"I also hope we can, John. It would be far better to part as friends, and without bloodshed."

135

"Without further bloodshed," Gonzales corrected. "Captain Austin, somewhere in your camp there is a man who should confine himself to rifles . . . not shotguns."

"I have one question before we begin, gentlemen," Austin said. "If we reach an agreement, is there any assurance that Bradburn will honor it? I have no trust for your commander."

"I only know that he says he will abide by our decision," Cortina replied. "In this case he must consider himself as representing the government of Mexico. And, as you have stated, Colonel Suverano is present at the fort."

"I hope he does, Colonel. There will be bloodshed if he does not." Austin spoke not as a threat, but simply as a matter of fact. "You know me, Juan, even if Colonel Bradburn does not. And you know and understand the men with me."

Williams was back at the table now, hovering over the group. "Gentlemen, please," he said, "let's not talk of bloodshed, but of peace and honor." He looked at the faces around the table, and they each met his gaze evenly. They were not baiting or threatening one another. They were speaking of fact, and they all understood the situation. It suddenly occurred to Williams that he was out of his depth. He went back to the horses.

As he turned away he heard Cortina say, "Now let's get down to business. Colonel Bradburn has sent a proposal for a mutual resolving of differences . . . one I think you will find acceptable."

The commissioners, seated there in high-backed chairs around an oak table in the center of a burned-over South Texas prairie, worked for nearly an hour under a sweltering sun. A rifle-shot to the south was Fort Anahuac, the walls lined with armed soldiers. An equal distance to the north, and spread through the fringe of wooded land, were more than a hundred and fifty armed

Texians, their firearms loaded, their patience thin.

The agreement they reached, finally, was simple and to the point. First, the Mexican cavalry patrol held prisoner by the civilian Texas militia would be released. Second, the militia and its followers would retire to Turtle Bayou, leaving a commission at Anahuac to receive civilian prisoners. Third, the civilians imprisoned at the Fort of Anahuac would be released the following morning, and delivered to the commissioners.

As he rode back toward Anahuac, John Austin was wondering what had finally softened Bradburn. He doubted that a bunch of settlers with rifles had achieved that effect. Maybe the man had decided to cast his lot with Santa Anna, and was in his own way making peace with the settlers.

At his window in the fort, Colonel Juan Davis Bradburn watched the commission ride away and smiled. He was thinking of the powder magazine in Anahuac.

There was considerable rumbling in Anahuac when Austin's commission reported back on the agreement that had been reached. The second condition bothered many of them, as did the day's delay in release of Bradburn's prisoners. And a good many felt let down. They hoped the problem was solved, and were willing to expect the best, but they had gotten themselves all geared up for a shooting war and the simple piece of paper in John Austin's hand seemed miserably anticlimactic. They mumbled, and they griped, but no one among them suggested not honoring the agreement. They began packing their gear.

"It just don't feel right," Jawbone Morris told Robert Williamson. "There's been too much get-ready and not enough do."

The first article was the release of Lieutenant Nieto's patrol. Williamson went with George McKinstry to attend to that detail. The soldiers, with the exception of

137

Nieto, were quite cheerful about the whole matter. They had been treated well, and considered many of their captors friends. All in all, it had been a pleasure and an honor to be the guests of the Texians. For three days they had done nothing but eat and sleep in what was, by and large, a pleasant confinement.

At the edge of the main camp, the soldiers' horses and arms were returned to them. As Nieto turned them toward the fort, a deep voice called from behind them. John Austin stepped forward and handed him his sword. Nieto's expression changed slowly from dismay to puzzlement, then to pleasure. On impulse he leaned from his horse and gripped Austin's shoulder. *"Gracias, señor,"* he said, then turned quickly, buckled on his sword, and led his patrol out of the camp.

As the Texian militia left Anahuac, a token force remained behind. Most of the men whose homes were in Anahuac dispersed and went home. Bill Russell, William Jack, and about thirty other Trinity and Brazoria men remained in town to receive Bradburn's prisoners the following day.

Wylie Martin made one more circuit of the little town, leading his horse and carrying his rifle, his eyes peering into each doorway and each narrow path. Finally he shrugged and mounted, then rode off to overtake the main party. Behind him, in a small building at the edge of town, a trap door was lifted and one man helped another out of a cramped cellar where the latter had spent three days hiding in mold and stench. John Manley Smith would live in fear the remainder of his life. At every turn, he would see the cold eyes and wicked rifle of old Wylie Martin, hunting him. Few noticed him when he rode out of Anahuac, disheveled and carrying a hastily packed carpetbag, heading east.

Frank Johnson directed the setting up of the camp on Turtle Bayou. James Taylor White, on whose property they camped, sent out a wagonload of supplies and a keg of rum. Austin, still feeling uneasy about Bradburn's sudden reversal, set guards on the camp perimeter and along the back road.

In the office of Colonel Bradburn, lamps burned late into the night as first one officer and then another reported to the commandant. Several of them were instructed to report again at dawn.

It was a reserved and silent group of officers who stood before Bradburn early the following morning. During the night, Colonel Suverano had been confined to quarters, and a guard was placed on him, by order of Colonel Bradburn. The big American-born officer was very much in command of this garrison, and he was going his own way. There was outrage in the dark eyes of some of the officers as Bradburn outlined his plans and gave his orders for the day, but there was nothing they could do.

At mid-morning a courier rode hard into the camp on Turtle Bayou, his horse lathered and wheezing, and headed straight for John Austin's fire. "Captain!" he shouted as he skidded the heaving mount around. "That bastard Bradburn came out of his fort at dawn with cavalry and infantry . . . full-scale attack on the town and the bunch you left there. Caught us flat-footed. Most of the rest of 'em's comin' in behind me."

Austin had been writing letters. Now he stuffed his materials away and pulled on his boots. "McKinstry!" he roared. "George McKinstry! Call the men to arms!" He turned back to the courier. The man was bleeding from a shallow wound on his leg.

Within minutes the quiet camp was again an army. But this time it was not a boisterous, bickering mob as before. Most of them were silent as they packed and saddled their horses. Wylie Martin's face was red and his brow lowered as he cinched a saddle on his roan horse.

"That blackguard," he fumed. "Gave us his word of honor, did he?"

Jawbone Morris was tying pack straps. "I knowed it, and I told ye so. You just remember, Wylie Martin, I told ye so."

One man in the busy camp was not quiet. William Jack, who had arrived just minutes after the messenger, was near to apoplexy. He stomped and shouted and berated everyone within range of his high voice. When the Reverend Mister Pilgrim tried to calm him down, Jack whirled on him and Frank Johnson had to restrain him from lashing out at the preacher in his fury.

Many faces in the camp were pale with shock. Most were dark with rage. Until now, most of them had thought it was over.

As they packed, the Brazorians pulled in around John Austin. They shared the rage of the Trinity settlers, but this was not their ground. They would follow the tide, but not carry it.

More of the stragglers from Anahuac were coming in now, some mounted, some walking, and some carrying wounded. There were women and children among them. Tiny, aged Maria Mendez de Almirante y Medoya was there, helped along by a tall man who walked with a painful limp. Her husband, Miguel Jesús Almirante y Medoya, was not there.

Doctor Labadie was tending the wounded as best he could. Someone shouted that Robert Williamson was being carried in with a broken leg. The doctor started that way. "Oh, he don't need you, Doc," the man corrected. "He needs a carpenter. It's his wooden leg that's busted."

Austin's Brazorians rode out to bring in the stragglers and to scout their back trail. They found Bill Russell and some Anahuac men trying to repair a broken wagon wheel. Several women and children were with them, and a wounded man was in the wagon.

"We didn't have a chance, Captain," Russell said. "They came on us all of a sudden, and they hit us hard."

How many dead? They didn't know—not many. Were the soldiers coming? No. They had taken Anahuac and the Plazuela de Maliche and stopped there.

"You know, Captain, most of those soldiers weren't aiming to hit. It's like they were just chasing us out. Some of them even helped these folks get away, when Bradburn's main guard wasn't looking."

Was Suverano with them? No, they didn't see him, at any rate. But Bradburn was there, mounted up on a big white horse, and shooting.

"This feller in the wagon, he's one. Bradburn shot him personal."

The Brazorians brought them in. They were the last.

At Turtle Bayou Frank Johnson had the reorganization well under way. To one side, William Jack had finally calmed down and had Hugh Johnson and several others in intent conversation. Austin and the Brazorians went to work, helping Johnson straighten things out. The women and children, and some of the wounded, would be sent off to White's ranch house for safekeeping. Several supply wagons had been emptied and pressed into service as ambulances.

Finally the leaders came together in conference. Austin went straight to the point. "We can't fight Bradburn as we are," he said. "We must have artillery. There are cannon at Brazoria, and I intend to go for them."

Hugh Johnson said, "William Jack has a thought that I believe has merit: that we declare our position and our intent in a resolution, legally agreed to, and that we declare ourselves in support of the Constitution and of General Santa Anna."

"You mean a written statement? For what purpose?"

"For a semblance of legality in what we do next," Johnson answered. "To justify ourselves and our actions, to act as responsible men, not as a mob."

"So we can blow down that damn fort and get my brother out of there," Jack said, and Johnson hushed him with a look.

"A resolution supporting Santa Anna," Austin mused, "and the Constitution of 1824. We are in the right, so we say we are in the right."

"And against Bustamente," someone offered.

"No," Johnson said. "Not against anybody. Just in support of our rights as stated in the Constitution, and in support of Santa Anna so far as he defends those rights. We don't know for sure there's a war on, and we don't know Santa Anna's going to win, if there is."

"John Williams thinks he will win."

"I hope to God John Williams knows more about Santa Anna than he knew about Bradburn, then."

"All right, Frank, set up your committee and write us a resolution, and then we'll see. And when it's done, we'll go after those cannon."

With William Jack wielding the pen, the writing did not take long. The "Turtle Bayou Resolutions" were dated June 13, 1832:

> The colonists of Texas have long since been convinced of the arbitrary and unconstitutional measures of the administration of Bustamente; as evinced
>
> 1st. By repeated violations of the constitution and laws, and the total disregard of the civil and political rights of the people.
>
> 2d. By their fixing and establishing among us in the time of peace, military posts, the officers of which, totally disregarding the local civil authorities of the state, have committed various acts evincing opposition to the true interest of the people in the enjoyment of civil liberty.
>
> 3d. By arresting the commissioners, especially Juan Francisco Madero, who on the part of the state government was to put the inhabitants east of the River Trinity, in possession of their lands, in conformity with the laws of colonization.
>
> 4th. By the imposition of military force, prevent-

ing the alcalde of the jurisdiction of Liberty, from the exercise of his constitutional functions.

5th. By appointing to the revenue department men whose principles are avowedly inimical to the true interest of the people of Texas; and that, too, when their character for infamy had been repeatedly established.

6th. By the military commandant of Anahuac advising and procuring servants to quit the service of their masters, and offering them protection, causing them to labor for his benefits and refusing to compensate for the same.

7th. By imprisonment of our citizens without lawful cause; and claiming the right of trying said citizens by a military court for offense of a character cognizable by the civil authority alone.

It was a catalogue of grievances, and as they put it together, as Jack put it to paper, none among them could dispute a word of it.

"All right," Robert Williamson said finally, "that tells 'em why. Now let's tell 'em what."

RESOLVED. That we view with feelings of the deepest regret the manner in which the government of the Republic of Mexico is administered by the present dynasty. The repeated violation of the constitution; and the total disregard of the laws; the entire prostration of the civil power; are grievances of such character as to arouse the feelings of every freeman, and impel him to resistance.

RESOLVED. That we view with feelings of deepest interest, and solicitude, the firm and manly resistance which is made by those patriots under the highly talented and distinguished chieftain Santa Anna to the numerous encroachments and infractions which have been made by the present administration upon the laws and constitutions of our beloved and adopted country.

"Ain't you spreadin' it a little thick?" Jawbone Morris inquired. "I might side with that Santa Anna, but I don't believe I'd shine his boots."

William Jack didn't even glance up from the paper. "If we are going to make an enemy," he said, "then we had better make a friend, too."

RESOLVED. That as freemen devoted to a correct interpretation and enforcement of the constitution and laws, according to their true spirit, we pledge our lives and fortunes in support of the same, and of those distinguished leaders who are now so gallantly fighting in defense of civil liberty.

RESOLVED. That all the people of Texas be invited to cooperate with us, in our support of the principles incorporated in the foregoing resolutions.

"Amen," the Reverend Mister Pilgrim breathed as Jack finished the draft with a flourish and leaned back.

Labadie carried the paper across to John Austin and handed it to him. "Sorry, John, but we decided if we are to support Santa Anna, then we should support him all the way."

Austin read over the work, then nodded. "Yes, I'll sign this," he said.

Several men were put to work making copies of the document, and when enough were done, they were signed. Riders were dispatched at once to various points throughout the colony, carrying copies of the Turtle Bayou Resolutions. Austin sent Henry Brown to the Neches and Sabine River settlements, and directed a copy to Gonzales for the settlers there. He urged Brown to make haste, then meet them in Brazoria. They were hoping that when they got there Henry's brother, Jerry Brown, would be in port with his schooner, *Sabine*. Heavy spring rains had swollen the streams in the area, and coming back overland with cannon might be nearly impossible. If Brown was at Brazoria, they could bring the artillery by ship.

John Austin stepped into his saddle and said to those around him, "We're for it now, boys. Right or wrong, we're gonna do it. So let's do it right." Then, in a louder voice, "I'm heading out for Brazoria. Anybody comin' with me, mount up and let's go."

Part Four

BRAZORIA

June 17, 1832

Small conflicts may be the work of many people, but
big conflicts seldom are. Local confrontations, regional
skirmishes, even pitched battles where honor and pride
flow red underfoot may be the combined climax of the
opposing wills of thousands. But the big events, the wars
which change the course of history, are more often, in the
last analysis, a matching of will and wit between two
men, each seeking absolute eminence over some one thing
of value.

The thing of value was Mexico. And in such a conflict,
the one who has possession is usually far more vulnerable
than the one who seeks it.

President Anastasio Bustamente had known this at one
time. A few years earlier, rallying the peasantry and some
of the military around him, relying on his wit to hold
together a strike force, and on his determination to guide
its destructive power, this fiery-eyed tactical genius had
smashed the regime of the tyrant Vincente Guerrero and
seized Mexico for himself.

There was a time when Bustamente knew very well how
to win, and for a time when it was over he remembered
why he had won. He had made promises to the common
people, and made them believe those promises. He had
made promises to the best young military officers of the
day and through zeal had stifled their doubts. And he had
studied his enemy. Before he made his move, Bustamente
had made very sure that he knew exactly what Guerrero's
weaknesses were, where his support was the thinnest, what

issues would most inflame the people against him. He had used every trick at his command, had acted on a strategically sound, philosophically attractive, and totally ruthless plan—and had won. He had drained Guerrero of everything he had, everything he controlled. And then he had, matter-of-factly, killed him.

For a time, Bustamente had carefully remembered all the skills of the revolutionary, lest they be someday turned against him. But from the throne, the view is different. As the years passed, other matters occupied his time and, one by one, he began to forget the essentials. He forgot that for every man in power, there is one who seeks power with all the talent that the first once used to obtain it. He forgot that there would one day be a nemesis.

For Bustamente, that nemesis was a young officer of Spanish descent, a man inflamed with ruthless ambition and a sense of preordination, a student of Machiavelli and the Sicilian Napoleon Bonaparte. This was General Antonio López de Santa Anna. Bustamente had taken Mexico from Guerrero. Santa Anna set out to take it from Bustamente.

Now on the 17th day of June, 1832, the game was in play.

Santa Anna's opening moves had been swift and brilliant. By preliminary threats, veiled but clear, he had caused the surprised Bustamente to withdraw most of his troops from peripheral areas of Mexico to strengthen the palace and inland garrisons around Mexico City. Bustamente had reacted precisely as Santa Anna had hoped. At the same time, Santa Anna had gained much support in these outlying areas—Tabasco, Chihuahua, the Yucatan Peninsula, Texas, and Coahuila—by maneuvering his chosen officers into places of importance where sympathy toward the oppressed—peons in Tabasco, Indios in Yucatan, and Anglo colonists in Texas—could be demonstrated. And Bustamente had inadvertently assisted him here. As unrest became apparent in those areas, Bustamente acted to suppress it. He chose officers whose characters were hard and callous, and set them in command positions with the power of martial law. He had forgotten the price of oppression.

Now Santa Anna was moving openly. He was in full command of Vera Cruz and held a tight perimeter around Bustamente's inland regions. And he was methodically drawing the cord closed. In a short time, Bustamente would go the way of Guerrero, and Santa Anna would rule Mexico. He promised himself he would never forget the lessons of his conquest.

In Saltillo, where the legislature remained in session although a feeling of hopelessness had descended over the representatives—Mexico would soon be under a new regime—the empresario Stephen F. Austin had received his first clear dispatch about trouble at Anahuac. John Austin and the Brazoria militia had gone to the Trinity Bay settlement to assist the Johnson brothers in obtaining release of the prisoners held there. Also, General Teran, whom Austin knew to be a fair and impartial man, had commissioned a certain Colonel Suverano, in residence at the Anahuac fortress, to exercise some authority in easing the tensions between Austin's colonists and the military commander of the place.

Austin felt a bit better about the situation now. He had confidence in the Johnsons, and even greater confidence in John Austin. For the first time, he felt sure the matter would be resolved without incident. He turned his attention to more important things.

At Matamoros on the Rio Grande, Colonel Mexía, acting on orders from General Teran, provisioned a fleet of five gunboats and directed them to positions along the coastal bend. He knew both purposes for the maneuver. Ostensibly, the ships were assigned to protect coastwide trade from New Orleans to Matamoros. In fact, they were also there to blockade the middle coast, to secure this upper portion of Mexico against any sudden flanking movement by Bustamente. Teran—and Mexía—were in full agreement with General Santa Anna about whose hands Mexico should be in.

To the northeast, on another part of the coast, Lieutenant Colonel Ugartechea was in a dilemma. The distance from Vera Cruz to his outpost at Velasco and the tedious pace of communications left him uncertain just how to turn.

Ugartechea had just received a copy of the Turtle Bayou Resolutions. But he had not yet received word whether there was, indeed, a war in Mexico. Like Teran and Mexía, Ugartechea was a follower of Santa Anna. But he was also a very cautious man and was nominally under the command of Colonel Juan Bradburn at Anahuac. He was fairly sure that Bradburn would not join Santa Anna if the general made a bid for power.

There was only one way to avoid a premature commitment. He dutifully forwarded the settlers' resolutions by packet to Matamoros, with a request for instructions—privately—addressed to Mexá. Meanwhile, he decided, he would carry out Bradburn's orders to the best of his ability. If the Brazorians attempted to return to Anahuac with cannon, he would stop them. His troops were limited, but flooding upstream would preclude an overland march with cannon. And Ugartechea's fortress at Velasco commanded the mouth of the Brazos River.

Inland, several things were occurring at once, as usual. A gaunt and angry band of men crossed Oyster Creek and spurred their tired horses toward Brazoria. To the west, Britt Bailey and his slave Bubba left the dressing out of a dozen deer and two black bears to slaves on the John Sweeny plantation and turned their mounts toward Brazoria. North along the river Jared Groce received word of the impending fight at Anahuac and sent men riding toward Brazoria. Farther north, word also arrived at the colonial capital at San Felipe.

At Brazoria, sixteen-year-old Benjamin Brigham was riding the woods and prairies east of the river, rifle in hand, looking for Indian sign.

Twelve

Five days of tender feminine attention is about all a wounded man can stand. Particularly when the female involved remains cross, aloof, and indifferent to everything about him except his wounds. Whatever ego Matthew Langley had salvaged from his near-fatal visit to Anahuac and the subsequent jolting ride in a wagon bed cross country to Minchey's and then to Blanchard's station had been neatly dismantled by the uninterested attentions of Miss Charlotte Blanchard.

Jeremiah Blanchard and his wife remembered Langley from when he had stopped for breakfast on the way to Anahuac. If their niece remembered him, she gave no sign of it. She just looked him over coolly and went for bandages.

"Have a rough ride in that wagon, did ye?" Blanchard asked, as he helped him to a hammock at one side of the house. "Well, Ma and Charlotte will fix ye up."

The nearest the man came to displaying curiosity right then was when Langley asked him to see to his horses. "Horses? Didn't remember you havin' but one. That mare's yourn, too, huh?"

"Yes. And my gear's in the wagon."

They put him to bed in the hammock. The boy with snakebite was given a pallet on the porchway, under the eaves, and the sick old man was taken into the house.

As he waited for his turn at ministrations, Langley rechecked his score since coming to Texas. His money was more than half gone, but he now had two horses and most of his gear. More importantly, he had recovered his land deed, and had it safely stowed away.

He also had a hole in his side where a pistol ball had nicked him, a deep cut on his right arm and another on his left shoulder, a shallow cut diagonally across his face from cheekbone to jaw and, the worst one, a deep puncture high in his left leg. All in all, he was not in too bad shape. He just couldn't seem to move around too well.

A doctor at Anahuac had sewed him up—he shuddered again, remembering that the man's choice of implement was an awl—and had cauterized the bullet wound. He had recovered consciousness again in a wagon on the road to Minchey's, and someone had given him a large dose of brandy. There was the Texian camp, then the wagon ride cross country to Blanchard's—nice folks on that wagon but not easy on their horses or their passengers—and now here. The Blanchard women got around to him eventually, cleaned his wounds, replaced the soiled bandages with fresh ones, and fed him hot venison stew. Neither of them said more than "roll over a bit," or "mind your arm, now," or "does seem like you coulda' got them cuts all closer together."

Blanchard came around and told him the old man they had brought in was dying. "You know him?"

"No, but I hear he's got kin over on the Neches River."

"Better bury him here, then, when he goes, and send word if we can."

For a day or so, Langley suffered from fever, and for another day from sheer weakness. After that he began to feel as though he might mend.

Riders came through from time to time, and he could hear Blanchard talking with them out front or behind the house. There were guests for one or two meals each day, and he tried to calculate how much money Blanchard was making at a dollar a head for folks and livestock. Good thing going here, he decided.

Mostly, he became more and more aware of Charlotte

156

Blanchard. She, or her aunt, was always there when he needed tending, but they ignored him the rest of the time. For his part, he stayed close to the hammock. At first, just getting to the outhouse now and then was about all he could manage.

Around the house, during the day, he could see Charlotte working at the stove, or carrying water, or serving guests. And he could hear her voice, and marveled at it. She seemed always impatient. Talking with her aunt or Blanchard she conversed quietly enough, although very little, but to anyone else—him particularly—she was abrupt and quarrelsome.

Then, on the third evening, when the sun was down and the stars were out, he had dozed and was wakened by a sound. Someone was singing, softly and in a clear, sweet voice. He raised himself and looked around, pushing back the veil of netting strung above the hammock at night to protect him from mosquitos.

It was a clear evening, almost full night, but with enough light that he could see the dark forest around the silvered clearing of the farm. Over by the nearest field, a figure was seated on a stump. Long hair hung loose in the light breeze, booted legs were outstretched and crossed, and she held a musket across her lap. Alone there by the field, in the last of the evening light, Charlotte Blanchard sat singing to herself. The tune was the sweet, sad "Jennie Rose."

Langley decided that he had never seen, or heard, anything quite so sweet. The haunting melody brought back memories from a long time before—memories he thought he had buried—of a quick-eyed pixie of a girl with golden hair.

Once before, some years ago, Langley had been seriously taken with a girl, had fallen in love, in fact, with the totality of one who had never before played the game of courting. He was not, by far, her only suitor. Half the young bucks in the county were after Langley's heart's desire, and she enjoyed every minute of it. Inex-

157

perienced in this kind of combat, Langley tended to retreat at the wrong moments, pursue in the wrong directions, and, in general, defeat himself in a game he might otherwise have won.

His clumsiness finally offended her, and a pair of her suitors took the occasion to narrow the field. On behalf of the lady they challenged him, and when he backed off in confusion, unsure of the art of deflecting a challenge, they made a mistake. They pushed too hard. Routine solitude had laid a veneer of patience over the natural temper of Matthew Langley, but beneath its finite swathing that temper was still there in full. On a dusty street of Mason, Illinois, he battered them mercilessly, both at once, then dragged them across the square and dumped them on the doorstep of his recent ladylove.

In the years that followed, he had made no further attempt at romance. The anger had faded, but the hurt remained, and he was in no hurry again to expose his soul to casual abuse. The few encounters he had had since then had been inconsequential and had posed no threat to a young man's pride.

The young man had grown older over the years, however, and had come to find the loneliness less easy to live with. The sweetness of Charlotte's voice, blended with the sadness of the tune she sang, touched Langley in a way he had not felt in some time. For a long while he continued to listen to it, until drowsiness finally overcame him and he went back to sleep.

By the time Langley awoke the next morning, the sun was high overhead. After he had washed his face and put his shirt on, Blanchard stopped by to talk with him. He reclined in the hammock, wishing the throbbing pain of the leg wound would ease. Blanchard sat on a sawhorse near him and chatted about the latest news. There had been some shooting at Anahuac, but apparently no one was hurt. And it looked as though Austin and Bradburn were going to negotiate peacefully for the prisoners in the stockade there.

Around the front of the house Charlotte's voice was suddenly raised in anger. Then there was a slap, sharp and loud, and the snakebit boy yowled.

"Youngster must be feelin' better today," Blanchard said conversationally. Charlotte came striding around the corner of the house. Her face was flushed and her eyes blazing. Langley had thought of her as having soft eyes, but right this minute he couldn't recall why he had thought that.

She stormed up to him and stuck a finger at his face, an inch from his nose. "You say one wrong word," she said, "or make one wrong move, and I'll upend that dang hammock with you on it." She marched away toward the rear of the house, and Langley watched her go with awe and admiration.

"Figgers you might git to feelin' better, too," Blanchard said.

That afternoon Langley walked around a little, somewhat stiffly but without undue pain. He stopped to visit with the boy and went in to talk to the old man, whom he hadn't seen since they were brought in. The man lay on clean bedding on a straw mattress, his face very pale and his thin white hair silvery on the pillow. He was awake, but seemed far away. The muscular old hands lay still at his sides. When Langley spoke to him he didn't answer.

After a while he went on out to the barn. His horses were being well taken care of. The bay mare looked sleek and ready to ride, and the Morgan was fat and frisky. Both of his saddles and all his harness were hung inside the barn door, soaped and oiled, and the rest of his gear was there beside them. He wondered what his bill was going to be this time, then decided it was worth it, whatever.

Back by the hammock, Charlotte was supervising as

159

two Negro women set a large wooden tub on the ground and began pouring pails of hot water into it. When there was five inches of water in the tub she handed him a bar of lye soap, pointed to the tub, and said, "Wash yourself. Give your clothes to Sheba."

She walked away, and Langley did as he was told. While the old colored woman carried off his reeking clothes, Langley climbed into the tub. The sun was hot, the water was hot, and his wounds were mending. Even the leg wound was well scabbed over, the strands of gut with which Doctor Labadie had patched him blending with the scab. There was discoloration around this and the bullet hole in his side, but it was the dark red of a bruise. It was healing.

He took his time washing, almost hoping that the haughty Charlotte might show up again while he was still in the tub. He imagined that embarrassment might be a refreshing change from her usual abrupt attitude. Then it occurred to him that he, in the raw, would probably embarrass her no more than a side of beef, and the likelihood made him angry.

By the time he had finished, Sheba was back with a razor, long flannel shirt, drawers, and britches from his pack. He put on the clothing, shaved, brushed back his hair, and felt better than he had in some time.

Two riders from the west pulled up at the house, and he went around to listen as Blanchard talked to them. They were on their way to Anahuac with news for John Austin. Santa Anna had occupied Vera Cruz and denounced President Bustamente. The government and the military were choosing sides. There would most likely be war, and it was the considered opinion around Brazoria that Santa Anna had the winning hand. The men stopped only long enough to eat a snack of fried pork, green beans, and cornbread, to fill their canteens, and to rub down their mounts and resaddle, and then they rode on to the east.

Blanchard charged them a dollar apiece.

160

"When do you think you'll be ready to buy Texas, Jeremiah?" Langley asked him.

"Wouldn't want it, son. Not enough money in it."

He ate with the family that evening, at the long table behind the house. The boy was there, too, hobbling on a badly swollen foot but looking fit enough. Mrs. Blanchard carried broth and cornbread to the old man in the house. When she came back, she was shaking her head.

"Don't know how that old codger hangs on like he does. Seems most ways dead, but he's still takin' nourishment."

There was one other guest, a trader from Harrisburg coming through with pack animals bound for Velasco. He was talkative and enthusiastic, and didn't need much help to keep a conversation going.

"That Harrisburg," he said, "now that's the place to put your money on. Goin' to be a sizable town one day, and that's a fact. Two—three hundred people around there already, and the commerce—why, it's a natural crossroads, sir. A natural crossroads."

Langley's scant knowledge of the dingy little town on Buffalo Bayou, at the edge of Tonkawa country, gave no clue to any reason for the man's enthusiasm, but he kept his peace.

"This whole end of the colony," the trader continued, "Harrisburg right on down to the Brazos port—maybe Galveston Island, too, if they ever get the Injuns and the blackguards under control—someday it's gonna be one sight to behold. Yes, sir."

He had seen Indian sign on the trail down from Harrisburg, but had no trouble. "The Kronks, they stay shy for a spell, then they all get together one night and play hell with somebody, then they disappear into the woods again. One thing sure, though, they always run in packs. Just like stinkin' big wolves. Ain't never heard of one of 'em doin' nothin' alone."

"I have," Langley said, but didn't elucidate.

161

"An' not a soldier on the road, all the ways," the man went on, unhindered. "Never seen the likes of it. Somethin's likely come up on down country. Lot of the greencoats movin' that way lately, and not many around here now a'tall."

Blanchard caught him between breaths and managed to fill him in on the latest news from Brazoria.

"Don't surprise me a'tall, sir. That there Santa Anna is a comer. A real comer. Has a head on his shoulders, too, and he ain't had a chance to go sour on us like Bustamente done the last few years. I expect things will be a whole lot better in Texas if he calls Bustamente out and wins. I believe Santa Anna's the kind of man Texians could get along with."

Langley had shoved his plate aside and was reaching for coffee. Charlotte came up beside him and pushed his plate back in front of him, then heaped some more pork and cornbread on it, and spooned honey onto the bread.

"You eat some more," she said. "It's good for you." Then she went back to the stove. Blanchard glanced around at her, then looked quizzically at Langley. The stranger went on talking.

After supper they dispersed, the women to clear away and clean in back of the house, the trader to throw his bed in the barn, the boy back to his pallet, and Langley to his hammock. He took a cup of coffee with him, and his pipe. Blanchard went off to tend the stock.

It was another beautiful evening. Blanchard came around after a bit to sit and smoke, and for a while they chatted about this and that and watched the stars come out.

"Noticed that land deed in your pack," the man said finally. "Ought to be real fine country up around there. You figurin' to work it?"

"Planned to, if I can ever get the title recorded. Seems like that's hard to do right now. It's a Spanish deed, so it won't clear through Austin's colonies. And that commander at Anahuac has all the patent magistrates closed up."

He had been thinking about going to Saltillo, or Mexico City. But now, with war brewing, he really didn't know which way to turn.

"Might be best just to stick around and wait," Blanchard said after a while. "Things are all messed up right now, but they'll sort theirselves out, given time. I reckon that pilgrim over there's right about at least one thing. Might do us all some good if Santa Anna was to take over in Mexico City . . . for a while, anyway."

Langley had been wondering about that, and felt as though Blanchard was right. When you get boxed in, and can't get out, it might be best just to wait for somebody to build a new box.

"You could stay right here for a while if you was a mind to," Blanchard said. "That old man in there, he's gonna die any time now, and that boy'll be ready to move on pretty soon. We have plenty of room."

"At a dollar a day?"

Blanchard chuckled. "I never charged anybody a dollar a day yet. I just charge a dollar. Day's got nothin' to do with it. It evens out."

"I don't know yet what I'll do," Langley said. "Might go back to Brazoria, or up to San Felipe. I'll think about it."

"You do that."

The conversation cheered Langley in at least one respect. He had been here five days now, and was beginning to worry about the cost.

At midmorning the next day a wagon pulled in from the east and the man driving it went straight to the boy on the porch, hugged him, patted him on the back, and then thoroughly cussed him out. His mother, it seemed, had been frightened half to death since he had left Liberty. It wasn't until a couple of days ago they had learned where he was. And what did he mean, packing off like that without asking permission?

The man got the boy and his baggage packed into the wagon, thanked Blanchard profusely for caring for him, paid his dollar and headed back east. Two mounted slaves followed behind, carrying muskets.

"Fine man," Blanchard said. "Cares a heap for that boy."

It was that afternoon that the Brazoria militia rode in, with John Austin at its head. Langley had seen the man briefly at Minchey's, but didn't know him. They had been riding hard, and they brought hard news. The commander of the troops at Anahuac had gone back on his word and had made an attack on the town. The negotiations were over, and the Brazorians were on the way home for more men and for cannon.

Some of them were stepping down to give their horses a breather, and Blanchard yelled for the women to put on coffee and cornbread. A man who looked familiar to him came toward Langley and stuck out his hand. "Don't know if you remember me," he said. "I met you back at Bell's Landing. Name's George McKinstry. I'm postmaster over at Brazoria. How's the cuts and scrapes getting on?"

Langley remembered him. McKinstry was one of the men who had helped him out when the soldiers and the bounty collector came for him at the sutler's store at Bell's Landing. Several others in the crowd waved and howdied to him, and he waved back. It seemed that more of them knew him than he knew. Then he heard a yell from the road and a small, bearded man on a gray raced up to him and reined in. It was Three-legged Willie Williamson.

"Howdy, Coonslinger," the man said. "Been wonderin' if you'd be up and around time we got here."

The bunch was as high-spirited as he remembered them, but there was less of the easy, careless joshing than he remembered from Minchey's—or even from

164

Anahuac. Even there, they had been basically a cheerful, vigorous people, but now, he noted, the cheerfulness was subdued and in its place was a kind of determined anger. Langley made another mental note about Texians. They would stand to be pushed around some, and they would bow to authority up to a point. But they didn't like being lied to.

Not all of them were Brazorians. Fiery little William Scates was there, with a few others from the Trinity.

Williamson introduced John Austin to Langley, who found himself awed at the intensity of the man. He had heard Austin described as a "born leader" and a "real, first-rate border captain." Feeling the firm handshake and looking into the level, appraising eyes of the man, Langley understood why Stephen F. Austin had chosen this New Englander as his second in command. He could follow John Austin.

"Heard a little about you," Austin said. "Glad you're feeling better."

As coffee was served around, the story took shape. The Turtle Bayou Resolutions were being distributed throughout the colony as a call to arms. Austin and the Brazorians were on their way to gather more men and pick up some cannon that were hidden away in Brazoria. There was much difference of opinion among them about just what they were after. Austin and George McKinstry steadfastly maintained that their aim was to raise whatever force was handy, return to Anahuac, obtain release of the prisoners there and suitable restitution from Bradburn, then go back to the business of running a colony in a wild land. But they were in a minority on this. Most of the men openly supported revolt — independence from Mexico. Their blood was up, and they weren't satisfied with the prospect of a small encounter.

Austin was firm about it. "There are less than six thousand people in all the colonies," he said. "We haven't the men, or the arms, or the money, to engage the Republic of Mexico in a war of rebellion."

"We done it before," an old-timer said crossly. "Kicked the British right out of America. And greencoats ain't near what redcoats is when it comes to fightin'."

"You weren't but five years old when all that was goin' on, Hiram," Williamson said easily. "How do you know?"

"But they ain't hardly no army at all in Texas right now, John," another said. "They mostly been called back down to Mexico City. They got other problems to worry about right now."

"And then they'll be back," Austin said. "Neither Bustamente nor Santa Anna's going to give up Texas without a fight."

And so it went. Nobody was convincing anybody. But in the meantime, there was a thing to do upon which they all agreed. They would take men and cannon to Anahuac.

It was a brief rest. Within an hour the Brazorians and the scattering of Trinity men were mounting up again. They would make Brazoria by tomorrow.

"You comin' with us, Matthew?" Williams asked.

For some reason he hadn't even thought of going along. Now he thought about it, and there seemed no question. "Yeah . . . yeah, sure I am. I'll pack and catch up with you down the road."

"Good. Thought you might."

McKinstry was approaching Blanchard with a handful of coin, and Blanchard waved him away. "This time's on me, George."

McKinstry went for his horse.

"Hold on there, dammit! I'm almost ready!" The voice was high and harsh, and several of them stopped and looked around. The old man who had been dying in Blanchard's house was scurrying across the porchway, hastily donned boots unbuckled, hat askew on his head, pushing his long shirt into his pants as he ran. He had an old musket cradled in his arm and a powder flask flapping at his belt.

"Waitin' five days fer somebody to come git me, and now ye try to run off an' leave me packin'!" he fumed. "Somebody git me that buckskin out of the corral over there."

Blanchard looked stunned, then began to grin. His wife was standing in the doorway, her mouth open, hands folded in her apron. Blanchard shouted to McKinstry. "That one," he laughed, "will cost you a dollar."

For several minutes after the Brazorians rode out, after the noise had died away down the west road, the silence at Blanchard's seemed unreal. Blanchard had gone off somewhere, and no one else was in sight.

Langley wandered around to where the hammock was strung and picked up his rifle and a few other belongings left there, then went back around to the barn. He changed clothes, putting on a fresh buckskin shirt and britches from his pack, and strapped on his broad belt with the long knife in its sheath. Blanchard came through the doorway and stood watching him, framed against the brilliant sunlight outside. "Sorry to see you leave, boy," he said. Lately he had taken to calling him "boy" and "son" although he wasn't more than a few years Langley's senior. "Aim to be back this way soon?"

"I don't really know. I'll follow along with them for a while and see what happens. Then I guess I'll either get back to my claim up the river or maybe head on down to Matamoros, maybe Mexico City. Depends on whether I can get that title registered."

Blanchard was quiet for a few minutes, then said, "A feller your age needs to be settlin' down. This is right good country to do it in, if a man's wise to the land, if he's got a feelin' for it. I been thinkin' you got such a feelin'."

"I don't know. Maybe." He was a little uncomfortable now, anxious to be away, but Blanchard still wanted to talk.

"Me and Ma, you know, we ain't original settlers here. We just drifted in from Kentucky on our own, and the colonists here sort of adopted us. We managed to buy this place, and been settlin' in ever since. Good life for folks don't mind a little work an' watchin' for Injuns." He paused a moment, reflecting. "You could do worse yourself, I expect."

"Expect I could, at that." Blanchard was skirting the subject. To settle and build a life, a man needed a woman. He had entertained fleeting notions about several in the past few years, but to no real purpose. Most recently, in the last few days, he had had some disturbing thoughts about Blanchard's niece, but he was trying to put those thoughts aside. Charlotte would be a little too much for anybody. In five days he had been nothing but courteous, and had kept his distance entirely, and yet she had managed to make him feel distinctly unwelcome. It was as though she had developed an instant dislike for him and was determined to let him know it.

Langley had very few illusions about himself. He had given up all his fantasies years ago. He was a large, clumsy, homely individual with an unsettled land deed and no bright prospects, and he was nearly thirty years old. He might find a comfortable woman some time, but it wouldn't be now, or here. It was a shame, though, about . . .

Charlotte walked in and gazed at him coldly for a moment, then turned to her uncle.

"He's going off with that bunch?"

"Appears like it. Man's gotta do what needs doin'."

She turned again to Langley. "None of my business," she snapped, "but there's some folks shouldn't be allowed to wander around loose, and you're one of them, Matthew Langley. Not even healed up from the last fool scrape, and already headin' out to another one." She was fairly choking now on her anger, and Langley could see no reason for it.

She started to say more, then stopped, her mouth

168

tight and eyes blazing at him, and turned quickly away. She walked out of the barn ramrod-straight, without another word. The men stood in silence for a moment, Blanchard lounging against the barn door, Langley with his mouth open and his ears red.

Finally he turned to the older man. "Jeremiah, what's she got against me? I didn't do anything to her."

Blanchard studied him for a moment, then shook his head.

"Son," he explained sympathetically, "I believe you're just plain dumb."

There was the problem now of one man with two horses, and Langley decided to ride the mare. She was a good mount, and should take the wooded trails well. The Morgan was a little skittish in trees. But riding one horse and leading one would slow him, and he had some riding to do to catch up with the Brazorians. Blanchard offered the solution.

"Why don't you leave the Morgan? I'll tend him, and you can stop by and get him when you're back this way. Only cost you a dollar, if you don't wait too long."

Saddled, packed, and mounted, Langley leaned down to shake Blanchard's hand and thanked him for the care he had received. He offered board fare, and it was shrugged off. They would square up when he came back for the Morgan.

"You take care of yourself now, you hear? And next time you run across a skunk, stand off and shoot him. Don't try to take him with a knife."

As he nudged the mare and turned into the trail, Langley recalled with surprise that Blanchard's contentious niece, in her anger, had called him by name. She hadn't done that before.

He caught up with Austin's men late in the evening, on the bank of a bayou. They had been slowed by a bogged wagon and were camped in trees on the far side. When he had turned the mare into their brush corral and had been introduced around, George McKinstry came over and got his signature on a roll he carried in an oilskin pouch. Then, standing by a campfire on the bank of a sluggish, unnamed bayou, he was solemnly sworn in as a member of the citizens' militia of the district of Brazoria, San Felipe de Austin Colony, State of Texas and Coahuila, Republic of Mexico.

For the time being, he was now a Brazorian.

Thirteen

On the west bank of the Brazos River a day's ride upstream from the Gulf of Mexico, John Austin established his town in 1828. Now, four years old and booming, Brazoria was the colony's second center of government and its first city in eminence. Despite the increasingly stringent trade regulations, embargoes, and military interference of the past year, Brazoria was still growing and thriving, seemingly running on its own vitality.

From the high cutbank of the river, extensive landing docks had been built out over the water where the growing fleet of small coastal schooners rigged for offshore navigation and river running could moor and unload and take on cargo. Here, too, larger sloops and an occasional brigantine could bring in the heavier cargoes the settlement demanded. Traffic had been badly cut by the Mexican embargoes, but the coastal schooners still traded here, some legally, paying tariffs downstream at Velasco, and some—with varied cargoes—running the blockades time and again. As often as not, when one of these runs was successful, it was because of the intentional oversight of the command at Velasco. Lieutenant Colonel Domingo de Ugartechea was known to be a fair man and not overly zealous in his pursuit of errant colonials.

Above the docks, on the river's edge, stood storehouses and sheds where cotton, sugar cane, syrup, and hides were amassed for export and where the varied imports of the little colony—everything from building materials to yard goods—paused briefly upon arrival. Behind the warehouses spread a burgeoning business district, still only a few small buildings but with more under construction. In offices, stalls, cubicles, and wherever roofed space could be found, a growing number of professions and trades were in full swing of commercial activity. Doctors, lawyers, dentists, merchants, and dealers in trade goods occupied most of the available commercial space, along with blacksmiths, carpenters, masons, harness makers, cobblers, and candlemakers. There were a gunsmith and two general mercantile emporiums, a weaver and a boot-and-saddle cobbler, and up the road, downwind, a small tannery.

And there was the recently opened but already highly esteemed social and business center of the town, the boardinghouse and tavern of the widow Jane Long. Two doors away stood the post office and between them a tiny but busy hardware store.

Brazoria's importance was further enhanced by the presence of John Austin. Although San Felipe de Austin—far upstream on the middle fork of the Brazos—was nominally the colony's capital, Stephen F. Austin was often not there. In his absence, the colony was run by John Austin from his home, Brazoria.

On this June day the sun was bright, the weather warm, and the river high from upstream rains. A hundred and fifty yards wide and churning, the river's red swell lapped at the Brazoria docks and lazily rocked the schooner *Brazoria*, riding high and empty at its moorings.

Benjamin Brigham, hunting a mile east of the river, could barely see the mast tops of the *Brazoria* off to his left, but ahead of him, north up the Bell's Landing road, was something of far greater interest. For several minutes he had been hearing the sounds of a large body of horsemen coming toward him. Now he could see them riding out of the woods. It was John Austin, riding at the head of the militia. Waving his hat, Ben Brigham spurred his horse toward them.

A few moments later, bursting with the news he had

received from the lead riders, he galloped again down the trail toward Brazoria. The ferry was on the far bank. Ben nudged his animal, scrambling and sliding, down the steep bank and into the water, kicked free, and swam with the horse to the other bank, coming out a quarter of a mile below the point of entry. Climbing the west bank, he regained the saddle and headed the wild-eyed horse into town.

"Get your guns! Everybody get your guns! There's gonna be a fight, and the whole town's invited."

He made a circle around the town, calling to everyone in sight, then reined in at the rail in front of Jane Long's tavern. Two of the colony's leading citizens, Dr. T.F.L. Parrott and the planter William H. Wharton, master of Eagle Island plantation, were coming out of the post office. Parrott stepped to the tie rail and looked down the block. "What did the boy say, Bill?"

"Something about a fight. Let's go see."

The front street was beginning to fill with men, all heading for the tavern. Ben Brigham, basking in his moment of glory, ignored the questions of the first arrivals, waiting for a suitable crowd.

"Ben, you whippersnapper, if you don't speak up, I might whale the daylights out of you right now," school master Bill Smith declared. "And I'll tell your daddy why I did."

Ben grinned, paused a moment longer, then relented.

"John Austin's comin' with some of the men, back from Anahuac. They're comin' for cannon and more men. We're gonna blow that damn fort down around them Meskins' ears!"

"Ben, you watch your language or your momma will paddle your young tail for you."

"Aw, Doc, I'm near about growed up now." The boy reddened.

The ferry had started toward the far bank, and the crowd could see Austin's men on the cleared ridge above the river. The barge would make several trips to bring

173

all of them across.

Austin came over with the first load, and joined the excited crowd in front of the tavern. Someone brought out a whiskey keg and started passing cups around. Several women had appeared at the back of the throng, and others were hurrying up, running to meet their men as they came off the ferry. At the tavern Austin and George McKinstry led the first group inside to the bar. Others trooped in behind them, waiting for Austin's comments.

Jane Long, tall and dark-haired, set mugs of cool beer before Austin and McKinstry. "Welcome back," she said.

"Jane. Kian. Been a long ride."

"Howdy, Mistah John." Kian was a tall, molasses-eyed Negress who was Jane Long's personal servant and, for many years, close friend. "Nice to have you back."

McKinstry finished his beer quickly and headed for the post office, anxious to see his wife and get caught up on the business of his office. His place at the bar was taken by Henry Smith, who didn't try to mask his delight at the news he had just heard. Smith wanted Texas free of Mexico and was impatient for it to come about.

"Whiskey, Jane, please. John, they tell me outside Bradburn is still holding his prisoners."

"That's right."

"And you're going back with cannon?"

"That's what I intend to do." Austin worried about Smith sometimes. The man was a firebrand, and a dangerously capable orator. He and Stephen F. Austin had nearly come to grips on several occasions—Austin preaching patience and tolerance, the doctrine of restraint, Smith arguing for independence and hang the cost. Stephen F. Austin was wary of the man. John Austin was wary, too, but basically he liked him. "Do you think the colony will go along with me, Henry?"

"Most of them will, I think." Smith sipped his whiskey. "You know, I believe most of them will be delighted. And with Stephen in Saltillo, he won't be around upsetting the applecart."

"Don't underestimate Stephen, Henry," Parrott advised. "He's a careful man and a patient one, but don't sell him short. When the time is right, he'll fight with the rest of us."

"But the time won't ever be right, dammit! Not for Stephen. How long are we going to be pushed around by a government that went back on every promise it made to us before we strike back?"

Doctor Parrott was standing near. "Stephen is striking back, but he's doing it his way. Legally, through the legislature."

Smith's glare nailed him. "And the legislature has no power, sir, not anymore. The country is under martial law."

John Austin was ignoring the exchange. He had heard it all before. And he, for the moment, was committed to a course of action. All philosophy aside, some of them would go back to Anahuac and do what needed to be done.

Smith was talking now for the benefit of the entire crowd. "All the talk and all the reason has gotten us nothing but more taxes and more restriction. The Mexicans have a gold mine in this colony, but they aren't working it — they're cleaning it out."

Several around him were nodding in agreement. Others were listening patiently, waiting for him to run down. Someone in the back, less patient than the rest, said, "Tell us about it later, Henry. You ain't been to Anahuac. Let's hear what John Austin has to say."

Austin put down his mug and turned, his elbows on the bar. "There isn't much to say. Santa Anna is going to start — maybe has already started — a revolution in Mexico. In my opinion, it isn't really any of our concern here, except for two things. First, Bustamente is no good for us anymore. Santa Anna might be better. Second, and more important, we have a stable to clean here in Texas, and Santa Anna has given us the broom to clean it.

"I am going back to Anahuac. I will take cannon, and any man who wants to come along. I will support the Trinity settlers to gain the freedom of their neighbors from Bradburn's stockade." He paused and surveyed the room with a cold gaze. "And I will speak further with Bradburn, one way or another. The agreement he broke was an agreement with Brazoria as well as the Trinity party."

He tipped his head toward the wall at the end of the bar where McKinstry had posted a copy of the Turtle Bayou Resolutions. "If anyone here has not read that document, read it now. It states our case and our justification. I expect now that we will fight Bradburn and his troops. And we will fight them in the name of General Santa Anna."

Bill Russell elbowed his way through the crowd and some of the latecomers slapped him on the back as he passed. "Been home yet, Bill? Eleanor know you're back yet?"

At thirty years of age Russell was already the father of seven children and his wife was expecting their eighth. It was the general opinion that Bill Russell intended to populate Texas by himself. Russell grinned at his hecklers and made his way to where Austin stood.

"John, I sent some riders out to call a meeting here tonight, and George is putting a notice up at the post office. Thank you, Kian." He accepted the mug of beer she set before him, and drank half of it. "Most of the boys have gone on home to see their families, but they'll be back. Talk is, most of 'em are committed to going back with us to Anahuac. Will the colony sanction it?"

"We'll see soon enough." Austin raised a hand for the attention of the crowd. "All right," he announced. "There will be a meeting tonight, here. Most of us who went to Anahuac are going back, prepared to fight if necessary. I'll ask for a vote tonight, whether the entire colony is to be committed, or whether we go on our own." He pushed away from the bar. "Right now, I'm going home

176

to see the wife and the boy. Read that document over there, think about it, and I'll see you all back here tonight."

When he left, several others left with him. Most of those remaining were townspeople who had not been with the militia at Anahuac. Only a few of the tired, dusty riders remained around tables at the back.

At the bar William Smith shook his head. The schoolteacher had not joined the conversation before, but he was worried. "I don't know about this, gentlemen. I really don't. Our colony isn't strong yet, and we might be biting off more than we can chew."

A bushy-bearded settler beside him shared his concern. "If we do back Santa Anna, and it turns out he loses, we goin' to be in a real pickle."

William Wharton, trim and dark, turned a solemn eye on the posted resolutions. "From what I hear, most of the Mexican army in Texas and Coahuila . . . at least most of the general officers . . . are declaring for Santa Anna. It looks to me like we can't sit this one out, and we can't stay in the middle. We have to choose a side.

"There is Teran, and Mexia," he enumerated, "and Cos. And a lot of others. Santa Anna is their choice, and they won't take it kindly if we stay too far out on the sideline. This is our country, too."

"Hell, yes, it's ours!" Henry Smith put in, a belligerent eye on William Smith. These two had often thanked God that, despite the same last name, they were not related. "And if we play it just right, we can cut off from Mexico entirely."

"Henry, we just aren't strong enough yet," Doctor Parrott interrupted with exasperation. "How many times must we go over the same ground?" Glancing at the fiery Smith, he softened his tone a little. "Besides, Santa Anna sounds like a fair man, and he favors the Constitution of '24. He might be all right if he gets in."

"Don't bet on it, sir. Just don't you bet on it!" Smith was scowling as he turned to address the room in gen-

177

eral. "Mark my words now, all of you! Santa Anna will win this revolution of his, and he will rule Mexico. And when he has the country under his thumb he'll turn on us. He will be another dictator, just like the one down there now!"

"For the good of Texas and Mexico," Parrott breathed, "I hope you're wrong in that last."

"I, for one," William Smith said, "wish John Austin would change his mind about going back to Anahuac."

"You know better than that." It was Wharton. "We all know Big John Austin better than that. He said he's going, so he's going. Whatever the colony as a whole decides, John Austin will fight."

"So will a whole lot of us," someone said.

Most of John Austin's militia had homes in Brazoria, but some didn't. There were men here from Anahuac and Liberty on the Trinity who had come back with Austin to help with the cannon. There were others from east on the Neches River and a few from as far as Nacogdoches who had joined up for various reasons. There were some from Harrisburg and a couple of men picked up along the way back from Anahuac, like Langley. And as swift riders carried the word north and west about the Turtle Bayou Resolutions, a few had begun drifting in from up the Brazos and from west on the San Bernard. Several also came in from Bell's Landing, Chenango, Peach Point, and Quintana.

As the day went on, more and more would come in from farther away, riding to the news of the Anahuac incident. Word would not reach San Felipe and the up-river colonies for another day or so, but with Stephen F. Austin away in Saltillo, the effective seat of the colony was at Brazoria, where John Austin hung his hat. Men from the little settlements of Velasco and Quintana, flanking the river's mouth, brought news that the Resolutions had reached Fort Velasco and that Colonel Ugartechea had called in troops quartered in the beachfront settlements to strengthen his garrison.

The extras in Austin's party and the new arrivals pitched their camps on the riverbank to await Austin's meeting. Some of them headed for the tavern to pass the time, and some just wandered around.

Choosing the latter activity for a while, Langley noted with interest that the town was bigger than it had been just a few weeks ago when he first passed through. He also noted that, among the freshly painted professional and commercial signs hung everywhere on buildings along the front street, there was an overabundance of lawyers. This fact brought to mind something that Robert Williamson had said. Williamson had observed that at least half the renegades, highbinders, and general good-for-nothings in Texas at the time were lawyers.

"It don't mean nothin' a'tall. There's lots of reasons why folks get to be lawyers. Some of 'em figure that's the only way you can steal legal, and some figure the best way to protect yourself from one is to be one. Most of 'em, though, get to be lawyers because it don't take near as much education as bein' a doctor or a carpenter or a planter or somethin' else useful." That, Langley realized, was very true. If a man could read, and did so for eighteen months, and proved it, he was a lawyer.

"Most of them prob'ly won't ever practice law," Williamson had pointed out. "Some will go into politics and some will take up land-sharkin', but most will just go on their own way and stay middlin' honest. But them that practices, they'll do all right.

"You know, you take a town and put one lawyer in it and he'll starve to death. Set up two of 'em and they'll keep each other alive. But you get three or more lawyers goin' in one town, chances are they'll all get rich."

Langley noticed, too, a deep and pervasive difference between the Brazos colonists and those of the Trinity. They were all the same breed and brand of people but their backgrounds were of different levels. Along the

Trinity, and in fact throughout the eastern Texas colonies, the people were a thoroughly mixed lot. There were aristocratic people and people from the gutters, wealthy people and poor people, people of breeding and bearing and people fresh from the woods. They were a grab-bag lot of the adventurous and the hunted, the resourceful and the resourceless, the pioneer looking for a new start and the fugitive gambling on a last chance.

On the Brazos, where Austin's hand-picked "Old Three-hundred" had taken root, they were more of a kind. Like the Trinity settlers, they came from all over the United States and some other countries, but unlike the Trinity people, those along the Brazos were principally eminent citizens. These were people who had held wealth and prestige in a dozen states as merchants, traders, congressmen, and judges. The base of the population of the Brazos colonies was made up of people who were well acquainted with power and wealth, who by choice had traded the comfort of a secure position in Virginia, the Carolinas, Tennessee, Mississippi, Delaware, the central coastal states or New England for the promise of a raw new land.

There were plenty of ordinary folk here, too—drifters and settlers, the people who go where there is a place to go because it's better than where they were. But there was a solid and deep underpinning to the culture growing along the Brazos. Moses Austin and his son Stephen had been very careful in their selections and very persuasive in their arguments.

Langley was surprised at the number of men who hailed him, waved and smiled, and stopped to shake his hand. At first he was baffled, until some of their passing comments began to run together.

"Mister, ain't you the one give that feller Whitlet whatfor? Proud to meet you . . ."

"I seen him when he come through with them soldiers. He sure ain't so pretty anymore . . ."

". . . 'bout time somebody got in ahead of that pistol of

180

his."

And the other story, the knife fight in Anahuac, was making the rounds, too. Next to drinking and fighting, Texians loved to talk, especially about each other.

His upbringing in the Illinois hills outside St. Louis had fairly well equipped Langley to look out for himself in most situations, and the time he had spent in St. Louis and New Orleans taught him that where there are a lot of people there is always a chance of trouble. But nothing in his background had prepared him for a reputation.

Like many a man with an ordinary face and a backwoods background, he was comfortable around the edges of civilization. He decided he would never get used to being in the middle of it. There was nothing handsome, dashing, or brilliant about him, and he knew it. He was somewhat oversized, strong enough when he had to be and fairly quick at times, but he had never noticed being noticeable.

Every reputation worth talking about needs an element of mystery, and this was added by his three-legged friend from the river. Passing the open front of a saloon, he heard a snatch of conversation from inside: "How come ol' Willie calls that feller 'Coonslinger'?"

"Damned if I know. Willie don't say."

Langley decided he appreciated Williamson's belated reticence. He didn't intend to elaborate, either.

As afternoon wore into evening, Langley stopped to eat at a little place with a sign and three tables, then went back to Jane Long's tavern. Inside, there was standing room only, and the air was filled with the smells of smoke and whiskey and the sounds of loud conversation. The meeting was about to start, and everyone was arriving. Many of them, in fact, had been there most of the day.

After a while John Austin came in, followed by McKinstry and Russell. Following some preliminaries, Austin bulled his way to the bar, applied a bung starter

181

vigorously to the bar top, and called the assembly to order. When they were silent he made a short and eloquent address in a low-pitched voice, which nevertheless dominated the room. He described briefly the situation at Anahuac and related his promise to return there with cannon and men. He outlined the latest reports from Matamoros on Santa Anna's stand against Bustamente and explained the colony's dilemma in the face of a revolutionary war in Mexico. It would be wise, he said, to support a winner, and deadly to support a loser. But, unfortunately, he considered it equally deadly to make no choice at all. He made it clear that he would return to Anahuac and that a lot of men probably would go along, but that whether they acted on their own or on behalf of the Austin colonies was up to the citizens of the colony to decide by vote.

Then he turned the bung starter over to George McKinstry and stood aside. A murmur of conversation throughout the room erupted suddenly into a multitude of quarrels, and chaos threatened the meeting. McKinstry used the bung starter on the bar and offered to use it on some heads. The meeting came to order again.

Then the speeches started. Henry Smith declaimed for a decisive action by the colony to rid Texas of Mexican rule and was ruled out of order midway through. Dr. Parrott urged careful consideration of the courses at hand and that whatever decision was made be considered unanimous. Robert Williamson thumped up to the bar and delivered a short, beautifully worded speech for intervention, which drew applause for its fluency and boos from some for its militance. William Smith argued against intervention because of the likelihood of retaliation against the relatively weak and undefended colonies. He spoke of the women and children whose security depended upon not angering the power of Mexico.

Some others argued, and well, that as the first and oldest authorized American colony in Mexico, Austin's colony owed a debt of honor to Mexico for the land they claimed and the right to develop it. Others pointed out that this was not the Mexico of 1828, the land that had welcomed them as equals under a just system of constitutional law, but had degenerated into the worst kind of tyranny and must be fought if they were to ever hold up their heads again. The strongest argument, repeated several times, was the strength of Mexico and the weakness of the young colony—the fear that rash action would bring about their expulsion from this, their adopted land. Part of this argument was the repeated reference to their wives and families, their homes—and thus, their vulnerability. Texas couldn't field an army, at least not yet, and certainly not to fight on Texas soil.

It was going against the militia. Dr. Parrott put the cap on it.

"Gentlemen," he said, with worry in his eyes, "I don't know whether I am for or against declaring this colony for Santa Anna. Neither do I know whether attacking Colonel Bradburn at Anahuac as a colonial action would be wise. But this I do know: if Steve Austin were here, he would be opposed to it. And all of you know that as well as I. If my own conscience cannot decide this issue for me, then what I know of the leader of our colony must show me the way. If Stephen F. Austin could be here now, I believe he would say stand, gentlemen, stand and wait. He would not favor hasty action, and I believe he would not favor this action."

William Scates pushed forward, fire in his eyes. "Were you at Anahuac, sir, when that madman descended on the town?"

To one side, William Russell faced around to John Austin. "For God's sake, John, we're losing it. Speak up, man. They'll follow you if you say so. Advocate action, and they'll take it."

Austin's eyes were level, his voice calm. "I can't do that, Bill. I explained the situation as best I could, and I've committed myself. It's up to the colony, now."

McKinstry, rapping for order, turned to Austin. "Have

you anything to say, John?"

"No, George, I've no more to say."

The vote was taken by secret ballot that night in Jane Long's tavern. The question was, "That San Felipe de Austin Colony endorse and actively support the cause of General Antonio López de Santa Anna for the overthrow of the tyrant Bustamente, and act accordingly by engagement of the tyrant's bastion at Anahuac on Trinity Bay."

All present voted, except, of course, the slaves. The question failed by one vote.

In the silence that followed the counting, Captain John Austin again stepped forward to address the crowd. "That, then, is the wish of the colony. As for me, I will abide by that wish. The colony will not be involved. But I am committed to return to Anahuac and I will, with any men who care to follow me . . . and with cannon and shot."

He took a long look around him, then smiled and nodded. There were no hard feelings, the gesture told them. They had done as they thought best. The meeting was adjourned.

It was late now, and most of them filed out, home to their families or back to the river camp. As Langley passed the table where Three-legged Willie and four or five others sat, empty mugs before them, he heard Williamson cursing in a low, all-inclusive monologue. For the first time since he had met the man, there was no humor in the little woodsman's eyes.

The summer air of coastal Texas was soft and warm, with substance to it. Sometimes at night it subdued the stars, letting only the brightest show on a field of slate gray. But at other times the heavy summer air became a crystal lens in which stars swarmed in brilliance against a velvet heaven. This was one of those nights.

There was a soft breeze from the Gulf of Mexico, adding the rustle of live oak leaves to the trilling of frogs and insects off in the woods. At the main dock, the schooner *Brazoria* rode sleepily at the end of her hawsers, only a watchman's lantern showing aboard. Few lights showed anywhere in town, and these were dim except in a barn near the end of the pier and a couple of sheds back in town. Here there was light, and men were working, unwrapping and assembling artillery.

Langley slept well, rose early and walked up to Jane Long's to find some breakfast. Mrs. Long, Kian, and another Negro woman also were up early, and the aroma of frying steaks met him at the door. A few men who had enjoyed last night's meeting too much lay sleeping at some of the tables, heads pillowed on their arms. In the back corner two tables had been pushed together and a man in buckskins lay atop them, snoring loudly, his hat over his face.

George McKinstry waved to Langley from the opposite corner, where he, Bill Russell, Henry Smith, and William Scates were having breakfast. He joined them and the dark, pert Kian brought steaming black coffee and said the steaks "were a'makin'." John Austin came in, wished Mrs. Long a fair morning, and joined the crowd. The conversation turned immediately to plans for the return to Anahuac, and to logistics.

Going overland with heavy cannon mounts would be difficult at this time of year. Between Brazoria and Anahuac lay miles of coastal forest and marsh, and recent heavy rains upland had turned the streams and bayous into wide, treacherous swamps. They had experienced difficulty coming west with just horses and a couple of light wagons. It would be far worse taking cannon and shot back. The alternative was by water, down the Brazos to Velasco, then into the open sea and east along the coast to San Luis Pass or Bolivar Pass, and finally up Galveston Bay into Trinity Bay.

Only one vessel was now in port, the *Brazoria*. Captain John Rowland had secured his ship after offloading cargo and had then headed inland to visit friends in San Felipe. The first mate of the schooner was in charge until his return. McKinstry knew Rowland. He allowed that, if the captain were here, he would be delighted to assist with the project. Rowland, he said, had no use for the Mexican government and even less for its coastal revenue stations. Bill Russell was slightly acquainted with the mate and offered to go talk to him about it.

Finishing his breakfast, Langley paid his bill and went outside to sit on the porch bench, smoke a pipe and soak up morning sunlight. Russell had already gone toward the docks, and the others came out a few minutes later. McKinstry headed for the post office, Smith and Scates set off up the center street happily talking war, and Austin stepped to the end of the porch, leaned against an upright and lighted a cigar. He gazed across at the masts of the *Brazoria*. "Take a week or so to get to Anahuac," he said, "but it's the only way we got."

For a while they smoked in silence, then Austin snubbed out his cigar, dropped the long butt in a pocket, said, "See you," and started across the street to the alcalde's office. He was nearly across when he glanced up at the sound of hooves on the packed earth, and stopped.

"Hey, Britt," he yelled. "You're right on time."

Three riders were coming in from the north, walking their horses. James Britton Bailey was in the lead, looming huge and forbidding above the solid mount he rode. Slightly behind him was a younger man, dressed in a buckskin jacket and cord pants, and a few steps back, straddling a saddled paint and carrying his big musket across the saddle, was the huge Negro Langley remembered from Bell's. Five long-eared hunting dogs and a brace of laden packhorses plodded behind the procession.

Bailey waved to Austin, angled across, and reined in at the hitch rail in front of Jane Long's. His buckskins were soiled and his hair unkempt, but he swung sharply down from his laden mount, big mulehide boots crunching in the stubble sod of the porchway. The long, coiled whip still hung from his shoulder, the two broad belts still carried their pistol and huge knife, and the rifle in his hand looked as though it had grown there. Coming up to the porch, he glanced at Langley, then stopped to scrutinize him more closely.

"Know you, don't I?"

"Yes, sir, we met. Name's Langley."

"Yeah, as I remember, it is. From Bell's place upriver. Put yer big foot in a bounty man's mouth, as I recall. Nice seein' you again."

He turned to Austin, who had come back across the street. They shook hands. The big slave, Bubba, and the younger white man were dismounting and loosening cinches on the horses.

"What's all this ruckus I hear about, John? You fellers go off and whip somebody without lettin' me have a piece of 'em?"

Austin's smile was quick and easy. "We haven't finished yet, Britt. Figured we'd save the best part for you. How was the hunt?"

"Jist fair. Went over on the Colorado for a while." He scowled. John Austin was a husky man, but Bailey matched him in height and far outweighed him. "Wished you'da sent word, John. I'd like to have come along from the start."

"Now, Britt, you know we couldn't have found you. The Colorado bottoms cover a lot of miles."

The younger man had come up to them. "God only knows," he said. "And if anybody knew where we were it was Him."

Bailey winced slightly, as though a flea had bitten him. "I knowed right where I was all the time, you young fool. We come back, didn't we?"

Austin chuckled. His eyes caught Langley, and he indicated him to Bailey. "You met Matthew Langley, Britt? Matt, this ol' bear is Mr. Britt Bailey. Owns about half of Texas and thinks he owns it all. And this is David Milburn, married to one of Britt's girls." He swept a

187

hand toward the slave. "And Uncle Bubba. Belongs to Britt, and one of the few men I know might lick him in an even fight."

Bubba nodded to Langley. "Yassuh. We's already met."

"Met this'un up to Bell's about the time we started for the Colorado. Watched while he kicked a feller in the face."

Milburn stepped forward and shook with Langley. "You must be the one Papa Britt was talking about when we set out for the Colorado. Nice to meet you."

"Don't call me papa, you damn whippersnapper," Britt growled. "I ain't your sire."

Austin's attentions were back with Bailey. "You serious about going to Anahuac with us, Britt?"

"Damn right."

"Well, you've probably heard most of it already. The colony voted against approving the resolutions, but some of us are going anyhow, on our own. I mean to carry cannon on the *Brazoria* there if we can. We will load the six-pounder and one of the four-pounders, and Russell's got a blunderbuss that we can take. And there's the ship's deck gun." The *Brazoria*, like most trading vessels in wild country, was equipped with a deadly sting of her own—a small, long-muzzled cannon mounted on a circular track on the forward deck amidships.

"We ain't eaten all mornin', John. Let's talk about it inside. Bubba, go tell Kian there's hungry men comin' in, so pile on the steaks. Come on, John. Set an' talk while we eat. You, too, young feller. . . ." He eyed him studiously for a moment. "You sure you don't rassle?

"Now, what's this about a vote?" Steaks were frying for Bailey and Milburn, and Bubba was in the kitchen being fed personally by Kian. The white men were back at the corner table, coffee cups steaming.

"Well, we brought those resolutions over there," Austin pointed, "back from Anahuac after Bradburn backed out on a deal and jumped the town. Colony voted on them last night—to favor Santa Anna's stand in Mexico and to

188

sanction force against Bradburn. It failed by one vote."

"One vote!" Britt roared. "By God, sir call another vote. Us Baileys are here, and we aim to fight."

"All of us who were at Anahuac are going back anyway, Britt. We just won't have the blessing of the colony."

"Blessing of the colony, hell," the older man growled. "Let's go git 'em."

"Britt," a gentle female voice cut through the old man's roar, and Jane Long appeared from the kitchen. "I do wish you'd speak quietly. You might wake up the customers." When she smiled, Bailey grinned back. Jane Long was a strikingly beautiful woman, and most of the men in the colony, one way or another, were smitten by her. Bailey subsided into his chair and poured more coffee.

"By Gawd," he rumbled, "what a woman."

Bill Russell came into the tavern, sat down and greeted Bailey and David Milburn. "How's the hunt, Britt?"

"Jist fine. No people around askin' dumb questions."

Russell grinned fondly at the fiery old man and turned to Austin.

"Here's the situation, John. Couple of men told me Captain Rowland ain't at San Felipe. No one's sure where he is, but he's gone inland somewhere. So I talked to the mate of the *Brazoria*. He don't much want to take the boat out without Rowland's say-so, but I told him to find his crew and rig up, because you would impress the thing if he didn't agree."

"What'd he say to that?"

"Said he's just a poor man with a large family and he don't want to go off fightin' with anybody. I told him don't worry, we'd look after him. Then I told the boys to go ahead and start loadin' them cannon."

Kian came out of the kitchen with steaks and corn and served Bailey and Milburn their breakfast. Her eyes were bright, and her mouth curved in a faint smile. She said nothing, but headed back into the kitktichen. Bailey

189

grinned. "That damn Bubba," he said. "He's back there gittin' him a free breakfast.

"John, how do you figger we're gonna git them cannons past that fort at Velasco? You know Ugartechea ain't gonna let that ship pass."

"I thought we might ride down there this morning and talk to him," Austin said. "He's a friend of ours, most ways, and I think he'll lean to Santa Anna when he needs to. I don't know; we might work something out. I'll tell you one thing for sure, he already knows what's comin' off."

"He might be a friend, but he's a soldier first," Bailey said around a mouthful of food. "But if you want to go talk to him, I'll ride along with you."

"Pleased to have you," Austin lit another cigar. "Dave, you want to go help George McKinstry get things on the road here? And Bill, you and the boys go ahead and get those cannon assembled and loaded. And, by the way, you might run home and get the blunderbuss you got hid out there. Maybe mount it up on the for'ard rail . . . I think port side, clear of the jib halyards." He turned to Langley. "You want to ride down to Velasco with us, see what's goin' on?"

"Sure."

Austin stood up. "See you out front here in a little bit."

Britt downed his coffee, picked up his rifle and yelled, "Bubba, let's go!"

Langley went to the livery, saddled the mare and mounted in the corral to top her off for riding. The horse had been unridden for a week or more and was fat and feisty. It was several minutes before she decided the rider intended to stay there. By the time she had quieted, Langley was swearing and smarting. Several men had gathered around the corral to watch the fun.

Finally the horse stood calm, satisfied. Langley leaned forward and hissed, "You ready, now, you bonehead? All right, let's go."

190

Back at Jane Long's, Bailey and Bubba were already mounted, and Austin was riding up on a striking black with a star face. Bailey had traded an empty whiskey jug to Jane Long for a full one, with a comment, "Man shouldn't ever go anyplace thirsty."

Austin said, "Jane, I'd take it kindly if you'd keep an eye out for Henry Brown. He might be in today, and if he shows up I'd like for him to meet me here when we get back."

They headed downriver toward Velasco.

Fourteen

Along most of the Texas coastline, a perimeter of flat, treeless salt-grass marsh spread between the forests and the beach, in most cases stretching for many miles in width. But in the Brazos valley the forest came down closer, almost to the blue water's edge. Only for the last two or three miles toward the big river's mouth were Austin and his group totally in the open, approaching Fort Velasco.

The road, like all roads in Texas at the time, was simply a well-used trail along the river. Brush and smaller trees had succumbed to the traffic of hoof and wheel, leaving a brilliant green carpet of short grass. In the woods on either side, oak and peach trees towered above a thick, at times impenetrable sprawl of semi-tropical vegetation.

Once, about ten miles out, the party spotted Indian sign, a sizable band of savages by the tracks, crossing toward the river. Opposite, on the west bank, lay the vicinity of Peach Point, home of Stephen Austin's kin, the Perrys. Beyond was a small wild creek running into scrub oak vegetation on its way toward the Gulf. Bailey studied the tracks closely and allowed that a band of Karankawa had crossed early that morning, with squaws and children.

"Probably heading for the creek," Austin said. "They've been gathering there lately, maybe a whole tribe. There's talk of taking an expedition in there to chase them out. Might be a good idea, before they get it in their heads to raid somebody again."

The day was bright and clear. When the men finally

came out of the forest at a long bend where the river turned southeast, a vast expanse of open grassland lay ahead of them, shimmering and waving in the sun. Birds of a hundred varieties soared, swooped, and sailed over this prairie, deer grazed near the forest's protective edges, and two red wolves darted across their path and disappeared into the tall grass. They also came across the tracks of a great cat that had hunted this trail the night before.

Bailey gazed around him. "By Gawd, I ain't decided yet which is purtier—them deep woods or this."

They followed the river more or less southeast a few miles, then left it at a place where it veered west to form a horseshoe bend. Another half mile and the river was with them again. Straight ahead, they could see a thin line of blue on the horizon, and when they topped out on a low ridge the Gulf of Mexico lay before them. There, where the river met the Gulf, sprawled two villages, one on each bank. The near bank was Velasco, and the most prominent feature was the fort.

Fort Velasco had been established by the Spaniards, nearly demolished by tides and neglect, then rebuilt by Mexico. Three hundred yards from the seashore and a hundred yards from the river's edge, the big stockade dominated the gateway to Texas's main water highway. The fort was a circle, three hundred feet in diameter, the outer wall a double row of large upright stakes, sharpened at the top. Six feet inside the first row was a second row of logs, with the space between filled with sand to about four feet from the top. The resulting barricade was nearly impregnable to small-cannon fire, and the final rise of the outer fence gave protection to defenders at the wall.

In the center of the compound was a high mound of earth, taller than the facing walls. Hollowed into the side of this was a powder magazine, and on top was a pivot-mounted nine-pound cannon, surrounded by a wood parapet. Elsewhere in the compound, their roofs showing above the stockade, were various buildings. A wide, waist-deep moat surrounded the entire fort at a distance of fifty yards, fed from a small bayou that entered the river here. The stream joined a trench canal that had been dug from the bayou to the mouth of Oyster Creek, a mile or so to the east.

All in all, it was a well-built and strategically located fortification. This was Mexico's customs house for all the inland trade on the Brazos. Barely visible across the wide river was the sketchy little village of Quintana, similar in size and appearance to the village of Velasco which ranged east from the fortification along the dune line behind the white sand beach. The party approached the fort from the north, crossing the bayou at a small footbridge.

Lieutenant Colonel Domingo de Ugartechea, a sleek five-foot-six in his polished boots and every inch a soldier, was going over personnel rosters in his little office in the headquarters building when a sentry reported that John Austin and three other riders were approaching the fort. He thought for a moment, then retrieved the latest communique from Anahuac from a neat stack of papers on his table and read it again.

It was a directive from Colonel Bradburn, delivered by a courier who had slipped past the Anglo blockade at Anahuac. It was brief and to the point. There had been armed resistance at Anahuac and probably would be more. It was expected that a force of Texians would march from Brazoria, and suspected that cannon would be shipped from there. He was to let neither the Texians nor their cannon pass his post. It was a direct order.

In his career as an officer, Ugartechea had never disobeyed an order. But since he had been under Bradburn's command he had been sorely tempted on several occasions. Ugartechea was both an officer and a gentleman, and he carried an intense dislike for the crude, tyrannical Bradburn. He knew that John Austin would come to ask passage into the Gulf, and he knew—despite

194

his deep respect for the tall, somber Yankee—that he would have to refuse. It was an unhappy situation.

He smiled ruefully at a passing thought. It would be a joy to see the Anahuac fort brought down around Bradburn's ears, and there was little doubt in his mind that these hot-headed settlers could do it. It would, indeed, be a fine thing to see.

But then there would be hell to pay. The situation in Mexico was volatile, with open war now being waged between Bustamente and Santa Anna. Whichever side won, it would not be good for the Texians if they succeeded in routing Bradburn. Bustamente, if he won, would crush them. Santa Anna, if he won, might welcome the interference for a time, but would then make an example of them in order to assure that no others would attempt a revolution in Mexico.

Walking out of the building, he called the sergeant of the guard and ordered a check of defenses. The compound was full of troops, the parade ground lined with tents. There were at the moment more than a hundred and twenty men in Fort Velasco, recalled to the fort when Bradburn's message first arrived. At the gate, a sentry signaled that the riders had come up. Ugartechea told the sergeant to admit them.

John Austin, Bailey, Langley, and Bubba led their horses through the doorway mounted in the main gate and were greeted by a smiling brown-skinned man with wide shoulders and sergeant's braid.

"Buenos días, señor Austin . . . señores."

"Buenos días to you, Jesús," Austin said. "How's the family?"

"Very fine, gracias." The sergeant gestured toward Quintana across the river. "But I think I go home too much. We are to be blessed with another little one soon. That will make eleven."

"Seems to me you get blessed about as much as Bill Russell does." Austin chuckled. "Where's Domingo?"

"The colonel awaits you in his office."

195

The Texians handed their reins to Bubba and went across the compound. A guard by the gate motioned for Bubba to come and stand in the shade of the awning with him, out of the hot sun.

Ugartechea's door was open.

"Ah," the officer said, coming forward, his hand out. "John Austin and Señor Bailey. *Buenos días, señores.* Come in."

Bailey shook hands and said, "This feller here is Matthew Langley."

"How do you do, señor? Langley? Ah, yes . . ." The colonel went to a file box on his desk and thumbed through. "I have heard of you, señor."

Langley's scalp bristled. "Yes?"

"Yes. Let me see. Ah. It seems one Señor Aaron Whitlet, commission agent for my government, alleged that one Matthew Langley entered Mexico without visa at the Brazos Port." He looked shrewdly at Langley for a moment, then shook his head. "I, however, cannot say whether that occurred or not. And, unfortunately, Señor Whitlet suffered an accident at Bell's Landing recently . . . a fall from a horse, I believe . . . and subsequently has been transferred to Matamoros." He smiled. "I don't expect he will be back. Sit down, please, señores, and have some wine. How can I help you?"

Langley relaxed and Bailey grinned. "Fell off'n his horse, you say! Lit on his face, I imagine?"

"Most precisely on his face. Times have been hard for bounty officers lately."

When they were seated Austin asked, "Things going all right with you, Domingo?"

"*Más o menos,* John. Not too bad, considering I must keep track of so many recent Americans in one small section of the country. By the way, may I ask that you have a word with the esteemed Captain Jerry Brown? Twice now he has run my blockade to avoid customs. There is a limit, señor. One time I will be obliged to fire on him, and it would be a shame to see the beautiful

196

schooner *Sabine* at the bottom of the river."

"He is a wild one, isn't he?" Austin chuckled. "You'll have to admit, though, the customs are pretty steep."

"I agree completely." The officer shrugged. "But I must enforce the laws as best I can, John Austin. I am only a simple soldier, and must do my duty."

"You are a soldier," Austin said casually, "but you are far from simple, Domingo."

"Salud, señores."

"Salud."

The wine downed, John Austin got to business. "We are here, Domingo, to ask that you pass the schooner *Brazoria* without question or inspection. I will give you my word it will carry no taxable cargo."

Ugartechea studied them. "Where will the ship be bound?"

"For Anahuac."

"There has been trouble at Anahuac."

"Yes, sir." Austin met his eyes and held them. "There sure has. Colonel Bradburn has thrown some citizens of Colony de San Felipe into prison, for civil offenses. He has refused to release them, or to hand them over to the legal alcalde of Liberty. His actions have been in flagrant violation of the constitution of our country.

"To put it bluntly, Domingo," he said slowly, "If the son of a bitch won't let them go, we are going to have to go in and take them."

Ugartechea pondered for a moment, then handed Austin the paper lying on his desk. Without comment, Austin read it and handed it back.

"What will be on the ship, John Austin?"

Bailey erupted. The polite talk was too much for him. "Cannon, by Gawd, sir," he mumbled. "Enough cannon to blow that fort down around Bradburn's dirty britches!"

Ugartechea looked pained. Austin glared at Bailey. "Britt," he snapped, "you're about as diplomatic as a hog at the trough."

"Hell," Britt subsided, "all we need to know is one

197

thing. Domingo, are you gonna let that boat pass, or not?"

Ugartechea's eyes were downcast. "I am sorry, my friends. I cannot."

They sat in silence for a time. Then Austin said, "Domingo, we have drawn up resolutions backing our actions. If approved, these resolutions would declare the colony's allegiance to General Santa Anna. I'm wondering now where you stand."

"I am a soldier, John Austin, and I have no alternative. I stand for México. At the present time, Bustamente is México and Colonel Bradburn is Bustamente's representative."

"Then you're backing a real loser," Bailey snapped. "But I got to respect a man as thinks he's right, even if he's wrong."

"Then there is no way around you in this?" Austin asked.

"I am deeply sorry, John, but no. I cannot let you pass to fire on the flag of México."

"You know we will have to do what we think best, anyway?"

"Yes. I know."

Austin stood and extended his hand across the table to the officer. "It's a damn shame, Domingo."

"It's a shame, John Austin. I would not have wished it this way."

Ugartechea shook hands solemnly with Austin and Bailey and turned to Langley as the others went out the door. "I wish you good fortune, señor," the little officer said sadly. "I would also wish you were not here . . . but you are following a good man. Welcome to México, Señor Langley, and welcome to Texas."

As they left by the main gate, the broad-shouldered sergeant waved to them and grinned. "Nice to see you, señores. Come back soon."

Austin waved to him. Bailey turned away. "Poor ignorant bastid don't know he's about to git hisself killed," he said. "Bubba, hand over that fresh jug!"

Somehow the glorious colors of the land around them looked less bright as they rode back toward Brazoria. A gloom had settled over the Brazos valley.

Fifteen

A lot of the men willing to fight at Anahuac had left Brazoria by the time Austin and his group returned. They had decided among themselves to go ahead, to get back to Anahuac, and to wait for Austin there. Henry Brown had returned from his ride through the colony and had tried to get them all to stay together, to wait for Austin. But some of the more anxious had seen no reason to stay in Brazoria when the fight was going to be at Anahuac. So the number of men in Brazoria had been reduced. But some others, in the meantime, had come in from other communities.

Jared Groce had sent men from his plantation upriver. James Gibson had come in from Gonzales and Bob Wilson from Caney. Also, a pair of crew members from the schooner *Navidad* had decided to join up. They had nothing in particular to do anyway until their ship returned.

Austin's careful report on what had occurred at Velasco, delivered to a packed house in Jane Long's tavern, drew a mixed chorus of angry shouts and jeering, with only a few of the older heads shaking in sympathy for the hard position Ugartechea was now in. Austin quieted them and suggested another meeting later in the afternoon, to vote on whether to attempt passage at Velasco. George McKinstry, always quiet and always thorough, was surveying the crowd. "John," he said, "I move we do more than vote on that at this meeting today. I move we vote again on the Turtle Bayou Resolutions." There was a barrage of cheers and "ayes." Austin agreed.

"I say we fight!" Henry Smith yelled. "And get about it now. We don't need to vote."

William Smith yelled back at him. "With all due respect, Henry, hold your damn tongue. We'll vote."

That settled, Austin went home to eat and visit with his family for a while. The crowd thinned. Occasionally newcomers from various parts of the colony would ride up, quench their thirst and their curiosity, then go about their business.

Suddenly a ruckus erupted out on the street, and several of those inside moved out to see what was going on. Riding into town from the north were three of the strangest-looking men Langley had ever seen. The one in the middle was a monstrous man, not as tall as the two flanking him, but so massive in bulk that he almost dwarfed the sagging horse he rode.

"Strap's comin' in!" someone yelled. "Strap Buckner's here. Got Milton Hicks with him an' somebody else!"

"That's Tecumseh! My Gawd, boys, Tecumseh is here!"

Aylett C. "Strap" Buckner was by far the biggest man in Texas at the time, and the largest man Langley had ever seen. He had heard claim of a legendary giant in the colony who was called "the only man alive—next to Bubba, maybe—that can whip Britt Bailey in a face-to-face fight." Now, seeing him, the legends made sense. Buckner was well over six feet in height, but was so proportioned that from any distance he would have appeared almost dwarfish. His immense shoulders were the span of a normal man's arm. The neck they supported was a huge, gnarled stump of muscle. His arms, bulging the tortured seams of a great buckskin shirt, were the size of another man's legs.

Buckner was one of the adventurers who, along with John Austin and some others, had come into Mexico with the Long expedition headed by the widow Jane Long's husband. It had been in that expedition that Dr. Long had died. Austin, Buckner, and a number of others had wound up for a time in prison in Mexico City, then had joined Stephen F. Austin's colony upon release.

To his right rode a gangling tent-pole of a man at least two inches taller than Buckner but only a fraction of his weight. Milton Hicks was something of an enigma among Texians. Indian fighter, scout, woodsman, and frontiersman, Hicks generally stayed clear of settled lands, preferring the lonely wilds to the realms of civilized people. About all anyone in the colonies knew of him was that he came from the Smoky Mountain area of Tennessee or Carolina, that he was a good man to fight beside, and that he would be a dreadful man to fight against.

Hicks wore his black hair long and his face clean-shaven. He would never be mistaken for an Indian—though he was, in fact, half Cherokee—but he could pass among them with ease. He rode a stubby, sure-footed Indian pony and wore cord pants, knee-high moccasins, and a buckskin jacket of Indian design, fringed and beaded in the style of the Cherokee. Light blue eyes took in everything around him: the eyes of a hunter, eyes that would never show pain, fear, anger, or humor, that were used only for seeing.

Both Buckner and Hicks were, at first glance and in fact, remarkable men and remarkable in appearance. But of the three riding in, possibly the one who held the eye the longest was Thomas Bell. The name he preferred, though, was Tecumseh, the name given him by the Shawnees. He was, Langley had heard, a cousin of the respected Josiah Bell of Brazoria, but the family didn't speak of him. The man called Tecumseh was tall, but not as tall as Milton Hicks. He was muscular, but not nearly so huge as Strap Buckner. The remarkable feature was his face. Dark brown hair streaked with gray framed a dark, stern face with forbidding eyes. When those eyes met his for a moment, Langley had the feeling that there was little this man hadn't done, less that he hadn't seen, and nothing he wouldn't do. The eyes of Tecumseh were the eyes of a killer.

The three dismounted in front of Jane Long's. As they

stepped down, a huge delighted smile hit Strap Buckner's face and he strode to the door and flung it open.

"Where is that highbindin', low-livin' Britt Bailey?" he roared.

Bailey looked up from the table where he was demolishing a plate of pork, gravy, and cornbread. He put down his knife and stood up. "Well, I'll be danged," he said, "if it ain't Strap Buckner hisself. Come to watch us fight."

"Watch you fight, hell, I'm gonna do it for you, old man, so you won't bust a gut tryin' to lift a rifle or somethin'." Buckner strode across the room the other way, the floorboards creaking under his weight, and grabbed Jane Long around the waist, raising her high off the floor in his two hands. He gave her a loud, wet kiss on the forehead and set her down, then reached out and slapped Kian on the behind as she passed him. "How's my gal?" he asked Jane. Then, to Kian, "You been keepin' this white gal straight and true to me, Kian?"

Kian giggled. "Jest as straight as I can, Mistah Strap. 'Course ain't nobody 'round to keep me straight."

Jane Long gasped in the mountainous man's embrace and said, "Strap Buckner, you overgrown ox, turn me loose." As he released her, she gave him a quick hug and then backed away hurriedly. "It's good to see you, Strap, it really is. But mercy, you took the wind out of me."

Buckner crossed the room again in long strides, inadvertently spilling chairs and men as he passed. "Britt, you ol' son of a coon, how you been?"

The hands of the two giants came together with a crack, and then they were straining, pushing, muscles bulging and faces turning red. For a moment they stood frozen, straining at each other's grasp, then Buckner gave a mighty heave and Bailey went over backward onto the floor. But with a flip of his arm, as he fell, Bailey pulled Buckner down with him. The entire building shook with the fall. The two rolled over, laughing hugely, and sat up. "Jane," Bailey yelled, "bring us a jug."

Buckner was dusting himself off. "By God, Britt, if you

weren't an old man I'd have a hell of a time throwin' you."

"Old? Hell, I just go easy on you so's I won't break your damn tender spirit."

On their feet again, Bailey and Buckner found chairs and a table. Buckner shouted, "Jane! Keep them jugs a'comin'. Britt and me's gonna have a few drinks together. Just leave us lay where we fall!"

Henry Smith, who had been sitting with Bailey, found someone else to drink with. Milton Hicks and "Tecumseh" Bell had watched the wrestling match solemnly. Now Hicks went over to where a group of woodsmen were gathered and joined them. Bell glanced around the room, then had a quick drink at the bar and left.

It was a while later when John Austin returned to the tavern, Bell with him. He howdied with Hicks and several others, then headed for the table where Bailey and Buckner sat, three empty jugs stacked between them, both still mostly sober.

"Hey, John Austin!" Buckner reached out a huge hand and shook Austin's. "Set down here, Cap'n. I want to tell you somethin'. You others, too!" He indicated the room in general. "Gather 'round. I got news for all of you!"

When most of the assembly was around him, Buckner stood up, now quite serious. "There's somethin' I been ponderin' on," he said, "and I think it's important.

"You all know where them Cherokee Injuns are up there above Nacogdoches? You know they're on a Spanish land grant. Well, the Mexican government has told them it will clear that grant for them if they ally with Mexico. Ol' Milton and Tecumseh, there, were up there with the Cherokee when they got the word from Colonel Piedras that you boys down here was givin' Bradburn some trouble. That's how come they lit a shuck on down here, an' how come I fetched up with 'em over by Gonzales.

"At any rate, they been tellin' me there's a U.S. Injun agent name of Sam Houston livin' with the Cherokees up on the Arkansas, and he's been workin' regular to ally the Injuns clean into Texas with the United States. Seems he's

204

workin' on all the tribes, tryin' to get them not to harass Americans comin' this way.

"Now this Houston has been in touch with Hicks and Tecumseh both, wantin' them to head over into the Kiowa and Comanche country and work out some kind of similar arrangement with them. Now you see what I'm gettin' at?

"Seems to me the United States is spendin' a powerful lot of attention on the routes into Texas, don't it to you? I'm thinkin' if things ever come to push and pull down here, the United States might just step in and help us."

There was a moment of silent thought all around, except for Bailey. "Strap," he said, "I got to tell you. It takes you a terrible lot of words to say somethin'."

"Sam Houston," Smith mused. "I know of him. Used to be governor of Tennessee, then went to Congress for a while. You know him, don't you, Britt?"

"Yep. I know him. Uppity so-and-so, but a purty good man, I reckon. Back when we was fightin' the Creeks with Andy Jackson he was in a outfit supportin' us. Got hisself shot up at Horseshoe Bend."

Austin was thoughtful. He hadn't known the United States was clearing the way for settlement up to Texas. That, and the increasing flow of Americans into Texas, might make a lot of difference.

When the assembly was called for a recount vote on the Turtle Bayou Resolutions, John Austin took a stand for passage. And this time the vote was nearly unanimous. The colony would support and act upon the resolutions drawn up in that sad encampment on Turtle Bayou.

There was silence when the vote was counted and the results announced; then pandemonium broke loose. The shouting resounded across the Brazos, as men poured out of Jane Long's tavern and spread in all directions, heading out to pack their gear, prepare their animals, and talk to their families. They were going to Velasco. Then they were going to Anahuac.

George McKinstry carefully entered the vote in the colony's logbook, signed it and dated the entry—June 24, 1832.

Down at the docks, men were hurrying to make a nondescript little trade schooner ready for war.

British soldiers had learned several lessons in the Battle of New Orleans in 1814. One of them was that no rifle in the world can propel a ball through a bale of cotton. The Americans had learned it, too.

Bill Russell supervised the installation of cotton bales along the railings of the *Brazoria*, forming a fence of deck armor four feet high around virtually the entire topside of the little ship. The men on deck would be protected from rifle fire from the fort. Only luck or poor artillery aim could protect the ship itself, but it was the best he could do.

Isaac Tucker, mate of the *Brazoria*, had been mollified by Russell's assurance that he would not be expected to take part in any fighting but only to help navigate the ship. Tucker was not a Texian, and it was not his fight.

The two cannons were winched aboard and tied in place on the deck The larger of the two, a six-pounder, was field mounted on a large-wheel wagon carriage. It was hardly a satisfactory arrangement for a naval gun, but here again, it was the best he could do.

"Lash that damn thing fast," he instructed, "and block those wheels. Get some tar under there, boys. If that thing busts loose it'll kill more of us than it does of them."

They had to choose a single angle of fire for the big gun. There would be no windage corrections. After some discussion, it was decided to mount the gun forward, on the port side, angled about fifteen degrees to the fore. "So's we can get 'em goin' in," someone explained.

The smaller cannon was an ornate brass four-pounder with a heavy swivel mount. They set it aft, amidships, to fire over the after rail, "to get 'em comin' back." They nailed it to the deck.

The blunderbuss, a huge long-barreled punt gun with a belled muzzle for fast loading, was mounted on the rail forward, almost over the bowsprit. Fitted with a recoil block stubbed into the deck, it could be fired, loaded, turned, and fired again.

The final gun was the ship's gun, a slight four-pounder installed midway on the foredeck on a pivot and circle track. It could be turned to fire in any direction. Powder, fuse, and shot were placed in kegs and boxes on deck to be handy.

When William Scates, the Anahuac carpenter, came on board to lend a hand and saw the mountings of the two field cannons, he shook his head in disbelief. "And here I was thinkin' Bradburn had cannon problems," he moaned.

On a trip down the gangplank to bring up fuse, Russell found two ladies waiting for him on the dock. One was a frail elderly woman leaning on a cane. The other, a strong solid woman of middle years, said, "Mr. Russell . . . please."

"Yes, ma'am?"

"We brought you something, Mother and I. We thought it might help." Her tone was apologetic, but she carried the folded package proudly. "I asked Anne Austin about it, and she thought it was a good idea, so we did it."

"You did what, ma'am?"

"This!" She unfolded the parcel she was carrying and displayed it. On a carefully made flag of the Republic of Mexico, letters had been stitched spelling out "CONSTI-TUTION" on one side and "1824" on the other. It was a beautiful piece of work, the dark brown material of the letters showing vividly on the orange, white, and green of the banner. "Can you use it?"

Russell's grin was one of pure delight. "Ladies, you bet your—beg pardon, we will be delighted to use it!" In his enthusiasm he kissed the older woman soundly on the forehead, and shook the surprised hand of the younger one.

"Hey, Bill!" he yelled, "Get this up there and run it up

that halyard on the spanker boom, where everybody can see it. And if that don't put it high enough, nail it to the masthead! We got ourselves a battle flag!"

The two ladies had just provided the little schooner with the best armor it would carry. Every soldier firing on the ship would be firing on his own flag.

Britt Bailey had assigned Bubba to take a head count around town of those who planned to go to Velasco. Now he looked up John Austin and reported that there would be about a hundred and twenty, maybe a few more or less.

"Not too bad," Austin allowed, "considering quite a few went on overland to Anahuac. How many troops did you judge were in the fort today, Britt?"

"About the same, I guess." The big man hiccupped. "Pardon. Me and Strap and some others got us a sort of runnin' drinkin' match goin' on."

Austin grinned. The old man would be sober when he needed to be. He found young Benjamin Brigham and sent him to round up Russell, McKinstry, Henry Brown, and some others for a strategy meeting.

They met in the back room at Jane Long's, a room normally reserved for eating and for ladies. Most ladies avoided the tavern. William Wharton was there, with James Perry and David Milburn. Henry Smith arrived, followed by McKinstry and Henry Brown, and Russell joined them a few minutes later.

McKinstry had produced a careful drawing of the fort at Velasco, its contents, defenses, and surrounding terrain. They spread it on a table and hovered around it, Austin explaining his plan in terse sentences, his fingers moving over the map.

The plan of attack was a simple one. Russell would be in command of the ship. Austin and Brown would lead forces on land. They would try to get one company close to the fort unobserved, under cover of darkness, and dig in to wait for daylight. This would be Austin's company. Brown would take his company around to the southeast side of the fort, toward the beach, and start a diversion to cover Austin's approach. Russell was to bring the *Brazoria* in as close as possible and give the two attacking companies support with the cannon. There was no chance of knocking down those sand-filled stockade walls, but they might keep that swivel gun on the bastion busy.

Wharton said, "John, I have some heavy timbers at my place. We've started building on our new house. You could use some of them to make portable breastworks for your men, and I don't think a rifle ball would penetrate them. Might save you some digging."

Austin agreed. They would stop by Wharton's Eagle Island plantation on the way to Velasco. "We'll need a couple of extra wagons, George," he added. McKinstry noted it on his growing sheaf of papers.

Henry Brown was concerned about James Perry going along, and finally, reluctantly, he said so. "I'm not worried about you, James, so much as I am about Steve Austin down there in Saltillo. You being his brother-in-law, well, you know how the Mexican government is sometimes. They might accuse Stephen of being in on this, just because some of his family was along."

Perry, it seemed, had been worried about the same thing, but was torn between his concern for Stephen and his desire to go along to Velasco.

Austin settled it. "I think Henry is right, James. It would be better if no one close to Stephen is in on this, at least right now. If we wind up in a mess here, it's going to take Stephen to get us out of it, and he'd better be like Caesar's wife . . . above reproach."

Perry conceded. He would stay home. But he would at least go with Wharton to Eagle Island to help with the breastworks.

"All right," Austin said finally, "now let's go over some rosters and get our companies made up, then get back to it. We head for Velasco in the morning."

Part Five

Velasco

June 25, 1832

Singly, and by twos and threes, the Texians were converging on Brazoria and Anahuac. In later years a man would be able to start a fight in Texas over the question: what is—or was—a Texian? And in those later years someone might resolve it by comparing a Texian to a Texan as one compares a pioneer to a farmer. But right then, they were Texians, and they were going to war.

For a lot of different reasons, they were ready to fight. Some had friends in the Anahuac stockade. Some had tried to get land titles cleared, and had been given the runaround by an unresponsive and distant national government. Some had felt the weight of tyranny under the final years of Bustamente's rule. Many had been insulted, harassed, demeaned, and injured by Colonel Bradburn and his infamous Texas military regime. Some were ready to fight to break Texas free from Mexican rule altogether. Some merely wanted to impress on Mexico the fact that free citizens have rights. Some would fight to erase their past misdeeds, or to gain citizenship in a country they had entered illegally.

Generally, they agreed they wanted fair—but not oppressive—taxation by the government of Mexico. They wanted individual status for their colonies, with separate local rule for, and by, themselves.

And some would fight just for the hell of it.

Britt Bailey was a frontiersman and a planter. He was also a Texian.

Uncle Bubba was a slave, and a Texian.

213

George McKinstry, John Henry Brown, Bill Russell, and William Wharton were colonists, members of Austin's "Old Three-hundred." They were Texians.

Strap Buckner was a giant, and an adventurer. He was a Texian.

Milton Hicks was a scout, frontiersman, and woodsman, more Indian than white, more recluse than colonist. He was a Texian.

Tecumseh Bell was an outlaw and a killer. Henry Smith was a firebrand and a troublemaker. Benjamin Brigham was a young boy barely through adolescence. They were Texians.

Hot-headed, erratic William Barrett Travis and the shrewd, unscrupulous, and elusive Monroe Edwards, languishing in Bradburn's brick-kiln stockade, were Texians, too, as was Matthew Langley, in Texas because he had no place else to be.

Jeremiah Blanchard was a Texian, as was his fiery, determined niece, Charlotte.

Jane Wilkinson Long, old Wylie Martin, Jawbone Morris, and little Kian with the coffee skin and laughing eyes; "Three-legged Willie" Williamson and the sober Dr. T.F.L. Parrott; powerful Jared E. Groce and patient Stephen F. Austin; and the dynamic John Austin himself—these were the Texians.

In a matter of days, word of the incident at Anahuac spread to the distant parts of Texas, and the Texians loaded their guns and saddled their mounts. From Goliad and Gonzales, from Fort Bend and Nacogdoches, from San Antonio de Bexar and the Kiowa country, they spurred toward Brazoria and Anahuac. There were only a few thousand Texians, scattered sparsely over seven thousand square miles of wilderness, and of these only a few hundred were men of age and situation to join a fight. But those who were able were ready.

The call went out, and the Texians came.

Sixteen

As John Austin stepped from the porch in front of the alcalde's office, two riders, Mexicans with broad hats and bright ponchos tied behind their saddles, reined in and hailed him. Alberto Ruiz and his son Rafael had come to fight. Ruiz was a settler near San Felipe de Austin, a rancher and cotton grower, and a successful man. He and the young man with him rode magnificent Arabian horses with fine Mexican saddles. They carried long rifles of the Pennsylvania style, finished in scroll-worked brass.

Austin was taken aback when Ruiz announced their purpose. "I don't know, Alberto," he rubbed his jaw. "I am very pleased you want to join us, but I don't understand why."

Ruiz's smile slackened and his eyes narrowed. "If you were not my friend, John Austin, I think I would challenge you for that statement. Are we, then, less than you?"

Austin hastened to correct the impression. "Lord, no. Alberto, don't get me wrong. You just surprised me, that's all. We're on our way to fight Mexicans, and you're a Mexican."

The smile returned, but the eyes remained narrow and shrewd. "Are we not all Mexicans here, John Austin?"

Austin grinned at the gentle slap. "Yes, of course we are, and none better than any other. But look around you, Alberto. All the rest of us are Anglos." Not ten feet away Uncle Bubba was stacking bundles of jerky in a wagon. The big black's sober eyes met Ruiz's for a moment and both of them grinned. Ruiz turned a withering gaze on Austin, then turned to his son. "Observe, Rafael.

215

For once, you have seen the great John Austin . . . how is it? Discombobulated. It is an occasion, is it not?"

"All right, Alberto," he said reasonably. "The only thing I'm driving at is, aren't you going to make a lot of trouble for yourself and your family if you show up fighting against your own . . . I mean other native-born Mexicans, on the side of a bunch of newcomers?"

The two Mexicans were stepping down from their horses. Ruiz gave his reins to Rafael. The older man was small and wiry, graying and with deep lines in his humorous face. The face was now very serious.

"I understand your concern, John Austin, and I thank you for it. But the family Ruiz is as involved as anyone else here in the welfare of Texas. All México has felt the heel of Bustamente. Santa Anna is our best hope, I think. And in Texas, you . . . we . . . are Santa Anna's best hope." His eyes caught the bright banner waving proudly atop the rigging of the *Brazoria*.

"There." He pointed. "that is why my Rafael and I are here. For México. For Santa Anna. For the Constitution. We intend to join you, John Austin."

Father and son faced him, proud and fierce, determined to join his fight. Finally he put out his hand.

"Welcome, Alberto and Rafael Ruiz. We are honored."

The last rays of the sun had faded to blue evening, and the crowd around the docks and on Front Street had thinned. Business was booming at Jane's place and at the other establishments on the street. Down in the campgrounds someone had skinned and cleaned a couple of steers, and these were roasting over open fires. At two or three points heavy drinking was under way.

Jugs had been uncorked at the fire where Britt Bailey and Strap Buckner sat with Bob Williams, John McNeel, and a bright-eyed young man named Joel Robison. A haunch of venison was roasting and Buckner was expounding on the virtue of bear meat over deer meat. In the near background Uncle Bubba sat dark and quiet, oiling the gleaming sixty-nine-caliber musket that had been his since a time long ago that neither he nor Bailey talked about, but that was part of the bond between them.

From time to time over the years in Texas there had been comment by a few about the propriety of a Negro being allowed to carry a gun. Those few, when the remarks came to Bailey's attention, had been summarily invited to withdraw them and, without exception, they had. There were no such comments in this camp on the eve of battle.

Joseph Rawlings had ridden in during the afternoon, rubbed down his horse, and ambled across to a shaded porch where he helped some of the boys finish off a jug. Now he was roaming the campsite looking for food and conversation. He spotted Bailey's fire and approached, a smile on his long, sardonic face.

"There is ol' Uncle Bubba," he exclaimed, "sittin' over there with that damn big cannon of his." His grin widened. "You know," he continued, squatting in the ruins of whatever conversation his arrival had broken up, "there was a fella back in Sage County toted a musket just like that there. Little skinny fella he was. Got caught out in the rain one time and to stay dry he hung that smoke pole from a snag and just skinned up inside the muzzle of it. But he forgot it was loaded . . ."

"Rawlings done got here," Bailey explained to no one in particular, mock exasperation heavy in his voice.

"I notice," Buckner said.

"Nice to see y'all, too," Rawlings said cheerfully. "Anyhow, this feller forgot his piece was loaded, and it was lightnin' somethin' fierce about then and a bolt hit that snag . . ."

"I know!" Joel Robison raised a hand. "The gun went off and shot him clean into the ground. Right?"

Rawlings eyed him slowly, full of scorn. "No, you damn fool it didn't go off. Where'd you get an idea like that? What it did was stiff him up so bad his folks rented him out to the New Hope Cannoneers to use as a ramrod."

They laughed at that, all but Robison, who reddened and stared into the fire. Rawlings lifted the jug again.

"Damn it, Joseph," Buckner rumbled, "that's my last jug. Why don't you buy your own?"

"Can't do it, Strap," he said cheerfully. "I lost damn near all I had in a game up at Bell's. I'm down to my last peso. Have to drink yours this time around."

"And last time, too, as I recollect. I'm wonderin' why you don't leave off gamblin', you damn fool. You always lose."

"You got powder and shot for tomorrow?" Bailey asked. "Or did you lose that, too?"

"I got plenty of ball and cap, but only about a handful of powder. Figured I'd borrow some."

"Bubba, give this feller some of that extra powder we got in the shed over there, first thing in the mornin'. Anything else essential that you ain't got, Joseph?"

"Not to speak of, thank ye, Britt. You want a chance to win that powder back?"

"I didn't lose it, damn it, I just gave it to you."

"Don't apologize, now, Britt. I understand. Wanta bet on somethin'?" The gambler's eyes suddenly turned very serious, and his bantering tone vanished. "You wanta make me a bet?"

Bailey hesitated. The change in the man, suddenly like that, was strange. "What do you want to bet on?"

"I will bet," Rawlings said slowly, "that one of us, right here by the fire right now, will die early when we come up against Mexican troops."

Bubba's eyes widened. Bailey glowered. "Come on now, Joseph. I don't like that kind of a bet, not at all."

Buckner laughed. "Why, hell"—he pointed a huge finger at Rawlings—"Don't you see what he just done, Britt? He just saved us all from gettin' shot. This feller never won a bet in his whole life."

Another jug was opened and passed around, and Bailey pierced the roasting meat with his big knife to check the

218

color of it. The strange mood that had settled on Rawlings went as quickly as it had come, and the banter began again. Of those at the fire only Bubba remained shaken by the peculiar turn of conversation. The old black man had seen men who had seen ghosts before. He had, in fact, seen a few himself.

The thought of shooting tomorrow was worrying McNeel, and he said so. A storekeeper, McNeel had led a relatively peaceful life. He had never in his days shot at a man, and had never been shot at. At the same time, he had no doubts about going along. He was resolved to fight.

"Most folks don't like killin' when they stop and think about it," Buckner mused. "But when you get right down to it, most folks don't have any trouble doin' it when they have to. I could tell you some stories about killin' men — so could Britt, for a fact — but I don't reckon either one of us has ever felt fondly about doin' that."

"Mainly it's the situation," Bailey added. "You go after a feller if you need to and down deep you go hopin' it'll end friendly. But sometimes it's you or him, and that sure makes a difference."

Rawlings added his thoughts: "People aren't like other animals, you know. Any animal, whether it's a horse or a dog, a cougar or a pig, will kill if it needs to, and think no more about it than pickin' up a stick. But a man, now, he kills just as quick as anything else, but then he frets about it. His conscience bothers him.

"I'd bet you," he added, "that there ain't a man in this town right now — and all of us gettin' ready to go off an' shoot folks — that can kill a man and not think anything about it."

"You'd lose," Robison said. "There's two, anyway."

"Who's that?" McNeel asked.

"Milton Hicks and Tecumseh Bell." Robison looked around at the other men. "You ever look either one of them right in the eye? I have, and had to look away. There ain't any feeling there except coldness. Especially ol'

Tecumseh. You look at Hicks, you get the feelin' there just ain't anybody in there. But you look Tecumseh in the eyes, and you feel like you might be gonna die."

The young man shivered noticeably. "Them two are just downright spooky. No offense, Strap; I know they're friends of yours, but I never seen none like them."

"No offense taken, youngster," Buckner said easily. "And I guess you're about right. Feller asked me one time would I fight Tecumseh, and the answer is no. I wouldn't wanta fight either one of 'em. You know, me and Britt here and some others, we tumble around sometimes, rasslin'; then we have a drink and laugh about it. Most folks are like that, but Milton and Tecumseh, they're different. I 'spect they don't know how to fight for fun. They only got one way, an' that's for keeps.

"You ever see either one of them set after somebody, you know for a fact somebody's goin' to wind up dead. They just haven't got any fun in them. Maybe 'ceptin' Hicks, and I wouldn't count on that, neither."

"There's somethin' else about them, though," Bailey put in. "If you ever need a couple of good men to ride with, them two are about the best. You give me ten more like Hicks and Tecumseh Bell, and Strap here and me could take that fort at Velasco without no problem a'tall."

McNeel's eye had caught a figure moving across the road a short distance away, and he called out, "Hey, Dan!" To those around him he said, "I'll tell you this, that young Dan Albert is another good one."

The youngster McNeel had called to turned toward the fire. At fifteen years of age Dan Albert was a man. His father, three older brothers and two sisters had died of blackwater fever four years earlier, and the youngster had bowed his neck and started working his land like a man, with his mother and one old slave to help him. Now, going on sixteen, he was master of a small, poor, but respectable holding just outside Brazoria. The years of toil and the shock of loss had broken his mother's health, and the youngster cared for her faithfully, planted and harvested his crops, did odd jobs around town for a little extra money, and accepted favors from no man. Lately he had been clearing land for two new fields, and had been seen frequently courting little Peggy Nolan.

Even among the toughest of the settlers there was a frank and open admiration for this boy who had become more than a man.

"Howdy, Dan," McNeel said when the young man stepped into the firelight. "Can you set a spell with us?"

" 'Fraid not, Mr. McNeel. I got things to do before tomorrow."

"You goin' with us, Dan?" Buckner asked, surprised. "Damn it all, I sure don't think that's a good idea."

The boy drew himself up a little, bristling. "I don't recall as how I asked you, Mr. Buckner," he said sharply, then slacked a bit. ". . . Not meanin' disrespect, sir, but I am goin'."

McNeel said quickly, "Strap wasn't questionin' your right to go, Dan. But you know there's liable to be fightin'. How's your mother gonna take to that?"

"Who's stayin' with her?" Bailey asked.

"She's stayin' with the Williamsons tonight and tomorrow, sir. Then Peggy . . . Peggy Nolan . . . she's gonna take her home and stay there with her 'till we get back."

McNeel wasn't satisfied. "Son, you're all your mother's got. I do wish you'd not go."

The young man's features clouded briefly. "I know that, Mr. McNeel. Better than anybody else, I guess. But this is my home, just like the rest of you, and I'm the only man my family's got to fight for it. I thought a lot about it, but I just have to go."

And they understood, every one of them. Dan Albert was still a boy, but he was a Texian. When he had gone, McNeel said, "I hope my boys grow up to his measure, I shorely do."

"They could do a whole lot worse," Buckner said. "Bailey, you ol' he-coon, pass that jug back here."

Across the way another youngster, Edward Robinson,

was staggering drunk and brandishing a rifle. At the age of nineteen, Robinson was generally considered worthless, and seemed to have set his mind on proving the point. Right now he was howling drunk and ready to go to Velasco and shoot whatever moved. "Three-legged Willie" Williamson had wandered down to the waterfront to look around, and watched the swaying youngster lift his rifle and pretend to shoot it at a jug in another man's hand. He walked over to him.

"Is that thing loaded and primed?"

"Hell, yes," Robinson slurred, looking at the little woodsman blearily. "Ain't we goin' to a fight?"

"I wouldn't bet on your makin' it there right now."

Robinson peered at him and brought the rifle around. Williamson's Kentucky was cradled in his arm, muzzle down. "Boy," he said quietly, "I hope you're sober enough to understand me now, 'cause if that gun lines up on me, even just once, you're gonna be dead."

It cut through the fog in the youth's mind. He swayed, lowered the rifle and grinned crookedly. "No harm, Willie. No harm done."

"Not yet," Williamson snapped. "Now put that thing down somewhere and go home to bed. If I see you around here again tonight I'll whale the tar out of you."

He turned away. After a moment, Robinson started trying to figure out which way was home. Drunk or sober, he knew he was no match for the little man with the peg leg.

At the north end of town Dan Albert called at Peggy Nolan's house, and they went walking. Peggy was a pretty girl of fourteen, just beginning to be a woman, and although Dan had been calling on her for more than a month, he was still tongue-tied in her presence. They walked a short way on the darkening street, then paused beside a new picket fence, each trying to think of a way to begin a conversation.

Finally Peggy looked up at him and put her soft hand into his hard, callused one. "Dan," she said, "I just wish you wouldn't go."

They stood there for a long time, it seemed, before he answered.

"I got to, Peggy. There's work to be done, and the Albert family hasn't no men but me to do our share of it."

The tone of his voice made her proud, but the finality of his decision frightened her.

"That's the whole thing," he added after a moment. "Some fellas my age have got dads to do the fightin' for 'em. I ain't, so it's up to me. Peggy . . ." He paused. Then, "Please understand."

"I know." She averted her eyes. "I guess I just had to argue one more time. But I do understand. But, Dan, please, please be awfully careful. You are all your mother's got in the world. And me too. I want you to come back."

It came now in a rush, and he blurted it out, "Peggy, I want to marry you. I want us to get married just as soon as I get back. Will you? Will you think about it, anyway? Please?"

There was no hesitation at all in her response. "Of course I will, you dummy. Did you ever once think I wouldn't?"

After a moment they went on, hand in hand, and Dan Albert walked taller than he had ever done before in his life. Off toward the docks and the militia camp they could hear the voices of a hundred or more men laughing, joking, shouting, and talking—getting ready to go to war. In the near darkness, as they walked, a horseman passed them coming in from the north. As his tired mount shuffled through the patch of dim light from a gate lantern, he turned and tipped his hat, then rode on. Both the horse and its rider were long, lean, travel-worn, and tired.

Leander Woods had done some riding to get here in time for the big fight, and when he reined in his horse in front of Jane Long's, the animal just stopped and stood, its head down, not wanting to move again for some time. George McKinstry was seated on the porch, a lantern by his side, checking off lists of supplies.

"Reckon I made it here right on time," Woods allowed, studying the turmoil around him. "Where's John Austin?"

"Be here in a little bit, Leander," McKinstry said. "Set a while and have a drink."

Leander was one of the Woods boys, a son of old Zadock Woods, one of a half-dozen younger duplicates of the old man. Zadock and his sons were known throughout Texas on several counts—one of them being that they would ride a hundred miles for a good fight, no matter who as fighting. Tough, wiry, and rough-cut, Leander ran to length and extremities. Well over six feet tall, he was a rawhide hank of a man, wide in the shoulders, long in the jaw, narrow in the hips, with large, rough hands and big feet. As far as anyone had been able to compare, he looked just about like all the other Woodses, including old Zadock himself.

"Where's the old man and the rest of the crew?" McKiostry asked. "They comin' in, too?"

"Naw, reckon I'm it this time," Leander drawled. "Pa and the rest is up the other side of San Antonio some'ers chasin' Comanche. You know how Pa is." He loosened the saddle girth on the beat-down horse and stuck a wad of tobacco in his jaw. "This ol' hoss has carried me many a mile last couple-three days."

"Where'd you come in from?"

"San Antonio. I was in town pickin' up supplies when I heard about a ruckus down to Anahuac, so I come ahead on." He sat on the porch, pulled off his boots and rubbed his feet. "On the way down I heard they was gonna take some cannon over there. So I figured they'd have to go by water this time of year, and I figured you weren't gonna get past that fort at Velasco without a fight, and I was lookin' for a fight, so I came on to here."

"You figured that out, did you?" McKinstry was fascinated.

"Yeah. Figured ol' Ugartechea's too good a soldier to let y'all pass his fort with cannon. No Mescan soldier's gonna set by while somebody hauls off to blow hell out of another Mescan soldier, even if that other'n is a bastid like Juan Bradburn. Ugartechea's a fine feller an' all, but he's a soldier."

"And you figured all that out."

"Yeah."

"Well, Leander, you figured right, sure enough."

Woods stretched and yawned. "I know that."

McKinstry got out his roster and added another Texian to it.

Down in the camp area Matthew Langley spread his bedroll and started sorting his gear, packing light for the next day's excursion to Velasco. Deep in his pack he came across a piece of paper, folded and sealed with wax. He had not noticed it there before. It was a letter, addressed to him. It read:

Sir,

I am of the opinion that what my uncle said about you is exactly right. You are just plain dumb.

However, if you are still alive when you read this, then please know that we would be honored to have you call on us again at your next convenience. Maybe the next time you might be all in one piece and not all cut up from brawling.

Until such time as you may be back this way, if you are still alive, please take care of yourself. If not, please disregard the foregoing.

In any case, in the bottom of your pack you will find a package of salve which I believe to be restorative of cuts, gunshot wounds, snakebites, and other irritations. Use it.

Respectfully,
Miss Charlotte Blanchard.

He looked, and the package was there.

Later, packed and ready for the morning, Matthew Langley rolled into his blankets and dreamed confused dreams of silken hair and soft eyes, a small form pointing a large musket at a great bear, and a very short skirt that barely covered a girl's shapely knees. And, oddly, he also dreamed of soft hands on an aching head, firelight, and a passenger stage standing near a bunch of trees.

In the dark hours before morning Bubba mounted up and rode out, across the river and the few miles of forest to Bailey's Prairie, where he reported to Mrs. Dot Bailey that her husband and son-in-law were well and sleeping in Brazoria, and that her sons Smith and Gaines had joined them there. He explained briefly about the expedition to Velasco and assured her that Britt Bailiey had gone to bed early and gotten plenty of rest. She didn't believe a word of it.

Before daylight Bubba was back at the Brazos, a keg of beer strapped behind his saddle and a dozen eggs wrapped carefully in a kerchief at his belt. The ferry was across the river and the operator was asleep. Bubba awakened him by throwing clods across the river at him. In camp, Bubba counted blankets at Bailey's fire. The old man was there, as was Strap Buckner, enormous under a pile of blankets, and William Scates. Bubba collected four large mugs from around the camp, broke eggs into them, filled them with beer and then relaxed, waiting for Bailey to awaken.

As the sun came up, Bailey rolled over, sat up, yawned, and stretched his massive frame. Without comment, Bubba handed him a mug of eggs and beer. Without comment, Bailey drank it. Finally he reached over and whacked Buckner on the rear, bringing him around, and then nudged Scates.

The little carpenter sat up, moaned pitifully and grabbed his head with both hands. When Bubba offered him meat and biscuits he shook his head.

"Mistah Bill," Bubba said, "If you don't close them eyes you gonna bleed to death."

Scates groaned again and accepted a mug of beer and eggs. Bubba kept the fourth one for himself.

Strap Buckner sloshed down the beer and took a huge bite of meat. "Hoo, man!" he roared, and Scates winced. "That was some palaver!"

Brazoria, Texas, that early morning looked like a battlefield—after the battle. From the porch of Jane Long's tavern to the water's edge and from one end of Front Street to the other, lifeless bodies were strewn. Empty jugs, kegs, and bottles were everywhere. Here and there were signs of life, as early risers reluctantly greeted the new day, but many of them would remain dead until someone kicked, thumped, or doused them into staggering wakefulness.

Inside Jane Long's place, when John Austin arrived, there was a little more life. About half of the collapsed forms packed in the tavern had managed to regain a hold on life and had swayed to the bar for beer, coffee, or hair of the dog.

In the back room Henry Smith, Henry Brown, Bill Russell, George McKinstry, and Dave Milburn were ranged around the table that had become command headquarters. Dr. T.F.L. Parrott and Dr. Branch T. Archer were with them.

"Have we got any army left at all?" Austin asked, looking back over the sea of bodies in the tavern and outside.

McKinstry grinned. "They'll be all right in a little while. Lot of 'em had a goin'-to-war party last night."

"I can see they did."

They went over plans again, carefully and systematically. Austin questioned them on every point, then stood up.

"All right, men." He sighed. "Let's roll 'em out."

McKinstry, Brown, and Russell spread out through the town and the waterside camp, trying to shake men awake and get them organized. They had only limited success. Accurately estimating the situation, McKinstry reported back to Austin that it would be midmorning before they could expect to get the troops on their way.

Bill Smith, the schoolteacher, walked down to Front Street with rifle and pack. "I'm going, John," he said.

Another newcomer had driven into town from Bell's Landing in a wagon. This was Captain James Ramage, U.S. Navy. He asked Austin for permission to go along, as an observer. Ramage had been visiting relatives upriver when the word came.

"Will you travel in uniform, sir?" Austin asked.

"Yes, I will, and strictly as an observer. I believe the United States will be most interested in a report on this situation."

Austin welcomed him and assigned Henry Smith to escort him.

By midmorning Brazoria was bedlam. Men were scurrying around, doing last-minute things. Children and dogs were underfoot and women were saying tearful last-minute goodbyes to their men. Down by the docks three horses, one with a saddle, ran bucking wildly through the camp, their angry owners behind them yelling and cursing.

The disaster that was Brazoria's civilian army finally got itself organized and ready to go. The militia was ready to march into history or oblivion, whichever came first. Peggy Nolan came down to the dock to see Dan Albert off and, to his pleased chagrin, kissed him long and soundly in front of a cheering crowd of men. Bill Russell got his command aboard the *Brazoria* and prepared to cast off. Of the more than twenty men on the little ship, only four knew anything about sailing. The mate, Tucker, was aboard, as were Sylvester Bowen, who held a master's ticket, and Sam White and William Menefee, crewmen from the *Navidad*. Aligned on shore near the ferry landing, John Austin and Henry Brown were trying to get their joint command into a semblance of order.

"Come on boys," a man yelled. "Let's go fight Meskins!"

Alberto Ruiz, a few feet away, grinned wryly at his son. Si, Rafael." He chuckled. "We go fight Meskins."

"Hey, Jim! I bet I kill the first one!"

"You got a dollar on that bet, big mouth!"

Ed Robinson waved his rifle. "Hell, boys, I got ten dollars in American gold says I get the first shot in!"

Rawlings glanced at him with disapproval. "You're on!" he said.

Britt Bailey, Strap Buckner, Bill Scates, and Bubba didn't bother with the ferry. Jumping their horses into the river, they swam them across. Unlike the others, Bailey did not dismount when they got into the deep, swift water. The big man remained in the saddle, sitting straight and tall, while the desperate horse swam. Only the animal's eyes, nose, and ears were above the water.

Langley and Lander Woods had hit it off well on brief acquaintance during the morning, and now they joined Gaines and Smith Bailey, following the older men into the river and out on the other bank. Others followed them. The ferry, meanwhile, was creaking across the river with a load of men and horses.

Regathered on the east bank, they set off southward in a mixed command, Austin's and Brown's troops riding together. They would reorganize later, near Velasco. And no one was worried about riding into an ambush in the woods. Not with Milton Hicks and Tecumseh Bell riding scout.

A gaggle of young boys followed along, helping to tend the pack animals and glorying in their importance. They would go only as far as Calvet's upper landing, then would be sent home.

The conflict at Anahuac had been a skirmish. The real fight was about to begin, and it would begin at Velasco.

Seventeen

Eagle Island, William Wharton's plantation on the east bank of the Brazos, was the showcase among Texas plantations in 1832. Young Wharton, just turned thirty, was a shrewd and wealthy man, and his father-in-law, Jared E. Groce, was a powerful and wealthy man. Both of them, the older Groce and the young Wharton, adored pretty little Sarah Ann Groce Wharton, and the big new plantation house under construction on a high knoll a mile back from the river was evidence of it. When it was completed, it would be a gift to her from her father and her husband. And it would rival any house in Mobile, New Orleans, or Atlanta. It was to be the first grand house in Austin's colony built from milled lumber.

It was near noon when the Brazoria militia reached Eagle Island. The schooner tied up at the loading docks, while the two companies of riders came in by road.

Some of Wharton's slaves had loaded two wagons with big six-by-ten-inch oak planks, twenty feet in length, and hauled them up to the main house where Wharton met the settlers. Cut into four-foot length and doubled, the planks would make excellent breastworks for defense against rifle and musket fire. No small-arms fire was ever going to pierce them. Six pairs of sawhorses had been set up near the loaded wagons, and Austin assigned James Caldwell to take a group to assemble the breastworks.

Caldwell looked the planks over and shook his head. "Look at the size of them things!" he complained. "There ain't a man here can even get them off the wagons alone."

Strap Buckner grinned at him, his black beard flaring around big white teeth. "I know one that can." He looked around and spotted Uncle Bubba. "In fact, they's two of us right here can handle them things. I'd include ol' Britt Bailey too, but he's gettin' too old for heavy work."

"Too old, hell," Bailey growled. "I ain't too old, just too smart to bust my back when I don't have to."

"Haw!" Buckner bellowed. "Boys, give me some room." Striding to the wagon, he wrapped great hands around one of the planks and heaved it over the edge, then pulled another one down on top of it. Getting his legs under him, he raised the two upright, hoisted them, and carried them to the sawhorses, slamming them down there. The legs of the sawhorses sank an inch or two into the ground.

"Okay, Bubba," he said, dusting his hands, don't just stand there. Show these folks what a black-hearted scoundrel like me and a black-assed one like you can do."

Bubba shook his head sorrowfully as he strode to the wagon.

"Mistah Strap, you gonna work me to a early grave showin' folks how strong we is."

With a heave, the big black uprighted two planks on the wagon and carried them, ends high in the air, to another set of sawhorses. Between the militiamen and Wharton's slaves, working three to a plank, they got the rest unloaded, and Scates and some others went to work with saws, hammers, and spikes.

They worked in the hot sun, sweating and straining, and another crew transported the bulwarks to the ship as they were completed. Finally it was done, and Sarah Ann Wharton, young mistress of Eagle Island, served luncheon for the entire Texian army at long tables set with white cloths, silver, and china, on the lawn behind the main house.

Bill Russell had been watching the river closely for signs of tide. It was nearing its peak now, salt water from the sea rolling in along the bottom of the channel, the river's flow increasingly sluggish. Late in the afternoon it would be going out again and the flow would increase. This fit in exactly with Austin's battle plan. They would wait at Eagle Island until evening, then make the run to Velasco.

It was here, during the afternoon that Britt Bailey called together several witnesses and stated to them his last will and testament. "Just in case," he said jokingly, but his eyes were serious.

With Buckner, Langley, editor D.W. Anthony, Henry Munson, and Robert Williamson listening as witnesses, and Anthony taking notes, Bailey launched into an extensive itemization of his properties and holdings and their disposition in case of his death. It was an impressive feat. Bailey had large and small holdings ranging from near Brazoria north into the Tonkawa country and west into the Colorado basin, and knew each of them by title and description.

Finally he knelt by Anthony, peering over his shoulder. "Now, this next is the most important part," he said, "so get it right. It's how I want to be buried."

Buckner snorted. "Damn, Britt, everybody in the colony knows how you aim to be buried. Standin' up an' facin' west."

"I want it on paper," Bailey snapped. "Write it down, now, just like this. When I go I want to buried on Bailey's Prairie, standin' up like a man, facin' west, so nobody can ever say, 'there lies ol' Britt Bailey.' They'll have to say, 'there stands Britt Bailey,' instead. Now say I want a jug of good whiskey at my feet, my lantern in my hand, my whip on my shoulder, and my rifle beside me—with some powder and ball, ready to fire."

"Mistah Britt, I wish you wouldn't talk 'bout that right now," Bubba said, his eyes turning to Rawlings, some distance away across the lawn.

"I want the whole damn thing down and witnessed, just in case," Bailey stated. "I been havin' a feelin' lately like it's important."

"Don't talk that way, Mistah Britt, please."

"Oh, shut up, Bubba . . . and dammit, don't look at me like I was a ghost. I'm ready to whip my weight in

232

cougars. Or sassy niggers, for that matter."

Carefully, formally, those present all made their marks as witnesses, and Anthony folded the paper and put it in his pouch.

"One more thing, D.W., if I get through this shindig alive, I want that thing back. If Dot ever saw that will with them buryin' instructions on it, and I was still alive, she'd kill me."

While they waited for the last leg of the trip to begin, Langley wrote a letter, dated June 25, 1832, Eagle Island Plantation:

My Dear Miss Blanchard,

I am certain the salve you packed for me is an excellent medication, and I look forward to the occasion to make test of it.

Your invitation to call on you and your family again is indeed most kind and you may rest assured I will do so at the first opportunity that presents itself. Your uncle, Mr. Jeremiah Blanchard, has a good horse that he is keeping for me.

I remain in the best of health and spirit, and am in the company of the colonial militia, serving under the esteemed John Austin.

Hoping you are the same, I remain

Yr. Ob't. S'vt.,
Matthew Langley

Satisfied that this should keep the fires of romance burning—if there were any—until he returned, he imposed upon Wharton's chief steward to post the letter with the next packet.

It was a hot, sticky afternoon, with clouds rolling in from the Gulf. It looked, and felt, like rain. On the coast at Fort Velasco an excited soldier was galloping his tired horse across the last stretch of salt grass toward the gate.

233

"Los Tejanos!" he shouted as he neared the fort. *¡Vienen los Tejanos!"*

At the gate he slipped from the lathered horse and Jesús grabbed him by the arm. "The Texians? Are they coming now?"

"No, but I saw them," the man gasped. He was as out of breath as his mount.

"Come, Felipe," the sergeant ordered. "We will report to *el comandante.* José! Wake up, you donkey! Keep a sharp lookout!" The gate guard had been drowsing in the afternoon heat, but he was wide-awake now.

At the main building Colonel Ugartechea came out as they approached. He was buckling on his sword. The sergeant and the excited scout saluted smartly, and he returned it. "Give me your report."

¡Los Tejanos, mi Colonel! Cientos, cientos!"

"Hundreds? Indeed." Ugartechea had reports that there were only a handful of fighting men in Brazoria. The main body had ridden for Anahuac.

"At ease, man!" he snapped. "Now tell me, how many Texians did you see, and where?"

"Many, Colonel. Maybe three . . . no . . . four hundred. And they have a big ship, very long."

"Where?"

"At Señor Wharton's dock, sir. I have seen them there."

Ugartechea was thoughtful. "A long ship? The only ship upriver now is the *Brazoria,* and it is very small. Three or four hundred men, eh?"

"Sí mi Colonel. I think so."

"Gracias," Ugartechea said. "Sergeant, when the other scouts come in, I will see them immediately."

"Sí, Colonel." Jesús saluted, then grabbed Felipe by the arm and led him away, shaking his head. "Ass," he scolded. "Son of a donkey, hundreds of men, a big ship. *¡Hijo de burro!"*

Ugartechea could not help a slight smile as he walked back to his quarters. From the report, he had no idea how many Texians there might be, but he guessed no more than a hundred. And the *Brazoria,* far from being a big ship, was barely sixty-five feet in length. However, it confirmed what he had expected. The Texians would attempt an attack on the fort. The thought saddened him. He had good friends among those Anglo rascals. But if they launched an attack — well, he was a soldier. He would do his duty.

A little later two more scouts rode in. They had seen the *Brazoria,* her decks lined with cotton bales, at least two cannon visible. And they had seen a hundred or more Texians. They were all coming this way. He knew that the settlers had cannon at Brazoria. Although outlawed for civilians, they had found their way up the river in ships' holds — hidden in kegs, concealed in implement crates, or disguised as ballast. He had no idea how many.

He went to the armory, where two armed guards saluted and stood aside for him. Inside, he walked directly to a large crate, picked up a mallet and banged the top loose. There was no satisfaction in his eyes as he gazed at the machine inside. He had friends out there. He hoped they would not fire on him, but at the same time he knew they would.

He knew too well the man who led the Texians. John Austin was a quiet man, and a patient one. But when he made up his mind to do a thing, he did it. John Austin would not back down.

Outside the armory he gave orders to put the garrison on full alert, men at all posts and defense squads on standby. And he detailed a lieutenant to see to the unpacking and cleaning of the crated weapon in the armory — a weapon few of his men and none of the Texians knew about.

At a grove of pecan and hackberry trees beside the river, one of a few lonely groves dotting the wide coastal plain near the ocean shore, John Austin called a halt to the march and waited for the schooner *Brazoria* to come up with them. The tide was turning, and a wind was freshening off the Gulf. The men on the *Brazoria* had their work cut out for them. Overhead, fleecy clouds were forming ranks across the sky, crowding thicker and thicker in the rays of late sun. To the south, out over the ocean, thunderheads were packing up to move inland.

Just a few miles downstream now, at the river's mouth, waited an armed and ready Fort Velasco. The only element of surprise might lie in timing. There was no doubt in anybody's mind that Ugartechea knew they were coming.

When they were all together, John Austin called the men around him to go over the details of his plan of attack. It was a simple plan, depending largely upon an element of surprise and careful coordination of the three Texian forces.

Austin's group was to be the attack force, and the attack was to come from the north, from the mainland side of the fort. Henry Brown's men were to create a diversion. Under cover of darkness, Brown's force was to move east around the fort and spread out under whatever cover could be found. There would be drift logs, piles of driftwood, sand dunes, whatever offered cover. Brown was then to wait. At about three in the morning, he was to open fire in conjunction with the schooner on the river.

The critical element in the timing was the little schooner. At dark, Russell would bring the ship down to the bayou cut just out of sight of the fort. The masts might show, but it didn't really matter. Ugartechea knew they were around somewhere. The slight bend in the river at the bayou cut would protect the ship from cannon fire. In full dark—and Austin eyed the clouds speculatively— the ship was to move on down the river near the fort and lay a barrage about three in the morning, coinciding with Brown's attack from the beach.

This two-direction fighting, Austin hoped, would divert the garrison while his own troops moved in close on the landward side. They had to get close—close enough to make an assault on the walls at daybreak. Austin's force, coming in under cover of the firing from the beach and from the ship, would bring the wooden barricades with them. They would place them and dig in behind them, then wait for daylight. Russell was to take the ship back up the river after his cover mission, then bring it down again at dawn and move in as close as possible to the fort to cover Austin's attack.

Finally they were all ready. All that remained now was to wait for darkness. There was some jawing about it. Some who were in Brown's troop wanted to be with Austin instead, to assail the walls. Young Ed Robinson, mindful of his bet with Rawlings, wanted to change from Austin's force to Brown's so that he could fire the first shot. Austin and Brown kept the rosters as they were.

Bill Russell conferred with the mate of the *Brazoria* about wind and tides. The fates were not cooperating at all. The tide was coming in strong, and the winds were blowing from the sea. There would be no accurate timing for the ship. It might arrive in firing position at midnight, or sometime after three, or any time between.

Tucker reminded him of their agreement. He would help bring the ship to point, but he would not take part in the fighting. Russell agreed. When the firing began, Tucker could go below decks and stay there. Some of the settlers were irritated at this arrangement, but Bailey stepped in.

"Shut your mouths about that Yankee," he said bluntly. "He's got a family to take care of back home, and this ain't his fight. Now just let him alone."

Austin and Brown revised their plans on timing. It was decided the ship would be the time-peice and would open fire whenever it was in position. Brown would take his cue from the ship.

"Thing I don't understand," a man standing by the horses confided to another. "Looks to me like that ship has got to go right past that fort to get in position to start shootin'. Right?"

"Yeah."

"So if it can go past the fort to line up to shoot, why can't it just sail right on past and head for Anahuac and the rest of us take off across country and meet it there?"

"Guess we could."

"Then why are we gonna fight Ugartechea at all?"

"Why, hell, Sam, we got to fight him. How'd it look on his record if we just slip past him?"

Sam looked blank, so his friend explained further.

"Now, you see, we all know ol' Domingo's got orders to stop us from goin' to Anahuac. An' Domingo's a soldier, so he's gotta do what he's ordered, ain't he?"

"Yeah, but . . ."

"So John Austin asked if we could pass and he said no. So now we gotta fight. Ol' Domingo's a gentleman, and he never done nothin' wrong to us. So we ain't gonna humiliate him by sneakin' past. We gotta fight him honorable."

Sam scratched his chin, still puzzled, and the other added, "Well, then, Sam, if you cain't figure that, then look at it this way: if we don't whip Domingo here, he's gonna be right behind us when we get to Anahuac, and we gonna be in a cross-fire."

Understanding spread across Sam's rough features. "Oh, so that's why we gonna jump the Velasco fort first."

"No, that ain't why, but you ain't understandin' the real reason."

The cloud cover was solid and deepening by the time it was full dark. With some last-minute rechecking of strategy, Brown called his forces around him and led them off to the southeast, across the marsh. Within an hour or so they would be in position, southeast and south of the fort's walls. There they would wait for the opening shot from the *Brazoria*. This was the largest group of the three. When Austin's turn came to go at the walls, he wanted plenty of cover fire.

Russell's force had gone to move the schooner into position for the final run, and the men with John Austin sat around and waited in a cold, dark camp. The wind was turning, and there were brief flashes of lightning on the southern horizon where a rain squall was kicking up.

Langley was among Austin's troop, sitting with several men at the outskirts of the camp, watching the occasional flares of lightning to the south. Smith and Gaines Bailey were with him, and Leander Woods. Britt Bailey stood nearby in quiet conversation with Strap Buckner, while Bubba hovered about, cleaning his old gun, a darker shadow among the shadows.

"I got me a girl back in San Antonio," Woods said suddenly, à propos of nothing at all. "She's got black hair and black eyes and the softest hands you ever did see. Her daddy told me once he'd as soon shoot me as see me get near her, and I told him if I thought I was gonna do her harm I'd shoot myself first. We get along all right since then."

They sat in silence for a while and thought this over.

"Yeah," Smith Bailey said, quietly.

Woods nudged Langley. "You got a girl, Matthew?"

"Well, I don't rightly know."

Gaines regarded him. "What does that mean? Do you or don't you?"

"It means I don't know whether I do or not," Langley said evenly. "There's a girl all right, but I don't know whether she'd notice me or not."

"Well, hell, man, don't you think you oughta go find out?"

"I been thinkin' I might."

"What made you start talkin' about women all of a sudden?" Smith asked Woods.

"Shoot, I don't know. Couldn't think of anythin' better to talk about, I guess."

Just before midnight Russell sent word to Austin that if he was going to move into position under the fire of the schooner he had better start now. The incoming tide was pushing a current up the river that would be so bad by three o'clock that they might not be able to move. It would be different for the dawn attack, he said. The tide would be going out by then, and they could move easily.

Austin sent McKinstry to get the men ready to move out. He repeated his final order to be sure everyone understood it. There was to be no smoking, talking, or noise of any kind. And no weapons were to be carried primed.

"Do you want a weapons check, John?"

"No, just make sure the word gets around."

If Ed Robinson got the word, he chose to ignore it.

Eighteen

There wasn't much that Lieutenant Colonel Domingo de Ugartechea didn't know about combat. A career soldier, he had been a line officer most of his adult life. He had seen warfare and had learned from it. He had no fear of the settlers who were moving in to attack him, but he was a realist. He knew the shortcomings of his fortress here on this desolate river mouth—a cannon that could not be depressed, a shortage of powder and fuse, and soldiers who didn't really have their hearts in fighting people they considered neighbors. The only thing he had in plentiful supply at the moment was food, and the thought brought a wry grin to his seamed face. Maybe Matamoros expected him to persuade his enemies to eat themselves to death.

His forces were in place, squads at intervals around the walls, cavalry saddled and ready on the parade ground . . . what possible use could cavalry be if they were bottled up inside a fort? Well, he shrugged, that was the way the book prescribed.

Out on the east ramp, a group of soldiers were lugging a gun up to the wall. There was one weapon the Texians did not know about. It was a small swivel gun that could be mounted at any of several points on the perimeter wall. Smaller than a cannon, it could nevertheless fire a two-inch ball at great velocity and with deadly accuracy. Both the Texians and the Mexicans, most of them, were unaware of this weapon, but it just might make the difference. He was very sure that the Texians would try to get in under the range of the big cannon. It was here, at close range, that the swivel gun would come into play.

Walking up the ramp in the dim light of muted lanterns, he glanced back and saw the honorable Don Francisco Duclor pacing nervously in front of the main guardroom. Ah, he thought, Don Francisco is worried. Excellent! The tax collector's dismay brought a cheerful note to the colonel's otherwise dour thinking.

The past few weeks had been an unpleasant time for Don Francisco. First he had lost the services of his chief kill-dog, the Anglo Whitlet. Then the *Navidad* had run the channel at night and had been gone before the sentries managed to report its presence. Then the *Brazoria* had come in with cargo of such obviously American origin that there could be no question about it, and Captain Rowland had given Duclor an ultimatum: either prove to Rowland's satisfaction that the cargo wasn't Mexican, or accept a challenge to a duel, or stand a back and let the ship pass. Ugartechea's harbor guard, it happened, had been very busy somewhere else at the time, and Duclor had backed down.

Ugartechea thought there would be very little mercy for Don Francisco if the Texians should take the fort. The thought didn't bother him at all.

The night was very dark, with the look of a storm brewing. Suddenly a cannon boomed and a stable wall collapsed near the south stockade. Another boom, and ball whisked overhead. The Texians had arrived.

When the *Brazoria* opened fire from the river with her cannon, Brown's command on the beach, spread out behind driftwood and dunes, lifted their rifles and began a steady, withering fire upon the vague shadow of the fort, aiming for the tops of the walls. Several men aboard the schooner were adding rifle fire to the blasting of the cannons.

The sudden attack, coming from two directions, resulted in a moment of near-panic in the fort. Defenders were firing at random in all directions, aiming at imaginary targets or at nothing at all. It was several minutes before Ugartechea's officers regained control, directing the fire toward the sources of Texian fire. This left the north plain quiet.

The lull in his direction was what Austin had been waiting for. He and his men moved out in darkness, carrying the heavy wood bulwarks. Hurrying but stepping carefully, almost afraid to breathe for fear of being heard from the fort, they moved forward in a long line, two men to a barricade, to within fifty feet of the looming perimeter wall. Stringing out in a curved line about eighty feet long, they set the barricades upright on the saltgrass-clumped sand and began digging in, swiftly and silently. The firing across the stockade and the closer firing aimed at the ship was loud in their ears as they worked. From here the walls seemed to loom high above them, and the firing toward the river seemed almost overhead. The work went rapidly and well, trenches forming behind the wooden barricades, a sand embankment thrown up around them and then the barricades raised to the top of it.

Langley caught a quick glimpse of Bubba and Strap Buckner working side by side, doing the work of ten men. Bubba was humming a spiritual softly under his breath, and Buckner was cursing — quietly, monotonously, and apparently without ever repeating himself. Langley and Smith Bailey were sharing a bulwark. Gaines Bailey was off to the right. It was almost pitch-dark.

It was about this time that a shot was fired from Austin's ranks, and answered immediately from the wall. Ed Robinson may have been thinking of his ten-dollar bet with Rawlings. He may just have been careless. Whichever it was, he had ignored Austin's order to leave the rifles unprimed. His was ready to fire, and fire it did. On the wall above them an alert soldier heard the shot, spotted the muzzle flash, whirled, and fired toward it.

Ed Robinson was the first man in Austin's company to fire a shot at the Battle of Velasco. He was also the first to die.

The new firing on the north wall answered Ugartechea's

main question. He had recognized the first barrage as cover fire, and had realized almost immediately that the firing from the beach, at a middle range of seventy or eighty yards, was a diversion. Now he knew where "the real threat lay — to the north, almost under the fort's walls. Troops were moving around the walls and across the parade ground to bolster the defense there. Ugartechea called a lieutenant to him and directed the swivel gun to be mounted on brackets on the northernmost point of the perimeter wall. Within minutes it was there, and the gunners opened fire. In the dark they had no accuracy, but they fired where they thought a target might be.

On the Texian's left flank someone yelled, and the word passed along the line, "Down! Get down! They got somethin' that shoots through these planks! Tap Sanders got hit."

Word also was whispered up and down the line that the premature shot had been fired by Robinson, and that he was dead.

"Good!" Buckner hissed. He raised his rifle and fired at a muzzle flash above him, then ducked back down behind his barricade.

The swivel gun was almost directly over him, and the gunner saw his flash and brought it around and down. He fired, and the ball found the bulwark, ripped through the planking and took Buckner high in the chest. He gasped and grabbed Britt Bailey's arm, his hand crushing down on his friend's biceps, then relaxing. Even a giant was no match for a two-inch lead ball.

"Strap!" Bailey hissed, swinging around. He couldn't see the big man, but he knew the force of the blow by the way Buckner's body had been smashed backward. He felt for him and found him. "Parrot!" he yelled. "Doc Parrott! Git over here!"

Parrott crawled across to their trench, and checked Buckner's body in the dark. Finally he raised his head. "He's dead, Britt. There ain't a thing can be done for him."

Bailey sat dazed for a moment, then grabbed his rifle and stood up, shouting at the top of his lungs, "Robinson! Ed Robinson, you sonovabitch! Gawd damn your soul to hell!"

Bubba appeared from nowhere and lunged into Bailey, dragging him to the ground, holding him there. Bailey's rifle thudded into the sand at Langley's elbow and he grabbed it. Bubba was struggling to keep Bailey down, and Bailey was fighting him.

"Turn me loose, you black bastard."

"Nosuh, Mistah Britt." Bubba's voice was strained. "Won't do you no good if you git yo'self kilt!"

John Austin crawled over to them from the right. "What's happened, Britt? You hurt?"

"It's Mistah Strap," Buba said. "He's done kilt."

"Oh, Lord, no."

Bailey got an arm loose and swung wildly. "Let me go, dammit! I got to kill Ed Robinson."

"Robinson's dead, Britt. He died first."

It took a moment to soak in, then Bailey relaxed. "Good," he breathed.

Austin felt Buckner's dead face, and sighed. He had lost a good friend. And he would have to tell Jane Long. After a moment he turned and crawled back down the line.

The swivel gun had been silent for a minute or two, but now it began firing again. Whenever it hit a barricade it sent a shower of wood splinters flying behind it. Up and down the line, there were gasps and cries of men hurt. At Austin's passed command, all return firing ceased. In the darkness the gunners on the wall had no targets except muzzle flashes and Austin wanted them to have none.

A ball passed through a barricade at the east end of the line and a splinter plowed a deep furrow along the side of Henry Smith's head. Doctor Parrott was nearby, and he dressed the bleeding wound.

A sudden brief break in the cloud cover caught James

P. Caldwell, a Brazoria farmer, crawling behind the trenches between Britt Bailey's barricade and the one shared by Langley and Smith Bailey. The swivel gun was trained down the line to the right, but a soldier rose up behind the wall and aimed his musket. Langley saw him, grabbed the wooden barricade in front of him and heaved, his muscles cracking. The bulwark held for a moment and then flipped over and the sentry's ball thudded into it. The younger Bailey raised his rifle and fired, and the soldier toppled backward.

"Look, Matthew," he said, as they righted the barricade in front of them again, "you don't need to lift that thing for me to shoot through. I can just shoot over it if I need to." Caldwell had dived into their trench, and then as darkness descended again he moved on down the line.

Austin's men weren't the only ones having trouble with splinters. On the beach side, where Henry Brown's command was maintaining a steady fire, the splinters were flying from driftwood. Every time a soldier's aim found a driftwood pile, the slivers erupted like so many invisible darts. A splinter hit Bob Williams of Caney in the eye, piercing the eyeball. As Dr. Charles Stewart dressed the wound, Williams was mumbling, over and over, "There goes the Anahuac fight. There it goes down the river. There goe the Anahuac fight."

Brown's men dug in deeper, and those on the outer rank moved up. They were very near the range of the cannon on the fort bastion.

Milton Hicks and Tecumseh Bell eased up behind a pile of driftwood and Bell reached out a hand to explore it.

"Too small," he decided. "Let's move."

They found a new position with more cover, but couldn't get a good shot at the fort. "Come on, Iron Heart," Bell said, "let's move forward."

Both men jumped the pile and ran toward the fort, veering toward a clump of salt grass barely visible atop a wind-cut dune. As Hicks leaped for it a musket ball caught him in mid-air, throwing him off balance. He landed awkwardly and his left leg gave way with a snap, throwing him into a crumpled heap. He rolled into the shelter of the dune and felt his leg. A groan escaped his clenched teeth.

"You hit bad, Milton?" Tecumseh Bell was beside him.

"It's my leg. I caught a round along my ribs when I jumped, and fell and busted my leg like a green pilgrim."

"Which leg?"

"Left."

Tecumseh searched around and found two pieces of driftwood to use for splints. He explored Hicks's leg. "Hold tight, Iron Heart," he said calmly. "I'm gonna pull."

Straining and feeling in the dark, Bell set the leg and bound the splints tightly with strips of cloth. When he spoke again to Hicks he thought the man had passed out, but then Hicks answered. He had put a piece of leather thong in his mouth and had bitten down so hard on it that his jaws had cramped. Neither of them had thought of calling for Dr. Stewart.

Bell found Hicks's rifle and handed it to him, and helped him square around so he could face the fort. They fired only when they had a muzzle flash to sight on. Neither had any use for the "popping" many around them were doing, wasting powder and lead.

On the schooner *Brazoria*, William Russell was having his troubles, too. The premature firing from Austin's position had caught him off guard, and necessitated a change of plan. He saw immediately that the soldiers had Austin's group located, and did the only thing he could think of to do. Instead of completing his run and getting out of range, he dropped anchor in the river channel, four hundred yards abreast of the fort, and gave supporting fire. In this position he was a sitting target for the fort gunners.

Russell directed fire from all guns toward the fort, and the little ship shivered with the recoil. The wind had died and the tide was still pushing in. Then a lucky shot from the fort broke the anchor line, and the ship began to slide backward, upstream, past the fort. Helpless in the water, the *Brazoria* slewed toward the near shore and ran aground, at high tide, a hundred and thirty yards from the fort wall.

Russell was everywhere, directing a constant fire from the cannons and the deadly blunderbuss. The field piece tied to the deck bucked and pitched against its ropes and threatened to break loose with each shot. They kept shooting. Bill Menefee beckoned to him between rounds.

"Ain't we a little close to that fort?"

"Hell, we're just right. You can't miss at this range."

Young Dan Albert was having the time of his life, touching off charges in the bow gun. He laughed aloud as the cannon roared, and joked with the men realigning it for another shot. Sylvester Bowen smiled in the dark at the kid's enthusiasm, then his face contorted in pain. The master seaman fell to the deck, a ragged hole in his thigh. Dan Albert saw him fall and yelled for Dr. Peebles, who hurried to them.

"Where are you wounded?" he asked, straightening Bowen out on the deck.

"The thigh. Oh, Lord, that hurts."

"Dan, get his shoulders. Let's get him below."

Between them they eased the wounded man across the deck and into the aft hold. They put him down, lifted the blind on a lantern and gaped in surprise. There was a wide hole in the portside hull, a foot or two above waterline. A ball had gone all the way through the ship, smashing out the starboard side at almost the same level. Isaac Tucker lay on the decking near the starboard hole, dead. The cannon ball had gone through his chest. Dan turned pale and looked away.

Bowen followed the doctor's stunned gaze. "Well, I'll be damned," he said through clenched teeth.

"And he didn't want to fight," Dan Albert muttered.

They hung a blanket over the portside hole to block the light from the lantern. Dr. Peebles went to work on Bowen. After a while, Dan Albert went up on deck again.

Before dawn, firing from the fort slackened somewhat and Russell ordered the firing to cease on the ship to save the powder they had left, in case the Mexicans should attack outside the fort at daylight. The company on the schooner still fired their rifles now and then, but mostly they waited for dawn, when they would have to either defend themselves or support Austin's ground attack.

The offshore squall was moving in rapidly now, in the black morning hours. It was going to rain soon.

Nineteen

In the dark hours Colonel Ugartechea climbed down from the cannon bastion and called to his orderly, "Tell Major Moret, Captain Salvador, Lieutenants Rincon and Pillar and Ensign Pintardo to come to my quarters, immediately!"

"Sí, Colonel."

"Also"—he paused—"Tell Don Francisco to attend. I believe you will find him in his quarters."

Duclor was the first to arrive. He accepted the drink Ugartechea offered him, with a tight smile.

"Colonel, it seems to me you are taking a long time in dealing with that ragtag mob out there."

Ugartechea eyed him coldly and said nothing. Duclor toed up a chair and sat down.

"I believe I understand, Colonel. You feel I should take part in the fighting? Doing what, cheering your men on? I am not a soldier, Colonel. I am a tax collector."

Ugartechea's gaze had not wavered. "Sí," he said, "that you are. And that, I believe, is the crux of our problem."

Duclor's attention fastened on him.

"Don Francisco," Ugartechea said coldly, "do you believe these Texians are fighting only because Colonel Bradburn has antagonized them? I think not.

"No, I think they have become exasperated with him, and with you, and with others who have been systematically stealing from them and degrading them for a long time. They know, Don Francisco, and that is why they fight."

Duclor paled, and his hand shook slightly.

"Colonel, I take offense at your remarks."

Ugartechea smiled. "You take offense? Do not tempt me, Don Francisco. As you said, I am a soldier, and you are not. Be very careful in taking offense, Don Francisco, and do not even consider an affair of honor. I am an honorable man, Don Francisco. You are a tax collector."

Three officers entered the room and saluted Ugartechea. Major Juan Moret stepped forward. "Colonel, Captain Salvador has been killed."

Ugartechea nodded, closed his eyes for a moment, and muttered, "The saints be damned to hell!"

Duclor stiffened. "I do not think blasphemy is appropriate, Colonel."

"Blasphemy!" Ugartechea threw him a withering glance. "Blasphemy! Damn you, Don Francisco, don't you know plain cursing when you hear it?"

The two older officers smiled at this outburst from their colonel, and young Ensign Emanuel Pintardo grinned. Ugartechea pulled himself together and squared his shoulders.

"Gentlemen, let us review our situation," he said. "First, we are low on ammunition for both our cannon and our muskets. We have forty-five cannon balls, seventy-eight for the swivel gun and about six hundred musket rounds. And seventy cartouche boxes. Not much at all.

"Second, although we have the strategic position, we are defending with muskets against rifles.

"Third, word has gone out concerning our situation, but no relief can be expected for, say, six days at least. Now the questions is, what . . ."

"You would give up?" Duclor sputtered. "Sir, it is treasonable even to think. We must fight to the death to hold out. We must . . ."

Ugartechea silenced him with a raised hand, and sipped his wine.

"Don Francisco, I remind you that you are present at

this meeting only at my pleasure." He turned a look of scathing contempt on the tax collector. "Fight to the death, you say? And who would fight, Don Francisco? You?" He turned back to his officers.

"The question is what to do now. The answer is, simply, wait until dawn and hope for a miracle. Gentlemen, I think without one we cannot defeat the Texians.

"We have one thing in our favor. Those are honorable men out there, and it is their word that they do not fight against México, only for their rights under the Constitution and for General Santa Anna."

"Santa Anna," Duclor spat. "That dog!"

"If you interrupt one more time, Don Francisco, I will have you thrown over the walls." The voice was mild, the intention clear. "Now, if the Texians take this garrison, I believe we will be treated with honor and courtesy."

"Will we surrender at daylight, sir?" Lieutenant Rincon asked.

"No. We will wait, and we will do what is necessary. We will fight as best we can, but I will not call on soldiers to fight to the death against citizens of México, no matter what the tax collector wishes."

Duclor's face was white with hatred. "You are with Santa Anna," he accused.

"No, señor, I am for México."

The colonel finished his wine and walked to the door, then turned back. "Do not misunderstand, gentlemen. I will not bow easily to these Texians. No, we will conduct ourselves with honor."

Dawn of the 26th day of June, 1832, found the combatants on both sides damp, tired, and ill-tempered. Heavy clouds threatened in a bleak and ominous sky, and everything below was soggy with the humidity.

The most uncomfortable were the Texians huddled behind the wooden barricades, pinned down, unable even to stretch their aching muscles. Henry Brown's command was slightly better off. At least they could withdraw out of musket range and walk on the beach to ease their cramped legs.

Dawn also brought renewed firing, offering visible targets for the first time to both sides. The soldiers manning the swivel gun now went to work with new vigor, firing at the bulwarks, and each shot brought a cry from splinter wounds or worse. The Texians, however, could see now, too, and by common consent they directed their fire at the punishing gun on the wall. At first they were cautious, cringing behind the useless planks, darting a shot now and then, until Matthew Langley got fed up.

"To hell with it!" he shouted, rose upright on his knees and leveled a rifle ball through the brim of a gunner's shako, taking off the top of the man's head with it. As he dropped to reload, a dozen other Texians rose and fired as one, at soldiers who had stood to answer Langley's shot. The deadly fire cleared the wall, and probably saved the lives of most of Austin's command, as it started a rhythmic, steady stream of fire that for a while made the north wall a very unhappy place to be.

They fired, reloaded, fired again, taking aim each time and placing their shots with brutal accuracy. Two or three heads popped up and were shot down. The wall cleared again. Then the soldiers began raising only their hands above the wall, to fire blind. The arms and hands were simple targets for the Texians.

On the *Brazoria*, dawn brought a serious problem to Russell's men. Visible now, they were an easy mark for the big nine-pounder on the bastion. Realizing this, Russell directed all of the schooner's fire, cannon and small-arms, at the bastion itself. For a time it was effective. The Mexican gunners were pinned down behind their low parapet. Then the game changed.

A slim figure in spotless uniform mounted the bastion, in full sight of the Texian guns, kicked the gunner aside, and began loading and firing the big cannon alone. It was Ugartechea. Oblivious to the missiles spitting around his head, he fired, loaded, and fired again, a continuous stream of fire. His accuracy was poor, but his courage was exemplary. The Texians were thoroughly impressed. A cheer of applause went up from the *Brazoria* in tribute to the act. Then they got back to shooting at him. It was difficult, even at this close range, with the ship wallowing badly in a receding tide.

Jesús, the gate sergeant, ran to the northeast wall and found his squad cowering below the line of fire, awed at the barrage from Austin's men. The sergeant was dumbfounded. With a shout he ran up the ramp, raised his musket and fired at the line of Texians below. A rifle ball caught him in the chest and he toppled backward, over the rear wall, to the ground. He lay staring at the ominous sky. His mouth worked, but no words came out. A young private looked down at him in horror, then screamed for a medical corpsman.

Major Moret had come around the wall ramp and reached the sergeant as the corpsman looked up. "He will die, Comandante." The major bent to listen to the sergeant's chest. He could hear the wheeze of a punctured lung. "Plug up the holes," he said quickly. "Both front and back. Patch them so air cannot escape from the chest. Then take him to the doctor. Let him say if this man will live or die."

With a scowl Moret climbed the ramp and walked along the wall, in clear view, directing his men's fire. He had seen the acts of bravery of his colonel and now of this sergeant. He stood a little straighter for them as he walked. At his example the gunners at the swivel gun went back to work, firing one deadly round after another. Only furious firing from the Texians put them down behind the walls again. But in the meantime, the big balls took their toll.

Young Benjamin Brigham took a hit in the outer muscle of his shoulder, scoring the flesh deeply but missing the bone. Jim Caldwell was thrown against the back of his trench, an ugly wound in his side. A round ripped through a barricade and took Sanders full in the face. He crumpled without a sound. A splinter pierced Gaines Bailey's ear and another one gashed Bird Waller's wrist.

Henry Brown's command was hardest hit. When Ugartechea saw his men at the east wall stand and fire at the group southeast of the fort, he swung the big cannon around and began firing that way. He was still shooting after the soldiers on the ramparts had dropped to their knees and hugged the stockade walls for shelter. Brown shared the others' admiration for the spunky colonel, but he was doing too much damage. Concentrated long-rifle fire was leveled at him, finally driving him to the parapet.

A cannonball hit the pile of driftwood that Leander Woods was using for cover, and smashed its way through. Woods died with his discharged rifle clasped firmly in his hand. Thomas Chaudoin jumped to his feet to assist Woods and took a musket ball in the thigh. Matthew Hinds saw Chaudoin fall and crawled toward him. A ball hit him in the left side, shattering his spine. He was dead before his brother, Geron, could reach him.

Edward Robertson was shot in the face and died in his brother's arms a minute later. Arthur Robertson held his brother's bloody head for a moment, then jumped to his feet, screaming, and charged the fort, his rifle left behind him, a long knife in his hand. He was halfway there when Tecumseh Bell bounded over a pile of brush, caught him, and dragged him back to safety.

William S. Smith, Brazoria's quiet schoolteacher, died sprawled across a salt-grass dune, and Alberto Ruiz took a musket ball in the neck as he leaned across to hand some rifle caps to his son.

Job Williams was the last to die among the Texians that morning. A sailor for the schooner *Navidad,* on leave in Brazoria, he had joined Henry Brown's command to help with the fight. He had made his last trip to sea.

When the rifle fire from Henry Brown's command finally drove Domingo Ugartechea to cover on the cannon bastion, a cheer went up aboard the *Brazoria*. Bill Russell cheered with them, clapped his hands, and then turned to reposition the blunderbuss.

"Give me a hand, Danny boy," he called, then turned to look at Dan Albert, and the color drained from his face. "Oh, my God in Heaven," he whispered.

Dan Albert wouldn't be going home to his Peggy. He sat on the deck, his back against a cotton bale, his chin on his chest as though in sleep. A musket ball had taken him in the mouth. He had been dead since sometime before dawn.

At the barricades before the north wall, the firing had slackened. The Texians simply didn't have anyone to shoot at. And John Austin was trying to decide what to do next. He had planned a dawn assault on the gates, but that was out of the question now. The element of shock was gone, and the Mexicans were as ready to fight up close as his men were. He crawled down the line to check his wounded. At the fourth barricade Smith Bailey was trying to put a bandage on a long, wicked-looking gouge running halfway down Matthew Langley's back. The ball had deflected just enough not to ruin his spine.

"She ain't gonna like this," Langley announced, dazedly.

"Who ain't?" Bailey asked. But his question was unanswered. Langley had passed out.

It was nearly nine o'clock when the rain began.

It was a typical south Texas squall. It rolled and threatened for a while, making up its mind, and then it rained. Like pouring water from a boot. Within minutes the Texian trenches were full and overflowing. The fort was a gray, hazed bulk seen through a waterfall. Small-arms fire came to a halt, as powder was soaked in reloading. The few Texians using flintlocks were out of business immediately. The rest, and the Mexican soldiers

256

on the wall, got off one more shot from their percussion weapons and then were disarmed by the rain.

But the cannon was still firing, and the deadly swivel gun, using wrapped and waxed charges, was thumping steadily away, delivering its lethal missiles among the barricades.

Austin's position had been precarious. Now it was untenable. With the rain, Brown's troops pulled back unmolested. Ugartechca's command was concentrating on Austin, waiting to see what he would do. For a moment the firing ceased entirely, and the only sound was the rain, smashing against the barricades, flattening the sand and soaking the men.

The word *retreat* has implications that are usually cloaked in history by substituting more acceptable words. *Withdrawal,* for instance. Or the *retrograde.* Or *advance to the rear.* But when the swivel gun began talking again, there was no question of semantics involved.

"Get outta here!" John Austin's bull voice thundered down the line. "All of you! Run like hell!"

There was no argument.

Britt Bailey shoved Bubba half out of the trench, looking to see if his two boys were also moving out. "Run, Bubba," he shouted, "and pick up them feet or I'll run right over you."

All along the line men were coming out of the trench, cramped legs faltering, arms waving for balance, heading for safety. Henry Smith, a bandage almost covering his head, gained his feet, looked back to shout a curse at the fort, and fell flat on his face. Austin picked him up and propelled him onward. "Dammit, Henry, do your cussin' after we get out of range!"

They left their dead behind, giving their attentions instead to the wounded. Those who could walk or hobble did so, with help. Those who couldn't were slung over someone's shoulder and carried away.

As Bubba came out of the trench and stopped to help Britt Bailey get to his feet, a man staggered past with a

257

bleeding friend on his back. He stumbled and fell, and the injured man howled as he hit the ground. Bubba didn't take time to decide which one was wounded. Instead he scooped both men up and headed for the rear, long legs driving against the rain-packed sand.

They withdrew more than four hundred yards, and for half that distance they were visible to the gunners at the fort, in the lulls between sheets of cascading rain. But during that race no one was hit.

Aboard the grounded schooner Bill Russell saw Austin's command begin its hurried retreat and shouted at Austin. His voice was drowned in a barrage of thunder. Cursing, he ran up the ratlines to the fore masthead and shouted again, cupping his hands around his mouth. Austin heard him then, and veered to the left, toward the schooner, dragging Henry Smith with him. The man's soaking bandage had slipped and he was running blind, protesting bitterly and trying to push the mass out of his eyes. Several others followed them. They plunged into the warm river water and reached the ship, where they were hauled aboard. From the deck they could barely see the rest of the command, shadows in the pouring rain, running for the area where the horses and equipment were being held.

James Westall wasn't the first to leave the trench, but he was the first to arrive at the staging area, and when the others came up he was waiting for them, lounging against a wagon, rain pouring from the brim of his hat. Editor D.W. Anthony was among the first runners in.

"If you're gonna print the race results in the paper next week, D.W.," Westall said casually, "don't forget I won."

Uncle Bubba came trotting in with his double burden, the unwounded portion of it struggling and fussing. He lowered them gently, looked them over and went off to help set up some lean-tos. Dr. Parrott got busy tending wounds.

When the rain began to let up, Colonel Ugartechea

was standing atop the cannon bastion, an oilskin cloak wrapped around his shoulders, taking stock of the situation. Behind the rain came the wind, gusting and chill, kicking spray in sheets along the sodden ground. Major Moret ran up the bastion steps and handed the colonel a spyglass. He pointed toward the schooner.

The wind, whipping out of the south, was flicking the ship's flag up and out from the spanker beam. He saw it, studied it carefully, and smiled.

"Major, order all firing to cease. Call the officers to my quarters."

In his apartment the colonel selected a cigar, lighted it carefully and dropped into a chair. The officers arrived, followed by Don Francisco Duclor, bleary-eyed from brandy and interrupted sleep. Ugartechea looked at him, disgust plain on his tired face.

"Don Francisco, I will say this once only. Whatever is decided now you will answer in one of two ways. With agreement or with silence."

To the officers he said, "This is our situation. We are low on ammunition, we have sustained too many casualties, and we can expect no relief.

"The Texians have withdrawn for the moment only because their weapons would not fire in the rain. They will return, and this time they will take the fort. I see no other possibility."

The officers waited in silence, some nodding in agreement.

"I have seen the Texians' battle flag, gentlemen," Ugartechea continued. "It is our flag. The flag of México."

He looked at them each in turn, then at Duclor. "I believe these men will treat us with honor," he said tiredly, "even those who have cheated them, because we are all citizens of the same country.

"When the storm is over, I intend to surrender the fort. We have fought enough." He tapped his cigar on the edge of a basin, and added musingly, "Fifty-four casualties. A third of my command. It is enough."

Moret was studying the floor at his feet. Now he raised his eyes.

"What terms will you ask, *mi Colonel?*"

"None." Ugartechea scowled at the cigar, then abruptly stubbed it out. "We are defeated, gentlemen."

Twenty

The squall had blown itself out. The clouds were breaking up and bright shafts spilled through the breaks when the fort's small gate opened and two officers walked out carrying a white flag. They walked, stiffly erect, halfway down the beach toward the schooner *Brazoria* and stopped there, waiting. After a moment Russell and William Wharton went to meet them. John Austin, aroused from a brief nap, was waiting at the rail when they returned.

"The Mexicans have had enough, Cap'n," Russell told him. "They want to surrender the fort."

"On what terms?"

"None, they said. Only that they be treated as soldiers of Mexico by citizens of Mexico."

Austin looked around him at the rubble-strewn deck. On the aft deck, covered with a piece of sailcloth, were two still forms. Sylvester Bowen was sitting on the low coaming, his bandaged leg stretched out before him. Below decks Dr. Peebles was treating two painfully wounded men.

"Tell them to come aboard," he said finally.

The terms of capitulation were set down by Russell and Wharton, taking turns writing on a foolscap sheet spread on the deckhouse cover, while Austin dictated the terms. Juan Moret and José Maria Rincon, soldiers of the republic, stood by as he spoke.

The garrison of Fort Velasco, all those able and willing to go, would be permitted to march out with all the honors of war. They would be allowed to keep their arms, ammunition, and baggage. A vessel would be provided for embarkation to Matamoros, for which the commander of the garrison would pay to the ship's captain the sum of six hundred dollars for the voyage. All the wounded military of the fort able to march would carry arms. Those unable to walk would remain to be treated and cured, and would receive good treatment. Their food would be reimbursed to the Texians by Mexico.

"Señor," Moret said, "there is the tax collector, Don Francisco Duclor." At Austin's frown he added, "He is in our charge, señor."

"Very well," Austin decided. "Bill, make this item three and that last will be item four. . . ."

Duclor would be permitted to embark with the officers if he desired. His escort, a sergeant and two soldiers, would be permitted to go, as well.

"*Gracias, señor.*"

Fifth, the six hundred dollars the captain of the vessel would receive must be considered duty-free, and the troops taken by ship to Matamoros would be disembarked outside of the bar of the Brazos Santiago.

"What officers are in the garrison?" Austin asked.

"Only four remain, señor." Moret enumerated without emotion the two present, Colonel Ugartechea, and one ensign, Don Emanuel Pintardo.

"Take those names, Bill. And say that these four, by the instrument of this treaty, are obliged never to return to take up arms against General Santa Anna or his cause. Word it as it should be."

"What ship will be provided for us, Señor Austin?"

John Austin's tired face lifted in a sardonic grin, "This one that you're standing on, Major. It's the only one we have to spare right now."

The schooner *Brazoria* would be readied for departure immediately, and would be used. The schooner *Elizabeth* was due in that day or the next but probably would not arrive on time after the storm.

The big cannon and the swivel gun would remain at the fort along with all stores, extra arms, and ammunition. And finally, all remaining provisions of Fort Velasco beyond those necessary for the garrison's homeward trip would remain at the fort for the disposal of the owners. The agreement was signed by Juan Moret, José María Rincon, W.H. Wharton, and W.J. Russell aboard the schooner. Later, on the field between Fort Velasco and the staging camp of the Texians, Lieutenant Colonel Domingo de Ugartechea and John Austin met and signed their approval to the document.

Bill Scates and a crew were already at work on the *Brazoria's* battle scars, hurrying to make the little ship seaworthy. Austin wanted the soldiers loaded and on their way before some Texian who had lost kin in the fight let his emotions get the best of him and started shooting again. On the field around the fort, the settlers were cleaning up the sad rubble of war.

The cotton bales and cannon were carried off the ship, to make room for as many soldiers as possible. They wouldn't all fit aboard, but some could be taken across the river to Quintana. A lot of them had families there. They would be all right until Mexico got around to reassigning them. The Texians would wait here for the *Elizabeth*, then continue their journey to Anahuac.

There was a deep sadness over the Texian camp, the quiet mourning of those who had lost friends and relatives here and the quiet sympathy of the others. But the objective was still the same. They were going to Anahuac.

When the schooner was ready to set sail, Ugartechea led his troops out of the fort and turned the facility over to Austin. He saluted crisply, and they shook hands.

"*Adíos*, John Austin. And I hope next time we meet we are on the same side."

"If you elect for Santa Anna," Austin said, "I expect we will be."

"I cannot say for now." Ugartechea shrugged. "But maybe." He started up the gangplank, then turned back. "My swivel gun surprised you?"

"I expected you'd have something extra, Domingo, but it was a hell of a surprise when that thing started hitting us. It's a powerful gun for its size."

"At least I had you on something."

When they were loaded aboard, all of them who were going, the schooner's fore-and-aft sails were raised and they caught the wind. The ship edged away from the dock, seeming to slip backward until its wide jib sails billowed across the wind. Then it heeled slightly, righted, and headed for the open Gulf of Mexico.

Several Texians gathered on the dock to watch it go, and lingered as it passed the inshore breakers, climbed the waves, and headed out to sea. Those soldiers had put up a good fight.

It was some time later that a messenger rode in with news from Anahuac. Word of the fighting at Velasco, it seemed, had spread like a brushfire throughout the colonies, starting even before the battle had begun.

Austin read the written report, then called some of the men around him and read it again, aloud. After the siege at Anahuac, Colonel José de las Piedras, commander at Nacogdoches, had descended upon Anahuac to put an immediate end to the disturbances. The prisoners there had been released, and Colonel Juan Davis Bradburn had been summarily relieved of his command. Anahuac was now in the hands of Colonel Juan Cortina.

The Texians were stunned for a moment; then cheering broke out. They laughed, they joked, they danced around. They had beaten the Mexican army all the way around. Most of them, that is, cheered. A few didn't.

"Does that mean we ain't going to Anahuac, John?" one asked. "We ain't gonna fight?"

"Hell, sir," another laughed, "you already fought. Didn't you notice?"

Henry Smith was glum. "We oughta go anyway," he announced. "We oughta blow that Anahuac fort down just on general principles."

"Oh, hesh, Henry. And get that bandage up off yer face so I can see if it's you I'm talkin' to."

George McKinstry brought Austin an inventory of the

contents of the fort arsenal. There were thirty-five muskets in bad repair, and two hundred rounds of musketball. The big cannon on the bastion was there, with thirty rounds, and the swivel gun with forty-five. There were forty cartouche boxes and two brass blunderbusses and an inventory of parts and scrap. Two sergeants and five privates had been left behind, too severely wounded to travel. One of the sergeants was Jesús, with a hole in his right lung and a determination to live long enough to see his newborn son. The doctors had about decided he would see a swarm of grandchildren if he didn't get killed or something first. Of the seven Mexican wounded, only one was definitely dying.

McKinstry had a worried frown on his face as he stood with Austin and looked over the big circular stockade of the fort, which only hours ago had been raining death upon them.

"Now that we got it, John, what are we gonna do with it?"

The Texians' dead had been lined up down by the riverbank, each body covered with a blanket. One by one, as they went about their work, the Texians wandered over that way to stand for a few moments, looking down at them, remembering. After a battle, after the excitement and the terror, the shock and the confusion, when the world has stilled and the threat is gone for a while, that is the worst part of war. They looked around at the destruction they had caused, and at the destruction that had been repaid to them, and little by little it came to each of them that the friends who were gone weren't coming back.

Milton Hicks and Tecumseh Bell walked up the row of fallen Texians, Hicks hobbling on a crutch he had found in the fort, and looked for a while at the huge body of Strap Buckner.

"Old Hoss," Milton told his dead friend, "I shore hate to see you like this. But I reckon you never knowed about it when it come."

Tecumseh went over to where Leander Woods lay and

pulled back the blanket.

"This is gonna kill ol' Zadock."

"Reckon it will, 'bout," Hicks said. "But maybe he'll find some rest in knowin' his boy died with his rifle in his hand."

They stood for a few minutes, bareheaded in the sun, then turned to their horses. With a wave of farewell to their friends, living and dead, they mounted and headed north, not looking back. They would be well out of civilization before they stopped to make camp.

Four wagons were brought up, one for the dead and three for the wounded. Eleven Texians had died in the battle, and six were badly hurt. Eleven more had lesser wounds, and fully half the remainder would carry scars of some sort.

Rawlings walked over to the body of Strap Buckner. He looked down at the dead man for a long moment, then knelt beside him.

"That's one bet I wish I'd never won, Old Hoss." The sardonic face of the gambler softened and a tear glistened on his cheek. "God knows I never meant for any of us to die."

When the dead and wounded were started back up the road toward Brazoria, the remaining group divided up. Some would stay and look after the fort; some would go home.

John Austin gave a solemn word of advice to those who were staying.

"Take good care of the place, gentlemen. We just borrowed it for a while. It isn't really ours . . . yet."

Part Six

Texas

The Aftermath

In the early summer of 1832 there were two Mexicos, both sharing the same soil and each deadly to the other. Bustamente was Mexico—the solid, stable, cruel, and autocratic realm of the experienced dictator. And at the same time Santa Anna was Mexico—the impatient, ambitious, and ruthless destiny of the next dictator. The lines were drawn, the game of *coup d'état* was in full play, and Bustamente's clock was nearing its final stroke. Mexico had shuffled its deck before, and it would shuffle it again.

But for a moment, when news of the insurgence in Texas reached Mexico City and Vera Cruz, the game was suspended while both sides weighed and judged this unexpected turn of events. The reactions from both camps were surprise and hostility. All the powers of Mexico for a time believed that there was full-scale revolution in Texas. Neither the ruler of Mexico nor the man who would rule could countenance such a thing. Mexico's wilderness buffer was important to both of them. Santa Anna's forces acted first.

Communications being what they were, Santa Anna did not know that the colonists had declared for him. At the same time, the Texians had no way of knowing that the general's revolution was in an advanced stage.

When General Montezuma of Tampico, a supporter of Santa Anna, learned of the events of Anahuac and Velasco, he acted promptly to secure his general's northern flank. He dispatched Colonel José Mexía with a squadron of six gunships and four hundred soldiers to take decisive action against the Texians. Being a practical and methodical man, he also assigned Mexía a second task—to stop along the way and persuade as many military men as possible to join Santa Anna in his fight for control of Mexico.

Sailing north for Texas, Mexía put in at Matamoros, where he convinced Colonel Guerra Mansanares of the Bustamente faction that it would be in the best interests of Mexico if he could proceed unhampered by Mexican forces. His job, he said, was that of a policeman. The Texas settlers must be chastened, for the welfare of all concerned. Mansanares agreed.

While in Matamoros Colonel Mexía picked up a passenger: the founder of the Texas colonies and alcalde of San Felipe, Stephen F. Austin. Then he headed due east, far out into the open sea, then north. Swiftly and expertly, Mexía descended on the Brazos port.

Only a handful of Texians were left at Fort Velasco now, the second day of July, 1832, and they were staying there only to guard the installation against pilferage and vandalism. They had hardly any warning at all. Suddenly the near horizon was alive with warships, and then Mexía's armada was anchored at the mouth of the Brazos and armed troops were streaming ashore to set up firing units around the fort. Mexía also sent a letter ashore addressed to John Austin, demanding an immediate explanation of his actions in taking the fort. Stephen F. Austin was kept aboard ship.

John Austin's reply was a surprise. It was a copy of the Turtle Bayou Resolutions and a letter, in precise Spanish, inviting Mexía to a fiesta in his honor, to be held at Brazoria. Mexía scratched his head, read it again and believed it. He knew John Austin.

Detailing a unit to take possession of the fort, Mexía and an escort of officers brought Stephen Austin ashore and proceeded, with the jubilant Texians, to Brazoria. The chief alcalde of Colony San Felipe was quick on the uptake. By the time they reached Brazoria, Stephen Austin had convinced Mexía that this event, in his honor, would be a fine occasion to call in the subordinate officers of all the surrounding settlements and receive their pledges of allegiance to Mexico and Santa Anna. This was precisely what Mexía was here for.

In the meantime, of course, Texian scouts were riding hell-for-leather ahead of them toward Brazoria to make some fast arrangements for the party the colonel had been invited to. The reception was held at Jane Long's tavern. By the end of the evening, Mexía was convinced that the most loyal, most obedient and most courageous supporters his general would ever find were these fine people of the Texas colonies.

Colonel Mexía cancelled the rest of his visit to Texas and headed back to Tampico. Everything was fine in Texas, and he had the assurance of the Texians that any remaining Mexican forces in the colonies would either declare for Santa Anna's revolution or be kept mighty busy defending themselves.

The Texians, of course, intended to keep their word. In the name of Santa Anna and the revolution they visited garrison after garrison, and within a few weeks most of these installations were abandoned. The troops at Anahuac went off to join Santa Anna. The post at Gonzales was abandoned. The little detachment at Velasco was persuaded that they were urgently needed at home. Of the large garrison at San Antonio only seventy officers and men remained. Detachments at Tenoxtitlan and Goliad packed up and left for the revolution. The Texians helped them pack, and straightened up for them when they had gone.

One last stronghold remained in Texas, and the Texians took care of it. Colonel Piedras at Nacogdoches, seeing his garrison very much alone in the wilderness, decided he would stay. The Texians decided he would not. Three hundred settlers, Anglo and Mexican, descended on the stone fort at Nacogdoches and drove three hundred and fifty soldiers out. A small party of Texians led by James

Bowie headed them off. Surrounded at Angelena, the soldiers turned their recalcitrant colonel over to the settlers and headed for Mexico.

One guest at the Nacogdoches fort escaped. Colonel Juan Davis Bradburn, now back in civilian clothing and with a price on his head in Texas, headed for the Louisiana border.

By the end of August the Mexican army was gone from Texas soil — gone off to fight for Santa Anna, or to fight against Santa Anna, or in many cases simply to get away from the Texians. And with the army gone the Texians continued to pour in. They came with their Pennsylvania rifles and their Arkansas knives, their Tennessee debts and their Kentucky attitudes, Americans who intended to be Texians and weren't about to turn aside short of their goal.

The Mexican hold was broken. Texas was still Mexican soil, technically, but it would never again be dominated by Mexico.

Twenty-one

Two days' ride above Brazoria, the placid Brazos de Dios ran deep, green, and peaceful in the lazy heat of midsummer. Fitful eddies swelled and spread in ripples on the current's unhurried surface, flashing brilliant spangles of reflection from the August sun. Flecks of foam and bits of languid driftwood clung at the sandy shores, then moved away to cling again elsewhere.

At a wide bend, where the green cloak of summer crept down short banks, Matthew Langley and his bride tied their horses and stepped down to the water's edge to stop for a time and watch the ripples sliding by. They walked along the riverbank, uncramping muscles tightened by a long day on horseback. Charlotte carried a doeskin pack, which she placed on a drift log at the river's edge. Langley carried his rifle, a canteen, and a rolled blanket. The canteen and blanket joined the food sack on the log. The rifle he kept with him as they walked beside the river.

They walked a way, then walked back, Charlotte fascinated by the beauty of the wild river valley slumbering in the sun, her husband fascinated with this small creature who had become his wife. The change in Charlotte was remarkable, he thought. She was a quick, enthusiastic girl now, charmed with life and all about it, bright and cheerful as a kitten.

They stood on the bank and looked across the water. On the far side a lone deer crept through the screening brush, looked around, then leapt to the low bank to drink. Charlotte pressed her hands tight and stood still, enjoying the sight of the animal, afraid of frightening it away. Langley studied her clear profile and wondered if he would ever understand her. He decided he probably never would, and it didn't bother him in the slightest.

When a man has a long run of bad luck and then it finally changes to good, he doesn't question it. He just rides along and enjoys it. And for a hardscrabble farmer from the hungry hills of Illinois, Matthew Langley was doing very well. He was well clothed, well fed, well mounted, and well armed, and he was taking his pretty bride to see their future home. They would look at the land that was theirs and pick out a site to build a house on. And if he was thinking of a two-room cabin while she had dreams of a grand mansion, what did it matter? There was plenty of time to work it out.

"Oh, Matthew, look!"

A great bald eagle, dark feathers glinting in the sunlight and its beak a splash of yellow on its sleek white head, dived low over the shallows across the river and veered away from the bank, great wings carrying it aloft to dive again upstream. An Indian would have taken it for an omen. "An excellent omen," Matthew said aloud. He fixed his eyes suddenly on the far bank and squinted. Something about that cutbank . . .

It was the place he had found the little raccoon. And the Karankawa had found him. And Willie had found the Karankawa. An omen.

A crack like the breaking of a limb echoed away across the broad water and Langley jerked upright, his rifle coming up as he swung around. Charlotte gasped. In the foliage above him someone whooped and applauded. The voice that followed was choked with laughter.

"Hey, ol' Coonslinger! Jes' cain't leave that river alone, can ye?"

Langley had frozen at the laughter. Now he relaxed, a slightly irritated grin spreading across his face.

"Come on down, Willie! I oughta shoot you, but I won't. Might take a stick to you, though."

"Already got one, thankee." Robert Williamson's head appeared above the shrubbery, a delighted grin spreading

274

across his face. He eased down the high bank and walked toward them. "Howdy, Miz Charlotte. Nice day."

Langley stuck out a hand. "Willie, I swear! If you ever do that to me again, I am going to shoot you, right where you stand."

"Aw, Matthew." Williamson chuckled. "It ain't like it was every day. And if you'll recollect, there was a damn . . . pardon, ma'am . . . dern good reason that other time."

"Yeah, I guess there was. What was the reason this time?"

"This time I just couldn't help it. Say"—he pointed—"That bank over there, ain't that where . . ."

Langley's frown shushed him, and he glanced quickly at Charlotte and changed the subject. "You goin' up to Fort Bend for the meetin'?"

"Didn't know there was one. When?"

They walked a few steps to the drift log and sat, Williamson reloading his Kentucky rifle. Charlotte smiled, unrolled the blanket on the hard-packed riverbank, and started removing food from the pack.

"Would you like coffee, Matthew?"

"Uh, yeah. Sounds good. I'll build a fire."

He found some dry sticks and soon had a little blaze going on the open bank.

"Meetin's tomorrow," Williamson said. "Jim Bullock's over from Nacogdoches, and Jim Bowie's comin' in from the Neches, got a bunch of the Trinity men with him, too . . ."

"Anybody from Anahuac?"

"I reckon. You recollect Wylie Martin? Well, he's been up to Nacogdoches with 'em. Ol' Wylie just cain't miss a good fight, an' I hear that one is a dandy. And Bill Scates is along with 'em, and Morgan, and a couple of 'em that Bradburn had in the brick kiln over there. You remember William Travis, or did you ever meet him?"

"Saw him once. Fancy sort."

"Yeah, that's him. Well, some of us 're goin' up from Brazoria and Bell's too, just to see what it's all about. I reckon I know, though. Texas is plumb out of Mexican soldiers, so now we gonna have to start fightin' each other."

"I guess I haven't been keepin' up much lately," Langley said; then his ears reddened slightly, and he glanced toward his wife. She was spreading a dinner for three on the blanket on the ground, humming. Williamson chuckled.

"Heard you was doin' all right, Matthew. That scrape heal up all right?"

"Yeah, mostly. It's gettin' along."

"And you got your deed registered, I hear tell. Steve Austin give you any trouble about it?"

"No. I thought he was going to, but John Austin and Britt Bailey put in a word for me. Willie, is Stephen Austin afraid of Britt Bailey?"

"Ha!" Williamson slapped his knee. "Don't you believe it. That Steve Austin may not look like much, but I don't reckon he's scared of any man there is. Got more guts than you an' me put together, is my thinkin'."

"Yeah, I guess he must have. Anyhow, he coughed and sputtered some, but he cleared my deed for me. Charlotte and me, we're going up there now to look it over and see about gettin' it cleared to farm."

"That'll cost ye a mite. You got the money?"

"Got a note. I'll have to pay interest on it, but I can make that place pay off, given a year or two."

"Reckon you can, at that."

Charlotte had completed the unpacking and had put the coffee on to boil. She called them and they moved to the blanket, took off their hats and sat down. They bowed their heads while Charlotte said grace, and then they dug in.

"How'd you happen to find us here, Willie?" he asked, between mouthfuls of cold fried chicken and cornbread.

"Picked up your trail some ways back," Willie explained. "Just above Bell's, in point of fact, but I didn't spot that it was you 'til a mile or so back. That still the same mare

276

you brought back from Anahuac?"

"Yeah, and the Morgan."

"Yep, I reco'nized the Morgan's prints. Follered him before, once." The little woodsman helped himself to more chicken. "Anyhow, when y'all turned off into the woods here, I just tagged along. Wanted to say howdy."

"Well, you got one heck of a way of lettin' folks know you're around."

"Yep." Willie turned to Charlotte. "And may I say, Miz Langley, yo're a whole lot purtier than any wet coon I ever saw."

She was perplexed for a moment, then shrugged it off and treated him to a dazzling smile. "Thank you, Mr. Williamson, and the same to you."

Willie sputtered and almost choked as a bite went down the wrong way.

When they were finished they scrubbed out the few dishes at the river's edge, and Charlotte repacked them in the doeskin sack. "If you gentlemen will excuse me for a moment," she said. She picked up Langley's rifle, checked the prime carefully and climbed the bank, heading back toward the horses.

"She know how to use that thing?"

"You better believe she does."

They fired up their pipes, and Williamson filled him in on the latest news from Brazoria. The little town was growing by leaps and bounds since the fort at Velasco had been abandoned. There were close to a thousand people there, and more coming in every day.

"Seems like the whole province is busting with people," Langley mused. "Jeremiah Blanchard is gettin' rich takin' a dollar a head from the folks stopping at his place. You say the soldiers are all gone?"

"Yep, all that matters anyhow. All gone off to help Santa Anna finish up his revolution. Them at Nacogdoches was just about the last of 'em. Few left over at Bexar, but not many. Us Texians have got Texas all to ourselves these days, seems like."

There was something about the way he said it. *'Us Texians* are citizens of Mexico," Langley said.

"Oh, I know that, Matthew, but you know, there's somethin' invigoratin' about havin' all this to ourselves." He pondered a moment, his brows lowered.

"As I see it, Matthew, we was all Mexicans a year or two ago, and good ones. But that was before the big stir all come up. Now we're Texians. And that's somethin' a little different."

Charlotte reappeared at the top of the high bank and called to them. They got up and stretched, and Langley rerolled the blanket and picked up his canteen.

"Want to ride with us as far as Fort Bend, Willie? Be nice havin' you along."

Twenty-two

The village of Fort Bend was packed with people, but Langley found a night's lodging for them at a tiny inn by the river front. They had dinner, walked around for a while, and retired early. Out on the street there was drinking, laughing, brawling, and general hilarity through most of the night.

Langley awoke in the early dawn and dressed, careful not to awaken Charlotte. Outside, he strolled along the street enjoying the sweet air of morning, saying hello to a few friends. Henry Smith was there, out early, and Bill Scates. Both had been up far into the night, preaching revolution, and were out and around now looking for a cup of coffee and, if chance permitted, some more converts.

"I think John Austin's comin' around to our way of thinkin'," Scates told him as they sat in a tavern drinking black coffee from china cups. "He told me last week he thought Texas might be big enough to make its own way in a year or two if folks keep comin' in like they are now."

Smith wasn't satisfied at all. "A year or two! We could break loose right now, Bill, and nobody'd do anything about it. There isn't a soldier left in this part of Texas."

"They'll be back, Henry. That's what Austin's worried about. Sure, we could declare ourselves out right now, but we'd get pulled right back in . . . and hard . . . as soon as Santa Anna's done. You see, Matt"—he turned to Langley—"even the ones of us that agree don't agree.

"Henry wants to pull out of Mexico right now. I want us to pull out whenever the time's right. John Austin leans to lettin' matters ride until the war's over in Mexico,

279

then consider it."

"And Stephen won't even talk about revolt," Smith said sourly. "He's with Mexico all the way."

"Only as far as Mexico's with us," Scates corrected him. "Don't ever underestimate Steve Austin, Henry."

"Well," Langley said, "I expect it'll all work out."

"Hey, Matt Langley!" Jawbone Morris roared from the doorway, then came striding in and stuck out his hand. "You still alive? I thought you'd got killed back there at Anahuac."

"No, just cut up a little. Pulled out all right. How you been, Mr. Morris?"

"Fine and dandy, sir." He looked to the doorway where two other men were coming in. "You remember Wylie Martin, Matt? And James Morgan?"

Langley remembered Morgan very well—the livery stable owner at Anahuac. He greeted him warmly, then howdied with Martin. The old frontiersman gravely shook his hand, then sat at the table, his old flintlock rifle leaning at his side. The others sat, after introductions, and a Negro girl brought more coffee.

They talked for a while of the latest news from all over the colonies, Indian trouble at the mouth of the San Bernard, Jim Bowie's roundup of the last of Piedras's troops, the almost daily ship arrivals at Brazoria and Anahuac since the embargoes had been lifted, and such. Martin was quiet and sour-faced through most of it. He had missed the fighting at Nacogdoches's stone fort. He had been off with a detail wrapping up some patrols on the Gonzales road at the time.

"Ain't you had more'n your share of fighting anyway, though, Wylie?" Morgan asked him.

"That ain't it, exactly," Morris said, speaking up for his friend. "You see, Wylie's had business to do with ol' Juan Bradburn ever since that whole Anahuac ruckus blew up, and Bradburn turns out to have been at Nacogdoches when the settlers moved in on them there."

"Did they get him?" Smith asked, interested. A lot of

Texians had a score to settle with Bradburn.

"Naw, the polecat got away."

"Anybody know where he was headin'?"

"If I did," Martin said, quietly, "I'd be on my way there. It's a personal matter."

"Bradburn and a feller named Smith," Morris explained, then added hurriedly, "Not you, Mr. Smith. This was a different kind of Smith. Name of John M. Smith. Worked for Bradburn over at Anahuac. They likely be together, wherever they are, is my thinkin' on it."

Langley noticed that when Bradburn and Smith were discussed, Martin's face fixed in a solemn expression that set off about as deadly a pair of eyes as he had seen. They broke up finally, and he went back to wake up Charlotte.

She was up and dressed in a bright day-wrap. He kissed her and said, "I've been drinking coffee. Let's go find some breakfast." She smiled and nodded, but said nothing.

Over breakfast she kept glancing at him, then away, a slight, worried frown playing across her smooth face. But she said only, "Did you visit with some of your friends, Matthew?" and, a little later, "My, there are a lot of men in town. Will there be more fighting, do you think?" He decided to stay in town for the day, just to see what was going on.

About noon, he took her back to the inn to change, and heard a shout from out on the street. "You wait for me, Charlotte," he said, "and I'll be back in a little while to take you to lunch. I want to see what all the noise is about."

Another group of men had ridden in, coming from Brazoria. The *Navidad* had arrived there just before their departure, and they had news. An American party was being made up in New Orleans to come to Texas. A large party this time, several hundred families. Rumor also had it that President Andrew Jackson was encouraging migration of Americans to Texas, but discreetly, not to alarm

Mexico.

"Discreet!" One of the newcomers laughed. "Feller gave me fifty dollars to come to Texas. I'd have come for nothin', but he didn't know that."

"Maybe, but that feller wasn't Andy Jackson, I bet."

"No. Just a feller."

"That's what I mean."

There was other news, too. Anybody who could produce a cane crop this year in Texas would name his price in New Orleans. The market was wide open.

"And indigo, too. They're buying all they can get for any price they have to pay."

"You reckon they'd pay for palmettos in New Orleans?" a dour farmer scoffed. "I got more of them damn things than I got crops."

"Put coal oil to 'em, Job. That'll take 'em out."

And there was news of old acquaintances, family in the States. It was this way every time Texians got together. It was the way news was spread. Then a name caught Langley's ear.

"See one Texian there musta' gone back home," a man from the *Navidad* was saying. "Used to trade with him up on the Trinity. Feller name of John Smith. John M. Smith. Anybody know him?"

No one seemed to, but Langley saw a pair of Anahuac men edge away from the crowd and then walk, hurriedly, toward the river front. His curiosity got the best of him. He headed that way.

When he arrived, the men were talking animatedly with Jawbone Morris and Bill Scates. Wylie Martin was there, listening. For a few minutes after the news was passed there was silence.

"Is that the same fellow you men were talking about this morning?" he asked Morris.

"Ain't any doubt of it," Morris said. "And I say where he is, there Bradburn's gonna be too, now he's run out of Texas."

"New Orleans," Martin said, to no one in particular. It

282

was as though he were impressing it on his mind.

"Jawbone," the old woodsman said then, and there was death in his eyes. "I ain't seen New Orleans in a long time. Been thinkin' about goin' there for a spell. Want to come along and see the sights?"

There was no mistaking it. There would be some dead Texians in New Orleans soon, one way or another.

Langley wandered back into the heart of town. There was other talk, too. Comanches had raided far to the south of their usual haunts, into the settlements on the middle Colorado, and a company was forming up to go after them. With the Mexican soldiers gone, Indians were going to be a problem. The rifles were out, and the fighting spirit of the Texians was following in abundance. It was intoxicating. It was enough to make a man want to pack his gear, load his rifle, and join them.

Suddenly Matthew noted that it was well past noon, and the guilty realization hit him that Charlotte was still waiting for him at the inn. He hurried to get there.

When he entered the room she was standing, stiff-backed, looking out the window. She had put on her best dress and had been waiting. Now the stiff back and the averted face should have warned him that all was not just right, but excitement gripped him and he burst out, "Lottie, wait 'til you hear what's going on . . ."

The rush of enthusiasm ebbed as she turned to him. Too late, he saw the warning signals. Back arched and head high, she looked up at him, dark eyes slitted, lips white with anger.

"And just what is going on, Matthew? Another fight, perchance?" Her voice was soft, strained. Mock servitude framed the scorn in her. "And shall I begin tearing bandages now, so we'll have enough? What will it be this time—a cracked skull, possibly, or a rifle ball through the belly? Cuts to bind or maybe another bleeding furrow down the back with the bone showing through?"

As the words came out, the dam of constraint gave way and she blazed at him. "Just how much of you will be returned to me after this glorious battle? And how much after the next?"

She crowded him and he backed in confusion. His shoulders touched the closed door. "Lottie, I didn't mean . . . it's just . . ."

"Just another little fight!" She pressed in, furious now. "Just another opportunity to see you lying half-dead in a hide wagon, or bleeding all over a hammock. That's nothing much, is it? Well, I'll tell you right now, Matthew Langley, I'll have none of it. Those men out there . . . and you. Running off to one fight after another, just looking to get killed.

"Well enough for them, I suppose. They are other women's problems. But I'm not ready to be a widow, and I'm fair tired out from being a nurse."

"Oh, now, Lottie . . ." was all he managed. She wasn't finished.

"You can make up your mind right now, Matthew Langley. You can be a big man for those ruffians out there, and get your fool self killed"—her voice broke slightly, almost a sob—"or you can be a big enough man to let them go by.

"You might even be big enough"—the fury faded and she backed away a step, lowering her head—"to be standing on your own hind legs and all in one piece if I should sometimes need to lean on you."

She didn't really stop talking; she just kind of ran down. Langley was thoroughly abashed, and for a moment they stood in silence while his mind sorted out the perspectives of responsibility he had assumed when he won this pretty, fiery creature before him.

"Charlotte," he began, then had to begin again. "Little Lottie, I'm sorry I'm so late. I was talking. Now straighten your face, and let's go have lunch

"If we hurry," he added, "we can be packed and halfway to our farm by tonight."

The quick glance she gave him was skeptical, and she lowered her head again, trembling with vented anger. She

284

yielded only slightly when he put his arms around her. He would have to see to it there were more smiles on that lovely, somber face. He would see to it, and those smiles would be all he would ever need.

"Lottie," he tipped her face up and kissed her forehead. "I'm not a fighter. I'm a farmer."

There's always fighting if a man wants to look for it, Britt Bailey had said. And sometimes if he doesn't.

But there was nothing to say he had to look for it.

WESTERN STORYTELLER
ROBERT KAMMEN
ALWAYS DEALS ACES WITH HIS TALES
OF AMERICA'S ROUGH-AND-READY FRONTIER!

DEATH RIDES THE ROCKIES (2509, $2.95)

DEVIL'S FORD (3163, $2.95)

GUNSMOKE AT HANGING
WOMAN CREEK (2658, $2.95)

LONG HENRY (2155, $2.50)

GUNS ALONG THE YELLOWSTONE (2844, $2.95)

WIND RIVER KILL (3164, $2.95)

WINTER OF THE BLUE SNOW (2432, $3.50)

Available wherever paperbacks are sold, or order direct from the Publisher. Send cover price plus 50¢ per copy for mailing and handling to Zebra Books, Dept. 3097, 475 Park Avenue South, New York, N.Y. 10016. Residents of New York, New Jersey and Pennsylvania must include sales tax. DO NOT SEND CASH.

THE FINEST IN SUSPENSE!

THE URSA ULTIMATUM (2310, $3.95)
by Terry Baxter

In the dead of night, twelve nuclear warheads are smuggled north across the Mexican border to be detonated simultaneously in major cities throughout the U.S. And only a small-town desert lawman stands between a face-less Russian superspy and World War Three!

THE LAST ASSASSIN (1989, $3.95)
by Daniel Easterman

From New York City to the Middle East, the devastating flames of revolution and terrorism sweep across a world gone mad . . . as the most terrifying conspiracy in the history of mankind is born!

FLOWERS FROM BERLIN (2060, $4.50)
by Noel Hynd

With the Earth on the brink of World War Two, the Third Reich's deadliest professional killer is dispatched on the most heinous assignment of his murderous career: the assassination of Franklin Delano Roosevelt!

THE BIG NEEDLE (2776, $3.50)
by Ken Follett

All across Europe, innocent people are being terrorized, homes are destroyed, and dead bodies have become an unnervingly common sight. And the horrors will continue until the most powerful organization on Earth finds Chadwell Carstairs—and kills him!

THE SEVENTH CARRIER SERIES
by Peter Albano

THE SEVENTH CARRIER   (2056, $3.95)
The original novel of this exciting, best-selling series. Imprisoned
in a cave of ice since 1941, the great carrier *Yonaga* finally breaks
free in 1983, her maddened crew of samurai determined to carry
out their orders to destroy Pearl Harbor.

THE SECOND VOYAGE OF
THE SEVENTH CARRIER   (2104, $3.95)
The Red Chinese have launched a particle beam satellite system
into space, knocking out every modern weapons system on earth.
Not a jet or rocket can fly. Now the old carrier *Yonaga* is desperately needed because the Third World nations — with their armed
forces made of old World War II ships and planes — have suddenly become super powers. Terrorism runs rampant. Only the
Yonaga can save America and the Free World.

RETURN OF THE SEVENTH CARRIER   (2093, $3.95)
With the war technology of the former superpowers still crippled
by Red China's orbital defense system, a terrorist beast runs
rampant across the planet. Outarmed and outnumbered, the target of crack saboteurs and fanatical assassins, only the *Yonaga*
and its brave samurai crew stand between a Libyan madman and
his fiendish goal of global domination.

QUEST OF THE SEVENTH CARRIER   (2599, $3.95)
Power bases have shifted dramatically. Now a Libyan madman
has the upper hand, planning to crush his western enemies with
an army of millions of Arab fanatics. Only *Yonaga* and her in-
domitable samurai crew can save the besieged free world from the
devastating iron fist of the terrorist maniac. Bravely, the behe-
moth leads a rag tag armada of rusty World War Two warships
against impossible odds on a fiery sea of blood and death!

*Available wherever paperbacks are sold, or order direct from the
Publisher. Send cover price plus 50¢ per copy for mailing and
handling to Zebra Books, Dept. 3097, 475 Park Avenue South,
New York, N.Y. 10016. Residents of New York, New Jersey and
Pennsylvania must include sales tax. DO NOT SEND CASH.*